# THE SIDEMAN

## Caro Ramsay

This first world edition published 2018
in Great Britain and the USA by
SEVERN HOUSE PUBLISHERS LTD of
Eardley House, 4 Uxbridge Street, London W8 7SY.
Trade paperback edition first published
in Great Britain and the USA 2019 by
SEVERN HOUSE PUBLISHERS LTD.

British Library Cataloguing in Publication Data
*A CIP catalogue record for this title is available from the British Library.*

ISBN-13: 978-0-7278-8808-2 (cased)
ISBN-13: 978-1-84751-935-1 (trade paper)
ISBN-13: 978-1-78010-990-9 (e-book)

*All Severn House titles are printed on acid-free paper.*

Severn House Publishers support the Forest Stewardship Council™ [FSC™],
the leading international forest certification organisation.
All our titles that are printed on FSC certified paper carry the FSC logo.

MIX
Paper from
responsible sources
FSC® C013056

Typeset by Palimpsest Book Production Ltd.,
Falkirk, Stirlingshire, Scotland.
Printed and bound in Great Britain by
TJ International, Padstow, Cornwall.

# PROLOGUE

*Wednesday, 8th of November*

Costello pulled her car up outside the big house. It looked cold and dead in the bright winter sunshine, rays glinted off the ivy-covered slates giving a sparkle to the bricks of the red chimneys. She looked at the stained-glass window, the multi-coloured mosaic of Botticelli's *Primavera* was just visible through the reaching branches of the monkey puzzle tree. Behind the tall wrought-iron gates the grass was verdant, the pebbles still raked into the neat furrows that had impressed Archie Walker. On that day.

That dreadful day.

The trees were tall and mature, even devoid of leaves they cast long spindly shadows over the wide road, old-fashioned, gently cambered. The kind of surface that leant itself to roller-skating, so Costello's granny had once told her.

She turned the Fiat's engine off, slipping down in the seat, thinking about the night she saw Malcolm try to climb out the window above the porch, attempting to get away from his father. And Costello was convinced that *was* exactly what the boy was doing. The message Malcolm had left on her phone? A twelve-year-old wanting help to escape from a monster.

She'd got the voicemail the following morning. When it was too late.

Six hours later Malcolm's body had been found in this house, curled up on the beige carpet at the foot of his parent's bed, his mother's arms still wrapped round him, holding him close, giving her only son some solace as his short life slipped away. No doubt her own last breath had swiftly followed.

That image was seared into Costello's memory, the bodies and the speckles and spatters of crimson blood on the mirrored wardrobe doors. She could recall the events up to that, walking into the house, opening the unlocked back door; the first warning sign. Then the music floating from above; 'The Clapping Song'. The element of theatre. Then upstairs past the little teardrop of blood on the magnolia wallpaper, the stain he thought he'd cleaned away. Then into Malcolm's bedroom, too quiet. The Star Wars posters on the walls, the smooth R2D2 duvet cover decorated with a Celtic top, a pair of black leggings, two woollen socks, the trainers. They were arranged as if the child had been lying there, dressed and then spirited away, shedding his clothes and leaving them behind.

In the car, Costello wiped an angry tear from her eye, remembering how she had paused on the top landing, alert to the smell of blood. She had hesitated, not wanting to go any further but the door of the master bedroom was open, intriguing and beguiling. And all the time that song was playing.

*Clap clap.*

Standing in the doorway she had seen the blood on the doors, the walls, the ceiling. She had to force herself to carry on; she gripped the steering wheel. It was hard to think past the iron-rich stench of the blood, the sweeter mulch of faecal matter. Her last memory was of Abigail lying curled, her arm up and over the smaller figure of her son; his hands wrapped round her elbow, his fingers still gripping the lilac silk of her blouse.

She had presumed she would have tomorrow to sort it out.

She had been wrong.

What would happen if she didn't act now? What if they ran out of time?

She looked back at the gates, closed now to keep the media away from the 'Monkey House Of Horror'. What secrets had those gates kept?

Costello had only to wait twenty minutes before she saw some movement through the bare branches of the beech hedge. She had been following George Haggerty for a couple of weeks; she knew his routine. He would be going north to see his father in Port MacDuff now. She slid down further in her seat as the garage door opened, the gates swinging wide, the white Volvo rolling out majestically to park on the street. The driver's door opened and Haggerty, casually dressed for him in jeans and anorak, got out and walked back up the driveway, his shoes making no noise or indent on the gravel. True to his routine, he re-emerged a couple of minutes later, locked the gates closed behind him and walked briskly back to the car where he stopped and turned. He looked straight at Costello and smiled, clapped his hands together slowly twice, and climbed into the car.

*Clap clap.*

He drove away, without looking back.

George Haggerty was getting away with murder.

And Costello was going to stop him, even if it killed her. Or him.

# ONE

The house on the terrace was quiet on a Saturday afternoon, all week it had been like Glasgow Central
on Fair Friday, but everybody was out today. Colin
Anderson had the whole house to himself. He was lying on
the sofa, nursing a large Merlot and two sore feet after helping
Brenda make an early start on the Christmas shopping. He
was musing at the wine, as it swirled round the contours of
the glass, admiring the patterns it left in the light of the wood-
burning stove. His grandchild, Baby Moses, was asleep in his
basket at Anderson's feet. Nesbit, the fat Staffie, was curled
up on the sofa, ears tucked in so he didn't hear the rain battering
against the windows. *American Beauty* played on the DVD,
with the volume too low to hear.

It was almost perfect yet Anderson was not at peace. He was
still digesting the news that his partner for twenty years had
resigned. Costello was gone. No notice. No chat. No goodbyes.
She had walked into ACC Mitchum's office unannounced,
uninvited and slapped her letter of resignation on the desk right
in front of him.

Just like that.

Twenty years they had worked together, fought, made up
and fallen out again, shared laughs, heartache and a few broken
bones. She had always had his back. He had always had hers.
At times, their thinking was polar, opposite points of the
compass, balancing each other into a relationship that while
turbulent, was effective. Their track record proved that. Now
she was gone. Brenda, his wife, had explained it simply. The
events of the last few months had been too intense. Costello
had found Archie Walker. Anderson had found Baby Moses.

Both of them had moved on and maybe George Haggerty
had been the catalyst that finally separated them.

But then Brenda would say that. She had never really liked Costello.

He checked his phone. He was meeting the guys tomorrow for fish and chips, a long-standing arrangement. Costello had been invited. She had declined.

Anderson could accept that she had resigned in a fit of pique, saying she could do more about Haggerty without the restriction of the badge. She thought 'killing the bastard' would do her more good than any counselling.

And she had been furious when her request to form a task force to investigate the murders of Abigail and Malcolm Haggerty had been refused. The case had been transferred to Complaints and Internal Investigations, purely for clarity and transparency, but to him, and Costello, it felt they themselves were being scrutinized and judged. The first two people on the murder scene were members of the law enforcement community, and not just any members; a DI and Chief Procurator Fiscal. And as the fiscal's goddaughter was the victim's sister, the press were having a field day.

Haggerty was now talking to the media, playing on the 'Monkey House of Horror' crap. The case had rarely been out the papers for the last six weeks. Every day there was another tasty morsel revealed by the press. One thing they were all agreed on: the police weren't coming out of it well. George Haggerty was the obvious suspect and he was the one man who couldn't have done it. Even ACC Mitchum let slip that he too, had taken a very close look at that alibi. He had personally interviewed the two police officers who had caught Haggerty speeding in his white Volvo on the A9. One obvious suspect. Police Scotland were his alibi.

Yet, Costello had persisted that George Haggerty had killed his family.

He looked down at the bundle of pink skin in the Moses basket. His grandson, his link with Haggerty, the one reason they kept in touch. Anderson didn't like Haggerty, not the way his daughter Claire did. God, she had even drawn him a portrait of Baby Moses in pastel and had left it for him, signed and wrapped. Anderson wished she hadn't bothered. There was nothing he could define, nothing he could specify, just a very intense feeling of dislike. If he himself had one tiny piece of physical evidence against Haggerty, Anderson would have brought him in and every bone in his body would have told him that he had the right bloke. Every time, he was in Haggerty's company, Anderson could sense smirking guilt.

Anderson watched the Merlot, tipping it to the left and right. 'He has a watertight alibi,' he said out loud, 'and no motive at all.' He looked at his grandson, blowing bubbles in his basket. 'Well, none that we have found.' Moses ignored him but Nesbit cocked an ear. 'George Haggerty did not kill his wife Abigail or his son Malcolm. He couldn't have done it.'

To his mind the best way of getting Costello back was to prove her wrong and get DCI Mathieson and her team to prove that somebody else did kill Abigail and Malcolm. Then maybe Costello could get closure and move on. And then she might come back into the fold as it were. He could see how the lack of progress in the case might have frustrated his colleague. The killer had ghosted in and out the house, without leaving a trace. Or a trace was there because it had a right to be there. The Haggertys were not a social couple so the only 'other' DNA in the house was Abigail's sister, Valerie Abernethy, and she had stayed overnight only a few days before the killings. No fingerprints, no footprints but the blood spatter had left a clean zone where the killer had stood and that indicated they were slim, five feet ten or more. George was five seven.

It had also really annoyed Costello to learn that Dali Despande's proposal to pilot a new fast-track child protection service had been side-lined, again. Looking back, Anderson thought, maybe she hadn't been right since the Kissel case, that child being starved to death, neglected by a mother who didn't care, let down by a failing social work system. It had taken that little boy weeks to die. Costello had sat in the court and relived every minute of the harrowing abuse. Then Malcolm? Costello had in her head that Malcolm was a vulnerable child.

Then she had walked into that scene, a scene so awful, it was reported that the crime scene photographer on duty had been off work since with stress, unable to cope with what he had seen.

Still none of it was any of his business. He had to walk away and leave it to Mathieson and Bannon. He had his cold case rapes to work on. Mitchum had given him one more week before the file went back to the freezer.

ACC Mitchum had been very clear; Anderson's loyalty was to the force.

Not that there was any conflict of loyalty, Costello had not been in contact for twenty-one days.

*The Monkey House Of Horror.*

The tabloids hadn't been able to resist that.

Valerie Abernethy looked up at the familiar ivy-covered eaves, the two red chimneys, the big, stained-glass window all hidden from the road by the majestic monkey puzzle tree. Had it been a happy family home for her sister? The gutter press thought so. A happy family home that became a scene of slaughter.

Valerie took a deep breath, trying to calm the panic. They wanted her to walk round the room where her sister had breathed her last, shielding her son from the blade of a knife. She was aware of the investigative team hovering at the bottom of the gravel drive, pretending they were giving her a little moment to catch her private thoughts. She knew she was under scrutiny.

Well, they could stand there, out in the rain, a little longer. Valerie placed her hand on a petal of the stained-glass flower, a delicate stem with Mackintosh roses. The glass felt slightly warm to her touch, almost soft under her fingertips.

The front door was familiar and welcoming, painted claret to match the colours of the roses. The brass knocker that Malcolm used to polish managed to shine, even in this God-awful weather. The door was open. They wanted her to go in alone.

She had no idea when she was last here. Her memory had large gaps.

A lump caught her throat. This was too difficult. She tried lifting her foot to get her up the step, one stride and she'd be in the house. Nothing happened. Her leg was leaden, stuck to the red tiles. Valerie recognized that feeling, an old enemy returning.

She needed a vodka.

She closed her eyes and stepped up. She had to do this for Abigail. For Malcolm.

She was now stock-still, one foot up, one foot down and with her fingertips still resting on the glass window. There was movement behind her. Archie Walker was about to intervene and offer his assistance.

She needed to do this on her own.

Valerie turned her face up to the sky and took a deep breath. The raindrops spat at her with disgust, stinging the skin of her cheek. She didn't think it would be as hard as this.

Did she remember that night six weeks ago? Could she remember, vaguely, walking out the hospital? Standing in the light rain in Great Western Road, watching the traffic? She was probably looking for an off licence. Then there was a smell of perfume she could recall, something familiar she recognized from Abigail's house. Was that merely an association of ideas, her imagination filling in the blanks?

Another pause.

A rustle of impatience from the drive.

That would be the boss, a small fascist detective with hard flinty eyes. That cop was mistaken if she thought her pillar-box red lipstick distracted from the incipient Hitler moustache. Her junior officer, the big bearded bloke, kept a good four paces behind her. Like Prince Philip.

Fascist and Beardy, it was easier than remembering their names.

Valerie heard footfall behind her as the cops and Archie, here in his role as her godfather, not in his professional role as the chief fiscal, were walking up the gravel driveway. They only moved because it was too wet for them to hang around outside but it still felt like harassment.

Bugger them. She would do exactly what DI Costello had done on the day she had discovered the bodies. Valerie pulled away from the front door and walked briskly round the house to the back garden.

Now she turned to confront Fascist and Beardy, wishing then away. They were standing across the path, blocking her way out. Archie gave her an encouraging smile. The rainwater ran down his face, to be cast off as he nodded his head. They were getting soaked through. Even better, Fascist had a sour look on her face, her lippy was about to run.

Valerie took a deep breath and walked in, recognizing immediately the stink of the forensic cleaning team, a scent she knew well from her days as a fiscal. This no longer smelled like Abigail's house; these rooms were no longer infused with the aroma of roses, fresh coffee and George's aftershave. She walked through the pristine utility room, the kitchen – everything neatly tidied away – to the back of the hall where her boots touched carpet for the first time. This was where Costello had spotted the tiniest smear of blood on the wall, blood that somebody had attempted to clean.

Valerie wondered how easy that had been to wipe away; probably easier to erase it from the wall than to erase from the memory. Fascist crept up behind her, and coughed in irritation.

'Is there anything missing that you notice?' she asked in her snippy voice. 'We have a comprehensive list of the items that Mr Haggerty has removed and we have the crime scene photographs and . . .' That earned her an elbow in the ribs from Archie, now standing beside her. Nobody wanted to be reminded of that.

'Anything missing?' confirmed Valerie, thinking that her sister's smile was 'missing', the hugs from Malcolm were 'missing'. The house was a mausoleum.

'Anything?'

Valerie looked around, climbed the stairs to the half landing and *Primavera*, resplendent in coloured glass on the west-facing window. The view east was totally obliterated by the monkey puzzle tree. It was an easy escape route; this window, down to the roof of the porch, a short slither to the ground. It was reported Malcolm had tried to escape that way once after an argument with his father. This was actually an easy house to gain entry and exit without being observed; the monkey puzzle tree hid a lot. She turned to look down at her companions, then up through the balusters to the upper landing, with its expensive Persian rug on an expanse of oak flooring. And a plain magnolia wall. Valerie screwed her eyes up to concentrate on what she wasn't seeing.

'Well, there was a picture there, a pastel. I suppose George took that, he always liked it.'

'What was the picture? I don't think he has mentioned it.' Bannon checked his iPad.

'A painting, it was a painting. A rowing boat on a canal, under willows, weeping willows. How fitting is that?' She turned to the other three. 'Uncle Archie? Did you say there was music playing when you . . . found them?'

Archie nodded, teary. 'Yes, that kid's song, it was on repeat on the CD. It had been playing for hours. "The Clapping Song", the one w-where . . .'Archie stuttered. 'Where the monkey got choked and they all—'

Valerie stared at the gap on the wall. 'They all went to heaven in a little rowing boat.'

Kieran Cowan drove along the loch side, through the dark night and the streaming rain. The engine of Ludwig, his 1977 Volkswagen Camper, hummed along nicely as the windscreen wipers beat a regular tattoo on the glass. The left one squeaking at the end of its sweep, the right one responding a millisecond later with a resounding *thunk*. He had been intending to fix that, but after a fortnight of constant rain, he had got used to the noise. It provided an irregular backbeat to 'Life in the Fast Lane', which blasted out the old Clarion cassette player at full volume.

He was used to this road. He would be able to drive even if the wiper gave up the ghost and fell off completely, spinning over the top of the van and flying into the night sky. He had driven Ludwig to Ardnamurchan once with a cracked windscreen, sticking his head out the driver's window until he could pull over and punch the crazed glass out.

Cowan kept his eyes on the road, the narrow stretches where he had to slow, the wider stretches where he could put his foot down and the nasty bends where he needed to hug the rock wall in case he met a HGV over the white line.

The clock on the dash was saying it was half eight. He wasn't in a hurry per se; he was a little concerned about time. As long as it was dark.

The job needed to be done, sorted and over with.

He drove confidently now, one hand on the steering wheel and the other steadying the rucksack that rolled and yawed in the passenger seat. The camera had been borrowed from the university. He had signed it out on Friday night to be returned Monday morning. It was an expensive bit of kit, a Macro Scub 4 underwater video camera. It was fully charged and ready to go, safely tucked in the rucksack along with his flask of tomato soup and some sandwiches. He had no idea how long he was going to be here. As someone with a gift for stating the obvious once said, 'It took as long as it took.'

Cowan drummed his fingers on the steering wheel in time with 'Life In The Fast Lane' as he waited for a short procession of traffic to pass, and when the road was clear he put his foot down. Ludwig's air-cooled engine whirred in protest. He turned onto the road that hugged the North-West side of the loch and accelerated, cruising along, singing tunelessly with Glen or Don, as he checked the clock again. He was probably a little early. He could have stayed at his laptop and got a more of his essay done but he wanted to be there first and check out the lie of the land, get a good spot where he could stay hidden.

Covert breeds covert.

He pulled into the deserted car park of the Inveruglass visitor centre, putting his lights off first so as not to disturb anybody already there. The car park was not entirely empty, there was a Mini parked at the front, looking out over the water. Cowan gave it more than a passing glance, his heart thumping, in case this was who he was looking for. But the windows of the other car were steamed up. He judged it had been there for some time and it looked as though there was still somebody in it. Or it might be two heads in the driver's seat, a lovers' tryst, a quiet night out on the lochside.

But he was mindful there was somebody there and he wished that Ludwig did not have such a distinctive engine.

Tonight could be the night.

He drove Ludwig into the far corner of the second car park, beyond the café that led to the other exit road. Nobody driving into the main car park would see Ludwig; he would be safely obscured by the dark and by the screen afforded by the single line of trees. He switched the engine off, letting the camper roll forward, closer to the pathway that went up the hill to the viewing point. That was where he needed to be. He lifted his rucksack and climbed out into the driving rain, glancing over his shoulder to see if he could memorize the registration of the other car. But at this time of night, at this distance, he couldn't even make out the plate but the car was of those new fancy Minis with the doors at the back, like his granddad's old Morris Traveller. They had tried to recreate a classic. A car that had been built as cheap transport for the masses had been reinvented as a lifestyle choice of the upwardly mobile professional with deep pockets, no soul and even less imagination.

As Cowan closed the door, he patted Ludwig as if parting with a faithful old horse. He tugged his hood up, pulled the rucksack onto his back and set off through the dark, rainy night up to the viewpoint to find a place to hide.


Valerie lay on the bed in the hotel. The banality of her surroundings leeched every bit of vitality from her.

She had felt the pressure since visiting Abigail's house.

It had left her unsettled, more depressed, but there was some comfort in knowing that this was the last day of her life. The knowledge many of us think we would like to have, but very few are brave enough.

Imagine Abigail not realizing that this was the last time she would stack the dishwasher, Malcolm not thinking that this was the last time he would do his teeth, pull on his Star Wars pyjamas and argue about staying up for another half hour. If they had realized that, they might have spent their final moments doing something less mundane.

Like saying goodbye.

Valerie had spent most of the morning rolling on the floor, lying on the tiles in the bathroom, or being sick down the toilet. Then out to the house before a sneaky foray to the off licence for cheap vodka, the quick consumption of which totally erased any memory of the walk round the house. But tomorrow the empty bottles would be lying in the corner. Silent, but ever present in their condemnation of her.

Well, she wouldn't be here to be condemned.

She lay for a few minutes on top of the bed staring at the ceiling, gradually pulling together the information she needed to place herself in time and space. Judging from the lunatic screeching of revved-up enthusiasm she could hear from the room next door, it was Saturday evening. *X Factor*. Or *Strictly*. Something awful. Anything.

On the ceiling was the familiar smoke alarm, the water sprinkler.

The last day of her life. She had done her duty, she had gone round the house. The feeling was one of overwhelming relief, all was as it should be.

She had a gun.

And a bullet in the chamber.

She turned on her side, pulling the pillow over her head and stared at the bland beige hotel room wall, thinking about the cleaner who was going to open the door to her mess, walking in to the room pulling her Henry hoover behind her then looking up to see a woman with her skull blown apart.

The bullet would do a lot of damage. Valerie knew it wasn't like in the films where the head lay intact, a neat trickle of blood delicately running down a sculptured cheekbone to leave a crimson teardrop on the pristine white sheets. The eyes, each lash point perfect with the mascara, the pupils open and staring into the sunset. Ready for their close up.

No, it wasn't like that at all.

Her head would open up like a flower, blood and brains would spatter all over the room, behind the headboard, behind the curtains. Over the fire alarm. Not pretty.

The crime scene pictures of Balcarres Avenue had been burned onto her retinas. Her sister and her nephew, bloodied and torn flesh entangled. And Abigail, her arms round Malcolm, a final, desperate attempt to protect him.

She would have been fascinated by it if it hadn't been so personal. The whole room was a gaudy abstract of cream and crimson, matching the stained-glass rose on the door.

That was another memory that wasn't going to go away.

She felt the weight of the gun in her hand.

No. She had to time this right, so it wasn't the cleaner who discovered her body.

Archie Walker? Yes, she'd time it so Uncle Archie would find her.

He could explain it to red-lipped Fascist and Beardy dogsbody,

She sat back up, looking at herself as her face passed in the mirror. A haggard young woman stared back out at her, seeming to move slower than she herself moved. A pale face haunted by the loss of her family, the loss of her career. Her loss of self.

Getting up and walking across the floor, she noticed she still had her boots on.

She should pick up the empty bottles of vodka from the carpet.

Why bother? She'd be dead. Oblivion was better than another AA meeting where they looked down at her, because she had lived a dream life. She had had it all. Yet they would stare at her as if she was some stupid addict, like she was one of them.

She pulled the curtains over the window, blocking out the night sky as she tried to remember. Glimpses of being wet, walking down the street, her hand had been sore. She had stumbled against the wall at some point, remembering the stinging pain as she grazed the skin on her palm. She looked at it now, seeing the bloodied scrape, a dark scab starting to form. Was that yesterday? Or this morning? This afternoon?

She had no bloody idea. This was the way of her life. Flashes of this. Glimpses of that. Nothing that ever made any sense. It was like listening to a foreign language, recognizing words here and there but never enough to pull together a sentence, never mind enough sense for it to form a story.

Memory lapse.

And she had no memory of what she was doing the day her sister was murdered.

But she had visited the house. It was over, closed. She could end it all now.

Sitting down on the side of the bed she took her boots off. Nobody committed suicide with their boots on. She wanted to be comfortable, lie down, and not leave the duvet dirty.

Dirtier.

She lay down again. Relaxing. Life owed her nothing except this one thing – this little bit of peace and quiet, save the whipped-up hysteria being broadcast from next door. Picking up the gun, feeling the weight of it in her hand. It was far heavier than she had expected. It smelled of oil, it covered the skin of her hands in something foul.

She wanted her last thoughts to be of Abigail. Of Mary Jane. And of Malcolm. She wanted to remember them as they had been in life. Abigail with her prim, controlled smile. Mary Jane pouting for the camera as every teenager had done for the last twenty years. And Malcolm laughing, both hands holding onto his most prized possession: his Lego Millennium Falcon.

All gone.

Had they all gone to heaven in their little rowing boat?

And what had happened to the Lego Millennium Falcon? It hadn't been at the house; well, she hadn't seen it. She had bought it for Malcolm last Christmas. Good times.

She felt the tears fighting to escape her eyes, but she refused to cry. There was nothing to cry about, not now. She looked back at the water sprinkler and the smoke alarm. Then heard footfall, somebody walking along the hotel corridor passing her door. They walked quickly with the quiet jangle of a key. A car key most likely, as all the rooms in the hotel were card operated, so he, she presumed, was going out to the car park.

Then the footsteps paused. The jangling stopped. Valerie's eyes fixed on the corner of the room, at the door, willing it to open, or not open. It seemed a long time before the feet moved away, going back the way they came. He had forgotten something. She wondered what.

Valerie tightened her grip on the gun, allowed herself a weak smile. Was that going to be her last thought on this earth? What had that man forgotten that was so important he went back for it?

She'd wait until he went away.

She made herself comfortable on the pillow, thinking about pulling it round and using it as a silencer. But it would be better if they all heard. Then they might be careful about who opened the door, especially if her forgetful friend outside happened to recognize a gunshot when he heard one.

She lay back and closed her eyes. The muzzle was cold against her temple, it jiggled around a little, the tremor of her finger round the trigger, the weight of the gun itself was heavy and unstable, holding it made her wrist ache.

She ignored a guffaw of laughter from next door. She said goodbye to the water sprinkler and the smoke alarm.

Valerie Abernethy closed her eyes and pulled the trigger.

Valerie Abernethy heard a click.


Donnie McCaffrey sat in his Mini Clubman on the north-west bank of Loch Lomond, at Inveruglass, alone in his car, slowly steaming up the windows. He was parked right at the waterside, the most obvious place. During the day, even on a cold winter's day, this place was alive and buzzing, but now, on a dark evening, it took on the mystical aura of shape shifters and moving shadows; the subtle movement of the water deceiving the eye into seeing things it had not seen.

Or had it?

There could be anything up here, hiding away from lights and prying eyes. He looked around again, cursing himself for having a good imagination.

Inveruglass car park was hidden by high trees, shrubs, a small signpost on the main shore road pointing to a concealed entrance that led to the observation viewpoint. He had been here a few times with Isla and the boys. A family day out at the waterside, time for a paddle and an ice cream. But now, waiting, he looked around the car park with different eyes. An easy drive to Glasgow. And easy drive up north. An easy place to find. But why here? Once through the thick bank of trees, the narrow entrance opened up to allow access to the small vehicle car park, the café and the lower viewpoint that looked over the metal pontoons and the plinth with its brass map of the water and every one of the fifty-four islands.

He looked at it now through the eyes of a criminal, an obvious entrance and exit, with the smaller secondary route at the rear, accessed through the narrow line of trees, well hidden in this dense dark night.

When he was here before, he had climbed to the upper level of the viewing point with his eldest on his shoulders, sweating his way up to the large wooden sculpture, An Ceann Mor, with its seats and standing areas. He remembered the sign, hanging at an angle, from a single nail, that said barbeques not permitted. The wood underneath was charred to ebony cracks you could see the grass through.

That day the car park had been bustling; tourist coaches stopping for comfort breaks and photo opportunities, boat tours dropping off passengers on the pontoon, bikers meeting for coffee, kids eating ice cream, little old ladies resting their swollen ankles and drivers stretching their legs, but everybody stopped to take in the breathtakingly beautiful sight of the long view of the loch. His middle boy had eaten so much ice cream, he had been sick on the way home. Twice. The new car had been three weeks old. He pressed the button to drop the window a little at the memory of the smell.

But this evening, Inveruglass was as cold and deserted as a Soviet winter. At nine p.m. on the twenty-fifth of November there were no tourists enjoying the view, no lights casting a shadow over the dark and still water. There were no coaches sitting with idling engines, no caravans tucked away behind the trees. The hills were silent against the dark, tumbling sky, and the rain was pissing down as usual, battering on the roof of the Mini where Donnie was trying to listen to 'Stay' by David Bowie, with the melodic shapes of Earl Slick on guitar, sideman par excellence.

He was enjoying himself in an exciting kind of way. He knew he had been early, leaving more time than necessary for his journey up from Glasgow and he was appreciating the solitude and the music. He had been happy to leave Isla muttering about starting her Christmas shopping, sitting there in her PJs with the Argos catalogue open and a worryingly long spreadsheet printed off at the ready. She had got as far as her brother-in-law's yearly subscription for *What Camera* magazine when Donnie's mobile had bleeped. He had read the text and had been intrigued, and a little frisson of excitement had brightened up his Saturday night in front of the TV. Isla hadn't questioned it; she had merely looked up from the spreadsheet and asked, 'Are you going out to work?' then a quick glance at the clock. 'You had better wrap up. It's chucking down out there.'

He had nodded, kissed her on the cheek and left the warmth of the family home, shouting goodbye to the three kids playing quietly upstairs, then closed the door of his three-bedroomed semi and climbed into the Mini; a man with a mission.

McCaffrey looked around him. It was a lovely, lonely site at the north of the loch, deeply inhospitable in this bloody weather. Why here?

Costello would have her reasons.

He checked his phone again, then the clock on the Mini's dashboard. Ten minutes to go, he gave some thought to Christmas; all that cooking, all that potato peeling, Isla's dad.

With a bit of luck, he'd be working.

He was turning that around in his mind when he heard another vehicle, bigger than the small Fiat he was expecting. The air-cooled whirr of an old VW? The oblong shape of a camper was highlighted for a moment as it swung into the car park. Its headlights illuminated the trees and the shrubs that surrounded the café, the arc of brightness shone on the empty shelves and the seats upturned on the tables before being switched off. The vehicle drove behind the line of trees, moving from his sight. McCaffrey looked in the rear-view mirror with professional interest. Was this what he had been summoned to witness? He slid down in the driver's seat, watching as a figure emerged from the bushes, thin and swift, moved quickly, driven by the weather but not furtive. He walked like a young man, an impression added to by long slender legs and bulky jacket. He was holding something in front of him as he walked in plain sight round the windows of the café, into the darkness, then reappeared as an outline on the secluded path up to An Ceann Mor. Then he disappeared.

McCaffrey stayed in the Mini, watching out the rear-view mirror, then twisting in the seat to look through the rear-passenger and then the front-passenger window, but the figure had gone, swallowed by the trees and the darkness of the sky. It was bitter cold and as dark as the devil's armpit, as his mum used to say.

At least the rain was easing. The windows of the car steamed up again. He wished he hadn't had that last cup of coffee. He'd need to brace himself, get out and have a pee in the bushes. And he'd be better doing that before she appeared. He'd need to be quick before his willy froze.

He switched the CD off, wondering about the owner of the campervan. The driver had looked young so McCaffrey's mind turned to drugs and God knew they had enough problems with substance abuse around here and in Balloch and Alexandria. And there had been a spate of killings of the wallabies that inhabited some of the islands on the loch. A couple of weeks ago, the carcass of one poor beast had been spotted by a tour boat. It had been skinned and pegged out on a small patch of sandy beach, a bloodied pink mass for the entire world to see.

That had made the front page of the papers and the drug issue was right in the public eye, now that it was affecting the middle classes and the tourists. And that guy from the camp-ervan had been carrying something. If he was one of the gang killing the wildlife then there would be a small boat ready for him somewhere. The waters of the loch were very dark now.

McCaffrey made a decision, his nagging bladder forgotten. No wallabies were going to be harmed on his watch. He got out the car, pulling up the zip of his jacket before winding the scarf round his neck. He dug his hands deep into his gloves and walked round the back of the Mini, ignoring the bite of the cold wind that scurried in across the water and the reminders from his bladder. It had stopped raining but the chill ate at his muscles. He felt as if he was wearing no clothes at all. He shivered, jogging across the path on to the soft grass and stared into the car park, seeing the distinctive outline of the two-tone Volkswagen camper. When he was a boy, these were the transport of vegetarian peace-loving hippies not animal-torturing psychopaths. He turned, cutting across the other car park to follow the path of the younger man, walking up to An Ceann Mor, the big wooden structure with its bench seats and central walkway was easily visible against the skyline.

Maybe if the wind had been quieter, he might have heard the small van pull into the car park, its headlights out, and the engine off so the vehicle rolled with the lie of the land. If McCaffrey had looked back to check his car, he might have seen the man get out the vehicle, dressed in black, black gloves, black hat pulled low. He might have seen the long slim blade as he too followed the path to up to An Ceann Mor.

Valerie had no idea where she was.

Something rough against her lips, her shoulder numb and her feet very cold, sticking out of her warm cocoon. It seemed she was bound in a cloud of cotton wool; soft and warm, but it bound her all the same. She tried, but couldn't move any of her limbs, or straighten up, or stretch out. She had no hope of getting up on her feet. Her head hurt. Her legs were burning, her thighs sticky with her own urine. And the room was reeking with the dull smell of faecal matter.

That was obvious at least. She had shat herself.

Opening her eyes, she looked across a green field that stretched forever, until it reached a piece of wooden fence, a flat solid white fence. As she allowed her eyes to focus, in the dark that wasn't really dark, she began to make sense of it all.

She had fallen on the floor, rolled off the bed taking her duvet with her. From the feel of it she had hit her head on the way down, probably off the small white bedside table and as she had lain there drunk, as her bladder and bowel had voided.

That wasn't a first.

And then the full horror of it. This was a hotel room, not her home.

Slowly she tried to unwind herself from the duvet, trying not to throw up and add to the mess of the bodily fluids. Another thought stuck her through the maze that passed for her intellect nowadays. If this was in a hotel room then house-keeping would be coming in sooner or later. They couldn't find her like this, in this awful state. Alcoholism is the most private of diseases. It hides in plain sight.

In the end, after about ten minutes of writhing and slow acrobatics, she freed herself and crawled across the carpet on all fours, leaving the duvet, soiled and wet, in a pile near the bottom of the bed.

She got to the door and, holding onto the handle, she pulled herself up on her knees and listened. There was a flash of a memory. Could she recall, vaguely, being here the night before, between the first and second bottle? Doing something like this at some time? She flicked over the plastic sign hanging from the doorknob. On the inside.

Do not disturb.

Not even sober enough to put the sign out.

Still not sober enough to have an accurate memory of it.

From last night or this morning? Or this evening? She opened the door as quickly as possible, peering down the corridor, to the right and to the left before she slid the sign out, the scab on the palm of her hand nipping as she slid it up against the wood to the handle.

She retreated inside the room and tucked herself in the corner of the carpet and the door. She closed her eyes and slid down a little more, her body folding onto the floor.

Her eyes were crusty and jaggy. She picked at her eyelashes with inaccurate fingers, missing the islands of scabs, poking herself in the eye a few times, making her blink. She could sense the solidity of the darkness outside the room now. It was very quiet, much later at night. Maybe midnight. Maybe not. Time was very elastic these days.

Closing her eyes again, she tried to stand, levering herself up between the door and the wall, and then she saw the bed, minus the duvet, with the expanse of rumpled white sheet with dark islands of staining, and in the middle, framed by wrinkles in the Egyptian cotton, lay a small black gun.

A gun.

And then, as she held onto the wall, she remembered.

She couldn't even kill herself properly.

She was a high-functioning alcoholic and had been for years. Her drinking never bothered her, it was life she couldn't really contend with. She had never suffered bad hangovers because she had barely ever sobered up. The constant top-ups gave her strength and kept that black dog from snapping at her too much, kept it from biting at her heels. She drank to be happy. Her drinking had brought her to this misery.

Why did she get a gun that didn't work? What was wrong with her that nothing, nothing ever went right?

She was too tired, and too sore to cry. What was the point? She picked up the gun and slid back down to the floor, her head thumping as she went. Crawling over the carpet, pushing the gun in front of her, she thought how bloody stupid it would be if the gun went off now and blew her leg off, or her arm off or half her face. Or if it went right through her brain, in the front and out the back, leaving her a dribbling incoherent vegetable, a bag on a drip in her arm putting nutrients in as the catheter took the metabolites out to fill another bag. She tapped it along a little more gently, slipped it into her suitcase using the zipped pocket at the side. Then she thought again, and stuck it into her handbag.

Her mobile phone was lying on the floor where she had flung it, so she slithered across the floor towards it. The black screen refused to swipe into life. She hadn't charged it up. Nobody had called her for weeks now, nobody except the police, and lawyers, and they weren't calling Valerie Abernethy the woman. They were calling Valerie Abernethy the victim. Or the suspect. No friends ever called her. No friends had called when Abigail had died. No friends had visited her in the hospital.

Alcoholics do not have friends. They use people so much that friendships wear away, slip away, here with the roses, and gone in the autumn.

It was winter now, the deep, deep winter.

# TWO

Old Salty's Fish and Chip Emporium was busy, and very noisy. Adding to the usual chattering and cutlery commotion was the family at table eight, who were having some birthday Jenga-with-chips competition. The very attractive Australian waitress was judging and the rest of the restaurant were clapping and taking bets.

All except the four men sitting at table nine.

Four men on a table set for five.

They were subdued, three of them picking at their chips with their fingers, the eldest of the four using a fork. Failure has a bitter taste that no amount of cheesecake can sweeten; they ate as if their food was choking them, totally oblivious to the birthday celebrations in the next booth.

The four men; three detectives and a procurator fiscal. It was the first time they had met since the brutal murder of Abigail Haggerty and her son Malcolm six weeks before.

Not something anybody with a human soul should get over quickly.

They had an unspoken pact not to talk about it. That had lasted until the first lull in conversation, between the fish and chips being cleared away and the arrival of the cheesecake. They had exhausted the 'how are the kids doing?' conversation for Gordon Wyngate, and the 'how is Baby Moses doing?' conversation for Anderson.

Archie Walker related the story of walking round the house with Valerie and the missing picture and Lego model. At that point they all tried to avoid talking about Costello when she was the one thing they really did want to talk about; she was their thread of commonality.

It was a puzzle that consumed the detectives, eating away at their core. At the heart of the case was a strange coincidence, which was later revealed not to be so much of a coincidence at all. The Blue Neptune Case and the deaths at the Monkey House, as the tragedy of the Haggertys had become known, were 'intertwined, but legally separate cases' as the fiscal had put it. And the Haggerty case was under the eagle eye of DCI Diane Mathieson. Those sitting around the table, as part of the original team at the Blue Neptune, had been debriefed, welcomed, tolerated and then told in no uncertain terms to 'bugger off and to stop trying to be helpful', according to DI Bannon or 'stop bloody interfering', according to DCI Mathieson.

While they had no reason to meet, none of them had wanted to be the one to call off a date that had been pencilled into the diary for weeks. And they wanted to know about the problem. Costello's empty chair.

DCI Colin Anderson, the blonde detective in the jeans and casual shirt, had had very little to do with the case professionally, but he had a declared personal interest. This personal interest, the discovery of a daughter he never knew he had, automatically precluded him from any further professional connection. And he was becoming aware that it wasn't in his nature to accept that.

Archie Walker, the fiscal, looked to be his immaculately dressed self, but the constant drumming of his fingers, the frequent glances at his watch, betrayed him. He might have been trying to fool himself that all was OK in his world but he was having no luck fooling the three detectives round the table with him. His goddaughter was suspected of murdering her sister and her son. And she had no alibi. No memory. Only now was he discovering the issue of her alcoholism, mostly from reading his online newspapers.

Viktor Mulholland was watchful, keen to enhance his career here. This situation was a mess and he knew Diane Mathieson. He might hear something round this table that he could casually mention to her. Indeed, she was already approaching him, not any of the others, for any information she needed. That might be a simple matter of rank, but Mulholland suspected something more political. Mathieson was a player and Mulholland hadn't quite come to a decision about which team to back. His present career trajectory was on shaky ground.

With Costello gone, and the increased likelihood of Anderson going, the solid peg he had pinned his entire career on was now looking very shoogly indeed. And Mathieson had a reputation as a two-faced wee bitch. Being a cop who investigated cops was bad enough, but her track record was worse than most. She was after Costello for harassment of George Haggerty. And that complaint was justified.

Mulholland didn't like being associated with Anderson's team, not now Complaints were sniffing around, but he didn't enjoy the thought of being exposed in a new team led by a woman with only her own ambition at heart, so he was watching both Anderson and Walker carefully. Both men seemed deep in thoughts that he would like to have access to.

However, Gordon Wyngate was happily eating his cheesecake, aware of the tensions round the table and easy in the knowledge that he would be the one who would unwittingly broach any forbidden subject. So he did. 'When's the trial starting?'

The silence fell like a rock through a cloud.

Wyngate wanted the ground to swallow him, Mulholland merely smiled.

'No date set yet,' said Walker calmly.

'Do you think—' Wyngate stopped as Mulholland accidently stabbed him in the thigh with his fork and interrupted with a question of his own.

'Is Braithwaite still blaming everybody else?'

'Yes, and he has Tomlinson defending. Well, I have heard.' Walker intertwined his fingers and placed his chin on the mound of knuckles.

'You have Valerie's testimony. She survived. You were out with her yesterday, she must be getting more . . .?' asked Anderson, the question had to be asked now.

'Sober? Do you mean will she be fit enough to appear as a coherent witness? Is that what you are asking?' Walker snapped. He was touchy on the subject of the darling goddaughter who had fallen from grace so spectacularly.

'No, that's not what I meant, not at all. I meant, can she stand up to that questioning.'

A roar of excitement went up at the Jenga table.

'She lost her niece, then her sister and her nephew.' The fiscal raised three fingers. 'The three people in the world she was closest to. How do you expect her to be?'

'Archie, I know she'll be in tatters . . .'

'Are you asking if she's stopped drinking?'

'No,' placated Anderson, 'I'm genuinely asking after her welfare. She was half-strangled and left to die in a cupboard, so I'm asking how she's doing.'

'She's doing OK,' answered Walker. 'Sort of.'

'You're her godfather, and that excludes you from having any place in the investigation.'

'And as Mary Jane's father, you can have no place in it either,' snapped Walker.

It wasn't like them to stick the knife in. Wyngate began to find the morsel of cheesecake on his plate mesmerizing as Mulholland slid back in his chair, enjoying this gladiatorial exchange. He found Valerie Abernethy fascinating. A successful young woman who had everything; a career, a Porsche, a £600,000 flat and then threw it all away when she tried to buy a baby. The investigation into her life had revealed a story much more sordid than anyone would have thought. Mulholland thought it had broken Walker. His darling goddaughter was a delusional drunk, and then Mathieson had actioned the investigation into Valerie Abernethy as a viable suspect for the murder of her sister and her nephew. As far as Mulholland knew, the only motive was sibling rivalry; Abigail hadn't fucked up her life quite as much as Valerie had. A thin motive, but they had all known addicts kill for less. Alcohol messed with your thinking, that whole compass of acceptable behaviour was reset to where the next drink was coming from. Mulholland had not voiced the opinion, but it was obvious Valerie being the wielder of the knife solved a few unanswered questions. The lateness of the night yet Abigail opened the door. The neighbour said they had been alive at one a.m. Who else would Abigail take up to the bedroom? Who else would take Malcolm's beloved Millennium Falcon? Who else but the woman who gave it to him? Strange trophy for a killer. There were six stab wounds to the woman, twelve to the boy. The weapon had come from the house, a new set of knives George had bought the month before at Abigail's request. Or so George Haggerty had said. And there was no witness left alive who could say whether Valerie had been in the house that evening.

That was all he knew, common knowledge round the station, there would be a whole other layer they were not privy to.

'God, those two arseholes still think Valerie had something to do with killing her sister.' Walker clapped his hands over his face.

Mulholland looked down, avoiding their eyes.

'Who? Mathieson and Bannon?' clarified Anderson.

'They are a couple of arseholes,' agreed Mulholland, playing along, 'well she is.'

'Too right.'

'But Valerie was in the hospital recovering. Braithwaite had a real go at her,' Mulholland asked, fishing for information, seeing Anderson rub his own neck, remembering.

'Somebody had a real go at her. She has blackouts. Had blackouts,' Walker corrected himself. 'And she was not in the hospital the night of the murders. She'd walked out at the back of seven that night.'

'Yes, I'd heard that rumour,' said Mulholland, a little too readily.

'Why?' asked Wyngate. 'Had she not just been strangled?'

'Yes, but she had recovered from that. There was no brain damage. No damage to her larynx. And she has other issues. It was very stressful for her to be in the hospital and as she needed peace more than she needed medical attention they came to a compromise. She was free to come and go.' Walker pulled a face. 'I wish to god she had stayed in, got herself a rock solid alibi.'

The table fell silent. One by one they looked at the empty chair.

'Diane Mathieson asked me where I thought Costello was. As if I would know,' said Wyngate.

'None of us know. I think we have all that quite clear,' said Walker.

'But you have heard from her?' Anderson wanted confirmation.

'Well, I get an odd text now and then. She asks about Pippa. Nothing else,' he snapped.

'Bloody hell. I knew she'd fallen out with me but I thought

she'd keep in touch even if to tell me what a fair-weather friend I was, if in less polite terms.'

'You thought wrong.' Walker was still spikey.

'What I meant was,' Anderson picked his words carefully, ignoring another cheer from the Jenga table, 'none of us know where she is and she's not one to go anywhere quietly. This meal was planned for five. She was icily polite when she refused the invite. She asked after Moses, said she was glad he was doing well and that I was to keep the baby away from George Haggerty as that man killed his wife and his child. And I was never to forget that.'

'How many times does she need to be told!' snapped Walker. 'She just won't accept the fact that George Haggerty has a cast iron alibi for that morning. They were murdered between four and six; George had left at one and was on the A9. The fact he looked at Costello "funny" at Mary Jane's funeral does not make him a murderer.'

'She told me he looked right at her and clapped his hands,' said Wyngate.

'She told me the same thing,' agreed Mulholland. 'And the "Clapping Song" was on the CD, on repeat, when she walked in and found the bodies.'

'That's the song where they all go to heaven . . .'

'Yes, I know,' said Walker quietly, closing his eyes, summoning some patience. 'I was there, about four feet behind her. Please, can we let it go?'

The table fell quiet as another table burst out laughing at some witticism.

Anderson said, 'I did ask George about it. He's round my house quite a lot these days to see Moses, so we do chat. He says he has no idea what Costello's talking about. He recalls seeing her at the funeral, he might have looked at her. He might have been brushing his hands against each other to keep warm. It was a cold day; he had just come out the crematorium. I was standing right next to him and there was bloody Costello hiding behind a Victorian gravestone like a ferret-faced Goth stalking the dead.'

The image made them smile.

'George Haggerty might not have been everybody's idea of

a perfect husband but he had cared, in his own way. I have seen his distress at the loss of Mary Jane—' Anderson took a deep breath – 'his adopted daughter, and my real daughter. He has been generous to me in that grief while his wife and his son were murdered. He's devastated; he's on some serious medication. And—' Anderson looked at them all one by one – 'he is Moses' grandfather, if not by blood. I am, as the DNA has proved. George has been dignified over that as well. That child was taken from him with little more than a glance at a test tube.' He nodded. 'When the court made that interim judgement, he said "do whatever is best for the boy". And he meant it. I don't think that's the act of a guilty man.'

'Sounds innocent to me,' said Wyngate. As the father of two wee kids, he felt he could judge that.

'And I bet Costello said that was exactly how a guilty man would act,' argued Mulholland.

'How does she think an innocent man should react to the murder of everybody he had loved in his life? Given her past, she should know the answer to that one,' said Walker. 'And there is the small issue of a total lack of evidence. As well as an alibi that can't be broken.'

'You checked?' asked Anderson, surprised.

'Bloody right I did. You?'

'Of course I did. So did Mitchum. I trust that bastard Haggerty as far as—'

'I thought you just said—'

'I know what I said, but that's not what I feel. I know exactly what Costello is going on about. Yeah, I asked around about that alibi. He's watertight. Police Scotland are his alibi. He was caught speeding up the A9. Dad in care home in Port MacDuff, care home phones the house at 1.10 a.m. George leaves after a bit of an argument. He stops on the road and texts the missus, she calls back. That all maps out. The mobile phone is where it should be. And then, thirty minutes later, he gets stopped by the traffic police. But Costello is . . . Well, George Haggerty is an itch she can't reach to scratch.' Anderson opened his palms, grasping for the right phrase. 'She's obsessed by him.' He caught Walker's eye, a shared thought that neither of them voiced. What the hell was she up to?

The Jenga tower at the corner table of Old Salty's got higher, somebody was clapping their hands together in delight.

*Clap Clap.*

'Have you and George really bonded over Baby Moses?' asked Walker.

'Well, Moses has Down's Syndrome, he's three months old. His mother sold him, the broker rejected him, his mother was murdered and he was abandoned in a stranger's car. I think the wee guy needs all the family he can get. He's great.' His voice was full of pride.

It was obvious to the others that while Colin Anderson and George Haggerty had indeed bonded over their loss, their relationship would fracture the friendship of Anderson and Costello. It explained her absence from the table.

'You can understand Costello being bitter. I'm bitter. I've known Abigail all my life,' said Walker. 'She would have loved Moses, if she had ever been allowed to know she had a grandson.'

*Same way I'd have loved my daughter if I had been allowed to know she existed*, thought Anderson, *but we don't make the rules.*

Anderson recalled the crime scene photographs, Abigail's arms wound tight round her son's body, just as she would have protected her, his own daughter, Mary Jane. She would have felt the same about her grandson.

Mulholland waved a sticky finger in the fiscal's direction. 'You have known the Haggertys all your life, and you accept that George is innocent.'

'I accept his alibi,' corrected Walker, carefully.

'And Colin, you share a grandchild with the guy, you know him, and you think he's innocent. Why the hell does Costello think she knows better?'

'Bloody female intuition,' said Anderson dryly, 'seemingly that trumps small things like evidence and cast iron alibis.'

'Well, she'll have to toe the line when she finally deigns to return to work, when she gets on with cases she's actually paid to investigate, not go off on a whim of her own. Yeah, a few days back and we'll sort her out.' Mulholland gave Wyngate an exaggerated nod, and got one in return.

Colin Anderson put his hands on the table then took a sip of his pint. Something about his manner, his quietness, cast unease over the rest of the table. 'She's resigned.'

'Fuck!'

'She what?'

Anderson looked at Walker, and gave him a slight shake of the head. 'Sorry Archie, I didn't know if you knew. She resigned on Friday the tenth. She wound up Haggerty at Mary Jane's funeral on the Friday, then spent all weekend asking you, me and the Baby Jesus for help. Then she hangs about Haggerty's house and he files a complaint for harassment. She gets short shrift and resigns, not wanting to be hampered by the legal restrictions of Police Scotland.'

'Resigned? Really? Resigned and didn't tell me.' The fiscal's face was etched with disbelief, that slowly morphed into hurt.

'She didn't tell me either,' said Anderson, 'I was told "formally".'

'Bitch,' muttered Walker.

'Stupid bitch,' added Mulholland.

'Brave though, that takes some balls.' Wyngate raised his glass, they toasted her.

'To Costello's balls,' said Mulholland.

The mother of the family in the next booth turned to give them a dirty look. The chip tower of Jenga collapsed.

A tourist bus crawled past, part of a new Explore Scotland initiative; Glasgow at midnight, on a bitter cold November Sunday; the open-topped upper deck was empty apart from the two drunks leaning off the back of the bus singing a song about where to shove your granny. The downstairs of the double decker was steamed up. Anybody in there would see nothing but glazed lights and a dense smirr of rain, which was probably just as well.

'I do worry about Valerie, she wasn't exactly stable before the murders. Something I have only become aware of in hindsight.'

'She was married though, so there was a somebody once?'

'He left her because of her drink, I know that. Now. She was like a robot walking round the house on Balcarres Avenue, no tears, no emotion. It all seemed too much trouble for her. Talking about a picture that was missing, where was the Lego model she had built at Christmas? Was George going to sell the house?'

'You know murder transforms those it touches. Valerie's not immune because she's part of the judicial system, she has lost everybody,' argued Anderson.

'I don't even think she sees George now.' Walker glanced at his watch, 'I suppose I should go and visit her. She's staying at the Jury's.'

'Really? It's very nearly midnight.'

'Alcoholics don't sleep, recovering ones sleep even less. And she's in a hotel because she's skint. She sold her flat to try to buy a baby, remember.'

Archie Walker wasn't ready to sleep and he wanted to clear his head. It was only a twenty-minute walk from Byres Road to the hotel where Valerie had been living for the last three weeks. She'd be awake. Insomnia was one of the reasons she had reached for the bottle. He'd get there and phone her. If she answered, fair enough, if not he'd walk on to his own house which was another ten minutes along Great Western Road.

It was one of his conditions to get her to stop drinking. He would pop in with no advance warning, and she had better be sober. So far, for him, it was fifty fifty.

As he watched the steady rain, the glow of the traffic lights, he wondered about her memory lapses, and the nagging doubt at the back of his mind. Valerie was a fiscal, she had been a talented prosecutor in court, fierce when she was at the top of her game. Would she know how to commit a perfect murder?

Since the incident at the Blue Neptune, Abigail had said Valerie could stay at her house, but Valerie said she had not been there, or if she had, she couldn't recall it. If she had been there, she was drunk and nobody else left alive could bear witness to what had happened. Valerie had been in the house on the eleventh of October, three days before the murders. Her prints had a right to be there. And the perpetrator had taken their time in the house, they had known the house, known the victims.

And in Mathieson's view, a fiscal would be well placed to do that, but whoever had committed that atrocity, had a clear and precise thought process. Not the Valerie that he now knew, the one who crawled around the floor, too pissed to stand up.

He watched two young women, giggling as they got off the bus, deciding walking would be quicker than waiting on the late-night traffic through Queen Margaret Drive clearing. Their laughter made him think of how Valerie had been his favourite, the quiet thoughtful one. Abigail was the loving wee girl then, a normal happy child, mischievous and playful, a free spirit. She was fun to be around.

Anderson nudged him. 'Now we are on our own, tell me, do you think she did it?'

'Nope, she'd have been so pissed she wouldn't have cleaned up, it was a cool methodical mind committed that crime.'

'OK, does she share Costello's suspicions of her own brother-in-law?'

'Valerie is the one with no alibi, not George.'

'Answer the question Archie.'

'Yes, she does.'

'Come on, let's walk up to Oran Mor,' Anderson suggested; it was too cold to stand still. 'So what was Abigail like?'

'I was just thinking that. She was happy. A GP, bright. She was happy then Oscar, her first husband, was killed in an accident, boating, I think. Car? No, drowning. She ended up going to court to get him declared dead.'

'That takes ages, seven years?'

'Indeed. Mary Jane was about six or seven at the time he went missing.'

'They seem to be a very unlucky family,' said Anderson thoughtfully, standing at the kerb, waiting to cross Byres Road. 'But I do see Costello's point that no family can be that unlucky, which suggests it was nothing to do with a lack of luck.'

'Maybe that's not true, maybe in a roundabout kind of way everything is linked.'

'A butterfly flaps its wings in Columbia and the number twenty-seven bus gets diverted through Clydebank? That kind of thing? Come on, let's cross.' They both jogged across the road, cutting between the four lanes. 'It's not a small world when the fish swim in the same small circles. I still don't

understand why Sally never told me she was pregnant. I'd
have stood by her. I'd have wanted to know Mary Jane.'

'Maybe she didn't know the baby was yours. Or she did
and didn't want you to know. She was with Braithwaite at the
time and we know what a psycho he turned out to be. Maybe
it was self-preservation.'

Despite the tragic ending to the situation, Anderson smiled.
'It was a drunken night in the park when her bloody boyfriend
had buggered off elsewhere. So yeah, not proud of it, but we
were young and, maybe not in love but in lust at least.'

'Well, there you go then, at least you are human.' Walker
stopped to put a pound in the box of a homeless person.
Anderson patted the Staffie cross that was snuggled under the
blanket and gave him two of Nesbit's treats. They walked on.
'I've been thinking,' proclaimed Walker.

'Be careful,' cautioned Anderson. 'You're a lawyer, it's
against your religion to think without getting paid by the hour.'

They walked on, up to Oran Mor, watching the remnants of
the rain fall as orange and golden tears, catching the glare
of the street lamps and the headlights of the traffic waiting at
the Queen Margaret Drive junction.

Walker spoke with a sigh, 'I really do need to go and see
Valerie, I'm feeling guilty. I think she's hiding from me. She
thinks that she has let me down, again. Especially at the house.
She could barely be bothered to put a comb through her hair,
or wash her face.' He shook his head, being as perjink and
neat as he was, this was a heinous offence. 'Maybe she became
a lawyer for all the wrong reasons. Who can cope with months
and months of working on child abuse cases when she was
yearning for a child she couldn't have. I'm her godfather. I'm
supposed to look after her spiritual welfare, so I buggered that
up good and proper.'

'She buggered it up herself. At one point, Valerie was on a
good career ladder if she was already in charge of a unit in
Edinburgh. She was doing OK. At one point,' Anderson repeated.

'She was, at least until . . . until her marriage broke up,
until she realized that she was going to have difficulty having
kids. Then she began to drink. It was the pressure of the job,
the pressure of going through every test in the book, with a

husband that thought it was all too much bother. Grieg, her husband, had more of a *que sera sera* view on the subject. I'd like to think if I had a fiscal in my office with failed IVF behind her, I'd have the sensitivity to transfer her away from a child abuse unit. I saw her falling apart, I tried to intervene, talk to her boss to get her moved, but they wouldn't do it unless she asked, and rightly so . . . well, I thought that was a shit decision. It had to come from her, but she was far too proud to say that she couldn't cope.'

'She was very well thought of at her job, and she's still young. She'll get back to it, once all this calms down. She'll get back on track, just needs a bit of time, a bit of support to get off the sauce.'

'I don't think I can be bothered with her nonsense tonight.' He sighed. 'Is George really round your house a lot?'

'Too much for my liking,' answered Anderson truthfully. 'At times I like him, other times he gives me the creeps. He walks about my house, he drinks tea with my wife, he cuddles my grandchild; the child of a girl he adopted so I can't deny him that, can I? Mary Jane was in his life for twenty years. I never met the girl, and then I waltz in and take the only surviving relative George has and claim him as my own. By rights that child belongs to him.'

'You need to think practically, you have a house, a wife, a bank account that can support it all, George Haggerty is bereaved mess, he lives here and in Port MacDuff, two hundred and fifty miles apart. He shuttles back and forth. Not exactly stable. I think you are doing the right thing, I don't know that I could do it.'

They stopped at the corner outside Oran Mor, beside the bus stop, a couple of Jack Russell terriers crossed the road, their double lead tied to the handles of a bike with no lights ridden by a Chinese student. She nodded at them in acknowledgement for clearing the path for her. 'Yet a woman whose judgement we both trust believes this so much she has resigned from her job.' Anderson smirked. 'Mitchum said that she told him to take a running fuck?'

Walker smiled.

'Does she say much in the texts?'

'It's all very civilized.' He pulled out his phone. 'She never told me that she has resigned though. I guess she thought I would talk her out of it.'

'Do you know what she's up to?'

'Nope, but I presume she's after Haggerty.'

'Do you think she's going to do anything stupid?'

'Yes.'

'So do I.'

Wilma Patrick laid down her knitting and fumbled for the remote before that dreadful reality TV show started, the one where the 'stars', who had spent their youth at the best public schools in England, couldn't string a coherent sentence together. Wilma had retired for health reasons having taught primary pupils for over thirty years, nothing wrong with a bit of ABC and 123 before they started all that vertical learning and companion studies nonsense. She had taken her package before she said something she really meant during a meeting. She blamed Alastair of course. Being married to him always gave her a different perspective on life. And the lack of it.

The remote had slipped from the arm of the wheelchair and had disappeared under her ample buttocks. She wriggled around and poked under the cushion, before shaking out her knitting. The remote went flying across the floor. It spun round and spilled its batteries under the dog basket.

Hamish the Scottish terrier opened one eye, judged there was no food involved in this disruption and wasn't for moving, so Wilma wheeled over and turned the channels over on the Sky box, poking the button with her knitting needle. There was a new Scandi drama starting on Channel 4 that she wanted to see. She had perfected the art of reading subtitles and knitting a complicated Fair Isle pattern simultaneously.

She reversed herself back to the sofa. The programme was starting in less than five minutes so she'd wait until the first advert break before she shouted at Alastair to put the kettle on. He always spent a Sunday night doing his guitar homework, though why, she had no idea as he had a tin ear. He had to stop the singing lessons when he made Hamish howl, so he had taken up the guitar now. It was no more tuneful but it was quieter. Wilma understood it was therapeutic for him to plunk away.

The programme started and she settled back. A young girl, in her early twenties, was walking through a field of corn in the windblown rain. She had the obligatory Nordic jumper on, her red hair and high cheekbones gave her the look of that young constable Morna Taverner. The jumper and the actress were being soaked by the rain, and would probably catch the death of cold, thought Wilma. But, knowing these dramas, the girl would be dead by the first advert break anyway. She knitted on, with one eye on her needles and the growing tapestry of colour spilling across her lap, the other on the screen. The girl was running now, her arms pumping. There was no music, only the sound of her ragged breathing, and heavy footfall. She was running for her life, obviously. Wilma counted her stitches, and listened to the rain battering on the living-room window. The noise deafening, then quiet as the wind changed direction. The weather had been foul all week. The Portree – Port MacDuff ferry had been off more often than it had been on. She turned her attention back to the television where a man was now watching the running girl. She was still in a cornfield. He was in a car, a Volvo of course, watching her through the raindrops on the windscreen. The wipers went back and forth, clearing both his and the viewer's vision of her running away with her wet red hair straggling after her. She was an elusive figure between the sweeps of the wipers. Each time she reappeared she was further away. She might just make it. The girl was obviously running away from him, terror filled, not caring where she went, not looking back. She did the obligatory stumble as she ran, her arms wind-milling to stop her falling. There was music now, helping the drama along. The man stayed in his car, watching as the camera angle swept in so it was right on the girl's shoulders, as if the audience themselves were chasing her down.

Wilma liked that effect, she had to resist looking over her own shoulder. She settled for a shiver.

The girl looked behind her, her small heart-shaped face stared right into the camera. The corn parted, swallowing her. She turned and ran straight into the arms of a big man.

There was a bang. Wilma jumped. Hamish woke up, ears alert. The screen went black and silent as the opening credits rolled and the image on the screen changed to a fat detective sitting in his office, swinging on his chair, drinking a cup of cold coffee. It always was in these dramas, they never had time to eat and they never went to the toilet. Wilma went back to her knitting, realizing she had dropped stitches, and tutting, unravelled it.

The scene with the detective moved on with no sound. The storm fell quiet allowing the sound of the guitar to float down, a few ragged chords, a song that got so far and then got stuck. It resumed but floundered at the same point. The detective on the TV started shouting down his telephone in Swedish. Or Danish. Or something. The music stopped again. This time it got far enough for her to recognize the song; one of Simon and Garfunkel's lesser known ones, the one about Emily. It wasn't one of her favourites, but Alastair had always had a fondness for it.

The scene on the TV returned to the cornfield. Filmed from a bird's-eye view that rose until the body of the girl appeared, lying in a small flattened area of corn, as if she was in a nest, comfortable and asleep. A few dots circled round her, policemen like vultures. The girl lay in the middle, a tiny spindle in a big spinning wheel.

Then the camera plummeted down like a hawk on its prey, crashing into the dead girl's eye, into the blackness and emptiness of one single pupil.

Wilma went back to her knitting as the investigation got underway. In forty-five minutes all would be well.

She heard another bang and looked up. Hamish growled at the front door, she thought she could hear the low rumble of a diesel engine. A car coming up the street, then doing a U-turn, there was a flash of headlamps and a squeal of brakes.

The music from the TV got louder, more dramatic.

She heard another bang, this time she knew it was the front door. She thought about ignoring it but that had been twice now. Maybe three times. She checked the clock; it was nearly midnight. Putting her knitting to one side, she wheeled to the window, pulling back her winter curtains by a fraction of an

inch to look out into the bitter night. She saw a Land Rover
bumped up on the pavement and flinched when she caught
sight of the man, dressed in black, barely visible, standing in
her front garden. He gestured that he wanted the front door
opened. Now.

She let the curtain roll back, tensed in her chair, gripping the
wheels, suddenly feeling like the girl running through the corn.
Her husband got the awkward chord change and the tuneless
song went on.

Jo and Walter had walked the same route every Sunday, around
midnight, except when on holiday and the twelve weeks when
Jo was off with her new hip. They sauntered mostly together,
side by side, chatting and watchful. They looked like any other
old couple, maybe a bit incongruous out on the streets of
Glasgow in the witching hour; Walter with his thick anorak
zipped up to his neck, a scarf tucked in to keep out the chill.
Jo wore a navy blue coat that nearly reached her ankles but
it did keep the cold away from her hips. Their faith and their
uniform were both worn quietly, their belief more obvious in
their compassion.

Over the years they knew who was on the street, who would
be in what doorway, who might need feeding, who might
kick-off, who was new and who might be saved in the Lord's
eyes. Nobody was beyond redemption. But mostly, they sought
out those who might be in need of a kind word and a bowl
of soup, if not the loaves and fishes of the Lord himself.
Though, they both hoped, that would come later.

Big Smout McLaughlin sometimes joined them. He was an
enigma of Glasgow city centre. Tall, thin with chiselled
features, articulate and well educated. They wondered, but
never asked, why he chose to sleep in an alley at the back of
the sheriff court. Sometimes he would come to the soup kitchen
with a young one in tow, showing them there was always
someplace to go if it got too scary out on the street. Smout
McLaughlin had only ever stayed in the night shelter himself
once in the twenty years he had been living rough and that
was because of a vile chest infection. Jo reckoned he had
somewhere to go when he needed, a safe haven tucked in his

back pocket somewhere. To Jo, the maths were simple. People didn't last twenty years on the streets of Glasgow; pneumonia, sepsis or more recently TB would take their toll. All on the backdrop of the chilling wind and the damp, damp air that picked off the weak.

On this bitter November evening Jo and Walter were heading east from George Square. They had walked the concourse of Queen Street train station, had a word with the transport police. All was good. Next stop was Buchanan Street bus station, the first stop for many of the throwaways and runaways finding refuge in the cold, hard streets of Glasgow, or as their overnight stop on the way down south, to the colder, harder streets of London.

Walter adjusted the holdall he carried over his shoulder. It wasn't heavy, just bulky. It contained a couple of clean blankets and about ten pairs of warm woolly socks. They were heading, vaguely, for a young lad living in a box outside the side door of the bus station. Until recently he had been overnighting on the ground floor of the multi-storey. That was highly prized territory in the depth of the winter. Last week, the boy had his cardboard boxes back out on the street, tucked underneath the overhang of the station roof. And he had a bruised, bloodied face and a red socket where a front tooth used to be.

Tonight they found him, nestled into his fleece against his flattened cardboard. It was three degrees outside, the boy didn't have a pick on him. They woke him with a gentle prod, knowing that he would lash out before realizing they were handing him a blanket. Then they gave him the socks, Walter handing them over one at a time trying to make some kind of human, and humane contact, letting the eye connection last as long as possible.

The boy had woken up, flinching, his fist up ready but he didn't pull away. Seeing the socks, he immediately kicked off his dirty soaking trainers, one toe pushing off the heel of the other. Even in the stink of the human waste in the alley, Jo could smell the stench of the boy's feet from here. His toes were translucent grey, the skin round his toenails white and wrinkled, fisherwoman toes. There were deep dark tramlines where the seams of the socks had put pressure on the skin. She thought she could see the red puncture marks through the dirt in between the toes, but it was dark except for the overspill of lights from the concourse; maybe she was seeing what she expected to see. It wasn't her place to judge. The boy pulled on a pair of fresh socks, then placed his foot on the ground, soaking the dry sock, then pulled on his trainers.

Walter was talking to him, taking a good look, thinking that he was in his late teens at the most. Jo stood back, pretending to give him space and remain unthreatening, but really keeping clear of the dreadful smell. Walter's voice, friendly but not overly so, was telling the boy how close the soup kitchen was if he wanted something to eat, giving him rough, brief directions, before adding, if he couldn't manage they did have a van and could collect him. The boy was ignoring him, going anywhere meant giving up his space under the overhang. He was too busy stuffing the other two pairs of dry socks into his pockets and down his trousers. They were a prize and he didn't want them taken from him by unseen eyes watching from the dark.

Walter asked him if there was anything they could do for him. The boy looked blank. Even if he didn't speak a word of English, as increasingly was the case, there tended to be some response. Those in the clutches of heroin tended 'to roll' as Walter put it. Cocaine addicts rarely stayed still enough to fall asleep but this boy gave a resentful closed look before he went back to his business with the socks, pulling back the cardboard bed into the shelter of the overhanging roof. Two sheets had worked their way out from the wall a few inches and were swelling with the rain.

The look was more than Walter had got the last time, and an inch was better than a mile in the right direction. A look, then a word, then a smile, then he would be looking out for Jo and Walter to come walking along the street. Then a conversation and information. Then the boy was not that far from being saved from the streets and hopefully safe in the arms of Jesus.

Jo and Walter walked away, saying goodbye, wishing the boy would shout at them to come back but he didn't. Not this time.

Their next stop was usually The Heilandman's Umbrella, a section of Argyle Street under the raised tracks of the railway.

The shops and pubs were busy with shoppers during the day and clubbers out on the bevvy at night, and with the homeless and the lawless in the small hours. They preferred to get covered in pigeon shit rather than the constant Glasgow rain. Jo and Walter had turned into Buchannan Street precinct when Smout appeared, out of nowhere. This time he had a saxophone as well as his rucksack, obviously been doing some busking.

'How are you doing my friends, still doing the good work of the Lord?'

'While there remains good work to be done? Of course.'

It was a familiar exchange.

Their conversation was light hearted; Smout was not a lamb looking for a shepherd. He was more a collie looking after his flock.

He fell into stride with them both. 'There's a new one you might want to talk to, she's hanging about the bottom of the Buchanan Galleries. Been there all evening, confused. Older, definitely older and somebody has had a go at her already. And drunk, can't get a word out of her, you'll know by the smell, Eau De Thunderbird. See ya.' And he nodded, slapping Jo gently on her back, walking his jaunty walk into the darkness of Dundas Lane where he melted to invisibility, the smirr of rain swallowing him.

Walter consulted his watch and looked up as the rain started coming down in stair rods, jagged spears of orange in the streetlight, a night bus crawled its way round Nelson Mandela place, windows steamed up, engine groaning slightly.

'Shall we?' asked Walter.

Jo nodded. There was only one thing more vulnerable than the young on the streets of a big city. The elderly.

Ten minutes later Jo and Walter found the woman huddled into the corner of the steps of the concert hall. Her dark blue jacket had the hood up over her head and pulled tight round her face in an attempt to keep the world out. It was Jo who approached this time, even from a distance she could smell the alcohol but as she got closer she could see the blood on the side of her cheek, dried in a leaf-like pattern. The woman looked up, then when she saw Jo looking at her hands, she looked down at them also.

Jo approached as if she was a frightened animal. It could be a mental health issue, she needed to be careful. Human bites could be very dangerous. She knew that. But the older woman stayed calm, staring at some point lying in the middle distance.

Jo tried a few opening lines: 'Would you like a blanket? Something to eat? A bed for the night? Someone to talk to?'

There was no response at all. But she didn't react adversely and Jo placed her hand on the woman's shoulder. Soaking wet. That jacket was giving her no protection from the rain. Jo turned and shrugged to Walter who pulled out his mobile phone and called the community police as Jo got a blanket from the bag and placed it round the woman's shoulders. The woman, maybe not so old now, had looked up, vague recognition in her eyes as she reached out, her bony fingers moving in the air, edging their way to the badge and the black epaulettes on Jo's uniform.

And with a trembling finger, she pointed.

Wilma sat at the doorway, the warm living room behind her; the hall had taken on the chill of the November air. She had called for Alastair but he hadn't heard. She opened the door.

There were three of them, all dressed alike. One nodded to her and invited himself in.

He said one word. 'Tonka?'

Another stood back watching the street, one hand holding a large torch, the other deep in his parka pocket. The man in the doorway pressed closer, his hands crossed in front of him, peering over her shoulders up the stairs, then followed his colleague up, giving her a nod in passing.

Twenty years of peace and quiet, away from the madness, and here they were knocking on her door at midnight. She'd had her mouth open ready to protest, to ask them who they were, exactly. But she had known, known from the minute she saw them. No point in asking these men for I.D., that was the last thing they would have given.

She tried to tell them there was nobody living here of that name, no Tonka. It was a forlorn feeble attempt, her words spoken to their backs as they went up her stairs, silent muddy boots on her lovely new stair carpet. She could have wept.

They knew who they wanted, and they knew he was here. Another two men came inside and closed the door, dwarfing her and the cottage in their bulky dark blue and black jackets. Small men, in their thirties she guessed, young enough to be her boys. Hard faces, wide shoulders, alert and light on their heavy feet.

'Evening missus. Sit quiet and we'll be out of here double quick.'

Glaswegian accent. They usually were these people; Glaswegians were violent, any excuse. The guitar fell silent on a protesting chord. She waited, staring up the stairs.

Wilma had known that this day would come, shattering life's illusion like glass. It was a relief. There was nothing like waiting for that knock that never came. She kept to one side, her chair against the living-room door, but never taking her eyes off the top of the stairs where she could see a sliver of the man's body through the spindles of the bannister as he spoke softly, a quiet monologue. She heard Hamish whimper on the other side of the living-room door as if he also knew. She was still watching as the men came back down the stairs, moving at speed. They both nodded to Wilma as they passed, avoiding her eyes and they went straight out the door, leaving Wilma, in her chair, impotent in the possession of her own house. She watched them disappear into the black night, the dark wind swallowing them. She didn't hear the doors of the Land Rover open or close. Just the gentle pit pat of her husband coming down the stairs, carrying what he called his ready pack from the top of the wardrobe. He took his boots from under the stair, his jacket and his scarf from the hall stand. He didn't say a word to her or look in her direction in case he read it in her eyes.

*Don't.*

She looked into the ebony night, her eyes catching the twitch of the curtains across the lane as the neighbours had a quick look. She sat there alone and stunned as the Land Rover tail lights retreated and then vanished from her view as the vehicle turned the corner, hearing the engine accelerate hard, then there was nothing but the rattle of the rain and the howl of the wind.

*      *      *

The woman had said nothing on her way to the hospital, sitting in the back of the police car with ease and a degree of comfort, as if the journey did not faze her or she had absolutely no understanding of what was going on. The two cops who had picked her up, Turner and Whitely, had tried a few opening gambits about the weather and how it was far too cold to be sitting on a stone step at this time of year.

Silence.

Trying for a bit of chit chat, Turner asked her if she was hungry because they were passing ASDA and they could pop in for steak bake. Much to their disappointment she remained quiet, so they drove on.

She looked out the window, watching the nightlife of Glasgow float past; through the Clyde Tunnel, her eyes became wild and frightened. The blood was still steadily dripping from her head. Every so often she would fist it away, then rub the blood onto her anorak. Then look at the anorak as if she had never seen it before in her life.

At the desk in Accident and Emergency, Turner gave the details of where they had found her, and that they had no identification. He pointed to the blood on the side and the back of her head and to the overpowering stink of alcohol, both he felt being relevant to her story. He confirmed, in response to the receptionist's questioning eyebrow, that as yet there had been no reports of any missing person in the system who resembled this woman, and repeated that she had no ID on her, but they had only checked her outer pockets.

'I'll leave it to you lot to get her undressed and have a more thorough look. She's still bleeding.'

'No phone? No credit cards?' asked the receptionist, battering at the keyboard while her eyes flicked between Turner and the blonde woman. 'She OK?'

'Head wound,' Turner confirmed needlessly, then added that the patient was perfectly compliant, and seemed fully conscious. But wasn't talking.

'Can she walk OK?' The receptionist nodded towards the doors to the treatment area. 'Or do you want a chair?'

'She's a bit unsteady but she'll get through there. We'll stay until she gets sorted out. Is your coffee machine still on the blink?'

The receptionist pulled a sheet of A4 out the printer. 'Take that through with you and if you smile very, very sweetly, some nice nurse might stick the kettle on for you.' She gave them a huge grin that took sarcasm to an Olympic level. 'Make sure you've signed all your paperwork before you go. All of it, mind. And can you take that through with you,' and she opened the glass partition to shove a huge file into his hand. 'Dr Russell is wanting it. Well, somebody is.' The glass partition fell shut.

The two cops waited for the receptionist to press the green button and the door to the treatment area clicked open.

'Oh, hello you two. Three.' The nurse, her uniform straining to contain her ample figure, turned to the woman who was standing between the two cops like a young child, slightly nervous and waiting to be told what to do. The nurse looked at the slow trickle of blood meandering down the woman's forehead. 'Come on, sweetheart, I'm Hannah, let's get you through and find out what's been going on.' She placed a cupped hand under the elbow of the woman, easing her through the second set of double doors to the receiving and assessment unit. The woman paused for a moment and turned, as if reluctant to leave the two policemen behind.

'It's OK,' said Turner, 'go with Hannah, she will look after you. And while you are in there, we'll get a wee cup of tea.' Turner thought he saw a flicker of a smile in the woman's face.

'You know, pet,' said the nurse, 'they'll be lucky, getting a cuppa in here. Now you come with me, you'll be fine.' And they both were consumed by the blue curtains of an empty cubicle.

'What do you think?' Whitely asked. 'Domestic?'

'Could be. She stinks of booze. She could have fallen and hit her head and got concussion. She's developing that panda-eyed thing, so she's bleeding somewhere. Might be nothing in it for us but it's bloody freezing out there and nice and cosy in here so don't be so quick to get going.'

Whitely sat down beside him. 'Do you think we should see it through to the bitter end?'

'Oh yes. She's had head trauma.' Turner stood up to retrieve his notebook from his jacket and sat down, got comfy and started to write it up. Despite his levity, it troubled him a little. The woman was confused, non-vocal and had a nasty head wound that, weirdly, looked clean. Had she already received medical attention? Had she gone voluntarily? Had she had the wound cleaned and then a deeper bleed, some unseen damage now leaking into her brain that was causing a slow reduction in function? He had been a beat copper for twenty years and had seen everything, been bitten, spat at, punched, nearly stabbed a few times. Compliance like that was odd. She was quite at home in the police car, she smelled of alcohol but her eyes were straight and seemed to focus OK. And, apart from the blood, she was clean, well dressed; some attempt had been made to brush her hair, so most likely somebody somewhere was missing her. He radioed back to the station checking that no more reports had come up on the missing persons, reading out his initial description: sixty-year old female, blonde, grey-eyed, slim, five four . . . But that was all he knew.

The station checked the log, the number of people who went missing each day was incredible. The percentage who disappeared was growing as well, if people wanted to go, they would go.

They had one report that might fit. A Peter Gibson of Lochmaben Road in Crookston had phoned in to say that he had spotted a woman sitting on one of the benches at the perimeter of the small park known locally as the Tubs. She was wearing grey trousers, a long black jacket, white blouse. He guessed she was about sixty. Gibson had approached her, thinking that her clothes were not warm enough for this time of year and that she must be disturbed. Or drunk. Or drugged. Gibson had seen the blood on the white of her blouse and called 999. When the cops got there, she had run off.

Turner read the description again. Right age, wrong clothes. Not their woman.

# THREE

Alastair Patrick did not say much to the three men. They said nothing to him; he was a package for delivery. A few curt words passed between them. Tonka cleared his dry throat.

*How far?*

*A few klicks.*

*Where?*

*You'll see.*

They were following orders. They didn't know any more than they were saying. They were being polite and they didn't have to be. They were tooled. Alastair Patrick had noticed the guns in the quick dash from the front door of his house to the vehicle. It was important to notice these things, the sort of things that made only stupid men argue. Even in the noise of the wind, he had clocked the thrum of the 2.5 diesel engine; he'd been struck by the dull reflection of the street lamp from the resin composite shell of the vehicle. He saw the protection over the front grille and the lights, the lack of number plate. Christ, it even had a snorkel.

A snorkel.

He almost smirked as he climbed in. Boys and toys.

It was black beyond dark once the vehicle pulled out of the street. Rain poured down making visibility difficult even in the bright glare of the Land Rover's headlights, the rapid thumping of the wipers on full throttle filled the vehicle. Once out of Port MacDuff, they were winding their way along the single track road to Applecross, the driver switched on the roof-mounted spotlights to aid visibility. He drove quickly, skilfully. His position was relaxed and comfortable, not leaning forward to peer through the windscreen. The demister set on screen roaring loudly, the Landie banging and heaving like a boat.

This guy, the Glaswegian, was a professional. He knew exactly where he was going. He drove with confidence as if he had driven this road before, many times in darkness.

Patrick knew they were skirting the coast, even with the blacked-out windows in the back of the Landie. As the vehicle swung round, he could see the sea out the front window, the sweeping beam of the Rua Reidh lighthouse between the swish thump of the windscreen wipers. He began to have suspicions as to where they might be going, and why, but he tried to dismiss the thought. Surely not even these three, the Glaswegian and his two gorillas, would be that stupid.

Patrick felt a tremor of controlled fear run down his spine, images darting across his eyes, ball bearings flashing past in strobing light. A sledgehammer thumped in his heart at the intense memory of his mate Zorba, caught between the crags, screaming at his missing legs. Patrick blinked the image away, wiping his lips with the back of a gloved hand, removing a telltale smir of nervous sweat. Never show them that you are scared, once they know that, they own you. Some things don't change. Even now, helpless, he couldn't help planning how to take them. Some things, like old habits, die hard. And he believed that he also, would die hard.

He hoped it wasn't tonight.

He looked ahead, examining the back of the men's heads. Identical thick necks, short haircuts, the dark blue and black jackets invisible in the hours of darkness, the pattern varied to disturb any outlines. Their woollen hats were pulled down, the rim tucked up. Rolled out, their faces would be covered, save for two round holes at the eyes.

As they turned inland, Patrick tried to work out what to do as the windscreen wipers battered across the toughened glass. He wondered how the Glaswegian could see where he was going, even with all the extra light that dazzled on the tarmac in front of them making spotlights dance on the road as rocks swerved, slid past and then vanished to darkness. The Landie occasionally bumping slightly as it impacted something unseen.

He looked at his watch. It was half one. Zero One Thirty Hours.

Instinct, training, made Patrick strap himself in tighter as the vehicle really began to bounce around with more force, the driver taking out the corners of the twisty road, moving faster than was safe. He tried to take in as many details as possible. He was sure he didn't know any of the three men. The Glaswegian, his Gorillas, the brains and the brawn, but he knew the type.

Holding on to his seatbelt with both gloved hands, he looked round the vehicle: military, operational. He swore as it veered a sharp right, he heard the gears grind in protest but the driver didn't let up as the incline suddenly steepened. Patrick gripped the seat belt tighter, trying to secure himself in the seat, his boots bracing against the brackets. It got darker outside as if the headlights had died and he could only see the small lines of prickly skin between the hat and the collar of the gorilla in front of him. He closed his eyes, wrapping himself in his waxed anorak, a thick woollen scarf, knitted by Wilma, pulled tight round his Rohan hat and his hill walking boots. He had put on his warmest Thermawear jumper.

He was freezing.

The Land Rover jolted again, a teeth-juddering, bone-shattering jar.

'You have got to be joking,' he muttered, looking right at the back of the head of the Gorilla, as the vehicle tackled a hairpin bend. The Glaswegian's black-gloved hands on the steering wheel pulled to the right, letting it slip through to return to neutral. Calm. Controlled. Then Patrick realized he recognized the road; he thought he caught another glimpse of the shimmer of water to his left; the Inner Sound, the deepest territorial water in the UK. He thanked a God he didn't believe in, that the Landie had turned further inland. There was a flash of domestic light ahead, engine screaming as it tackled another ascent. The driver had taken a left turn out of Applecross. And that could only mean one thing.

They were going up the Bealach Na Ba.

'No. No way. Are you ripping the pish?'

'Nobody's laughing,' growled the Glaswegian, moving the armour-plated Landie, an all-terrain vehicle, as if it was a Ford Focus.

There was no point in asking why, they wouldn't tell him, mostly because their orders only took them so far. After that, something else? Someone else? But the driver knew exactly where he was going, Patrick just wished he was in a bit less of a hurry.

He fell back into his own silence, memories coming back, how easy it had been to slip back in harness. Even after all this time to drop into automatic mode. 'Claymore'. His activation code had unlocked the door to the ghost world, a path to slip back into this way of life, a life of hard men and hard choices. No compromise. He decided to stop being brave, he was no longer a young man. He had left those days far behind him.

Or so he thought.

He shut his eyes and waited for it all to stop.

The Landie side shifted with the strength of the wind. They must be high up now, nearing the peak. This vehicle weighed tons yet it was being blown about like a toy car, buffeted by the wind as if the hills were pushing them away, they were not welcome here. Only a mad man would be up here at midnight driving around at altitude, in the dark, in fifty-mile-an-hour winds and driving rain.

He concentrated on the back of the heads of the two silent men in front, as they bobbled and lolled as the vehicle bumped and bounced. He was in the company of mad men.

It took one to know one.

It was past one in the morning when Colin Anderson let himself into his own house, the big house up on the terrace. He had left his own car in town, too drunk to drive back, so he immediately noticed the white Volvo parked in his space at the kerb. George Haggerty's car. Here to see his grandson.

Anderson closed the front door quietly behind him and let out a long slow breath. This was a difficult situation, and one that Anderson, while sympathetic, was getting more than a little fed up with. He slipped off his jacket and hung it up on the stand. Nesbit came running from the direction of the kitchen, looking innocent of any charges of fraternizing with the enemy. Anderson bent down and patted the velveteen fur of the dog's head as Nesbit leaned against his leg and twirled round and round, looking hungry. Anderson ignored him. It was an old ploy.

Anderson was sorely tempted to creep upstairs and go straight to bed, but that might be construed by his family as weak, or rude. And there was plenty of chatter coming from the kitchen, so somebody was up. He followed the noise and the dog's wagging tail, gritting his teeth slightly. The dimmer lights were on, the room was illuminated by a gentle amber glow more suggestive of a high-end café. His daughter Claire, and her friend Paige, were sitting round the table with George Haggerty, in between them was Moses, fast asleep in his basket on the kitchen table, snoring gently.

The first thing Anderson saw as he entered the room was George's little finger clutched in the baby's tiny, chubby hand. It was difficult to pull his eyes away from his grandson. If he had been slightly drunk when out with Archie, gently floating on a little sea of beer, he was grounded now.

'Hello. Do you three know what time it is?' Anderson said, consciously keeping his voice friendly.

'George popped in to see Moses, and to collect his drawing.' Claire waved a wine glass that seemed half empty of a full-bodied red, towards the parcel. Colin looked at it, then her. She was too relaxed to notice the dangerous glint in his eye, the one she called his 'look', the one that said *wait until we get home young lady*. He noticed the remains of Doritos, olives, bits and bobs of dips on saucers. Paige had a glass full of wine, the empty bottle beside her. Her peroxide hair was buzz cut, emphasizing the narrow snaky eyes that normally glowered at Anderson with suspicion and something that bordered on loathing. Now she was almost smouldering at him through her false eyelashes. Anderson ignored her, as he was trying to ignore that uncomfortable feeling he had about Haggerty sitting in his kitchen, pouring alcohol down the throats of two seventeen-year-olds. And then he felt guilty, as Haggerty stretched out an arm and shook him warmly by the hand. The man had lost Mary Jane, a young woman he had brought up as his daughter from the age of seven to twenty four, so maybe this round-the-table girlie chat was usual for him. Although, should the girls not be in their bed, or studying? Anything but drinking. Maybe he was old fashioned.

'Sorry, Colin. Once again I have interrupted.' George Haggerty, contrition glowing from his deep brown eyes, shrugged. 'I was about to go back up north to see Dad but I haven't heard anything and wondered if you knew of any developments. Anything at all, about Abigail . . .'

A huge tug on his heartstrings, then Claire joined in.

'Yeah Dad,' said Claire, her words slurring slightly. 'About Abigail? Surely they must have some news.'

'They are telling me nothing. And they will tell me nothing. I have a personal link to the case. Him.' He pointed to Moses.

'The case. The murder of my wife and child. The case?' George Haggerty ran his fingers down Moses' chubby cheek.

Anderson wanted to tell him to leave the baby alone. 'And that's why it's not allowed. If I don't think of it as "a case" and a job to be done, it would become personal and that can lead to mistakes.' Like Costello, he nearly added, then remembered who he was taking to, a man Costello believed responsible for the murders. He wished she was here now, smashing a wine glass across the table and stabbing him in the throat with it. At least then it would be over with. She would have the courage of her belief, not constrained by legality, decency and a lack of self-courage the way he was.

Anderson was aware that he smelled of drink so he walked round the table and switched on the kettle, feeling absurdly guilty. The man was innocent. He himself had been out socializing when George's wife and child had been killed and they had no idea who had done it, Police Scotland seemed to be doing nothing. He was aware of Claire's eyes watching him, wanting him to come up with something to comfort the man.

'Claire, have you not got uni tomorrow?'

'That's a polite way of telling me that I have to get up in the morning. Bloody hell, Dad!' She stood up, swaying slightly. 'And Paige's staying the night, if that's OK.'

*Yeah, turn the house into a hotel why don't you?* 'Why would it not be OK? There's plenty of room. And it's very late.'

Paige stood up as well, taking the last Dorito from a plate and slowly placing it on her tongue, seductively.

'You'll both want paracetamol and black coffee in the morning,' said Anderson, holding the kitchen door open, ushering them through.

George gave them both a smile, as they retreated to the hall. 'That Paige is worth the watching.'

'Indeed. She didn't have the best start in life so she's here getting some stability, if you can call this madhouse stable. You do what you can.' He watched as George closed his eyes, biting his lip a little.

'Nice thought, nice to try and make a difference.'

Anderson needed to be careful here. He kept reminding himself that this man had lost his wife and his child, and tried to wish him well. But somehow, he just couldn't empathize without immediately feeling a churning anger that it might have been him who killed them.

'Do you want a coffee? I'm having one,' said Anderson.

George shook his head, his arms out. 'No, no, I didn't want to interfere with your night. I popped in to see Moses and the girls invited me in. I had brought you a nice Rioja. They have drunk it. And I had a game of Zombie Gunship with Peter. He beat me, he absolutely wasted me.'

Anderson made an empathetic noise as if he knew what Haggerty was talking about, trying to hide the increasing unease that Mr George Haggerty was becoming so familiar with his own children. And a rage of jealousy that Peter had never, ever, asked his dad to play Zombie Gunship with him.

'Yet again I have abused your hospitality, but I did want to know if you had heard anything.' He sat back down, waiting and cautious, keen for any details. 'In case you didn't want to say in front of the girls.'

'I'm sorry, George, but honestly, you probably know more than me. DCI Mathieson is good. She will be working away but keeping it from public attention. The exact time of death is causing problems. The pathologist thinks very early in the morning, you know, around six a.m., so why were they both dressed. They should have been in their night clothes.'

George nodded. 'They asked me about that. They were

dressed when I left the house. That pathologist told me they had to reposition the bodies at the mortuary so they could line up the wounds; some blows from that knife had gone through both bodies . . .'

Anderson was sure O'Hare had said nothing of the sort. 'Mathieson wants to trace the CCTV, try and get a vehicle check. There's a lot about the case that doesn't make sense.'

'They keep asking me if Abigail had another man in her life. She didn't, just so you know.' He turned to look at Moses, running his fingertip up and down the baby's chubby cheek.

Anderson wanted to ask him not to do that, but had no reason to, apart from that vague dislike. He had no reason for that either.

George turned and looked up, as if he had read Anderson's mind. 'I hope you don't mind me being here.'

'Well,' Anderson struggled to be honest, 'the circumstances are a little weird.'

'I like to talk to Claire; she is so very like Mary Jane.'

'Well, they were half-sisters,' said Anderson mildly.

George was staring at the door, watching the space where Claire had left the room. 'Claire has got such brains, concentration, focus. She's so talented. Have you seen this picture of Moses?' He patted the unwrapped package beside him, smiling.

'She gets that from her mum,' muttered Anderson, pouring in the boiling water to the coffee.

'They have the same gestures and the same . . .' Haggerty paused, a wry smile played around his lips.

'Attitude?' offered Anderson.

'Well maybe, in your daughter, it's a well thought out . . .'

'They were both my daughters,' corrected Anderson, then softened it with, 'but I know what you mean, something in that DNA that you cannot deny. Claire is an artist, Mary Jane was a singer.'

'Mary Jane *thought* she was a singer, that's not the same thing. She couldn't sing, no talent at all, but wouldn't be told. What a disservice we do our youth by letting them believe that everybody is owed their fifteen minutes of fame. And Mary Jane was nowhere near as intelligent or as instantly likeable as your Claire. This portrait of Moses shows a maturity beyond her years.'

*Stay away from my children.* Anderson pulled out a chair and sat down. 'Claire has been through a lot, far more than somebody of that age should be, but I'd like to think that she regards Brenda and I as constants in her life. No matter what she does, we will always be here. Mary Jane might have felt rejected by her birth mother, then her adopted Dad died, and then she was rejected again, maybe that coloured her whole life. If she knew it could be as precarious as that, why shouldn't she go and try to achieve what she wanted? I'm sure you didn't want to dash her dreams.'

'And then she dashes every dream she had by getting herself pregnant. And not a word to her mother or me.' George's eyes narrowed, as if not being told was the bigger issue.

'You didn't know?'

'Not until . . . no, I didn't. I do wonder if Abigail knew though. But she would have told me.' He placed his hands behind his neck. 'Mary Jane was twenty-four, she should have been able to cope with it on her own. I suppose she was drawn to having the baby adopted, as she herself had been.'

Anderson did not know how much George knew. Mary Jane was not having her child adopted; she had sold it just as her own mother had sold her. Mary Jane had sold her baby to a couple who had really wanted a child, just as, twenty-four years before, Anderson's old girlfriend Sally had got pregnant with Mary Jane, not told him and sold their baby to Abigail and Oscar Duguid. Nobody knew who Mary Jane's baby been destined for as Moses had been born Downs Syndrome and had been deemed not fit for purpose.

And that made Colin Anderson very angry.

He presumed that there was a strange kind of karmic synergy in that. Did George really not know that; had Abigail kept the pregnancy secret from him? That would have rattled a control freak like him. Anderson sipped his coffee wondering how hurt he would be if Claire kept something like that from him. But she never would. Or would she?

No.

Anderson looked at the man sitting at his kitchen table,

drinking his coffee, talking about his daughter and his grandson. He could see how easy it would be to paint him as prime suspect, as Costello had done. His mouth opened before his brain could catch it.

'Did you report DI Costello for harassment?'

George had not expected the question. He had thought they were having a friendly father to father talk, not cop to witness, or cop to suspect. His dark brown hair fell over his forehead, giving him the appearance of a guilty schoolboy. His eyes darted around, he was thinking too long to answer truthfully. 'I think I did, I didn't mean to. I was sort of saying to some-body, one of your colleagues, that Costello was parking outside my house, watching me, when I had already been spoken to, my statement had been taken, my alibi confirmed.' He raised his finger to Anderson making his point. 'I had been cleared. Costello was annoying me for no real reason. It was Diane Mathieson I spoke to and she said to stop Costello, I really had to make it official, so yes in the end I did report her for harassment.'

Anderson nodded, imagining how that conversation would have gone down. He was about to ask if Costello had left him alone after that but Haggerty returned to talking about Mary Jane. Anderson had thought he had caught a moment's hesitation, when Haggerty had considered lying, lying as an afterthought. Haggerty was here to talk his own conversation; the mention of Costello had made him a little uneasy, scared even.

Had she been onto something?

He sipped his coffee, watching as George Haggerty rubbed Moses' head and for the first time Colin Anderson felt a little fearful of what might have become of his sidekick.

He dragged away the chair, pulling Moses' cot with it.

The Casualty officer had taken one quick look, checked the chart where the patient's vital signs were being recorded and then taken a closer look at the occipital wound. While noticing it was remarkably clean, he saw it was also very deep. Any pressure with his fingers caused the patient to pull away but not before he had felt a degree of cushioning under his finger-tips. He needed an X-ray to confirm what he already knew:

there was a fracture in there. The woman was sitting on an
examination couch. Hannah had patted the pillow, and gestured
in every way that she could think of, but the woman remained
sitting.

'She might not want to lie down with a head wound like
that, and I don't blame her. Can you get an X-ray organized?
It takes a hard blow to fracture an occiput, but I don't like the
feel of it. If we see a fracture, we will MRI. Or if her neuro-
logicals start to decline. They are fine at the moment but her
comprehension's slow and she's not verbalizing. Not in any
language. Weird. Keep her under close observation. Stay with
her, go with her to Radiology. Let me know if anything
changes.' The woman was co-operative but he noticed she had
latched onto Hannah, her eyes flicking back and forth. When
he asked a question, the woman would look to Hannah for an
indication as to whether the answer was yes or no. And then
let Hannah answer for both of them.

The doctor left, Hannah heard him talking to the cops, then
heard them ask where the nearest vending machine was.

Hannah talked constantly, explaining to the patient that she
needed to undress in case they needed a scan later and offered
her a gown so she could examine her for other injuries, old
scars, stitch marks that might show the site of a metal implant.
The woman was co-operative, not really following instructions
but not resisting as Hannah opened the zip of the anorak and
slipped the woman's arms out. It was soaking wet and stank
of alcohol. She held it under her nose, the smell was overwhelming, leaving Hannah to wonder if somebody had
smashed a bottle of plonk over the back of her head. She'd
seen that before.

Hannah leant over the patient to slip her arms out the wet
jumper; had she got wet through the anorak? Had she been
somewhere without her jacket? Hannah breathed in over the
patient's hair. It smelled of shampoo, coconut shampoo. She
sniffed at the patient's breath as she looked into her eyes. No
alcohol.

Hannah leaned forward again as she undid the top buttons
of the black jumper, checking. Definitely no smell of drink
on her breath. She stood back and looked at her, something

here wasn't right. Then she put her head out the cubicle and requested a plastic bag for the woman's belongings. The woman watched as her arms were revealed from the sleeves of the jumper, cold, pink skin with lacerations, cuts on the lower forearms, defensive wounds. The arms had been held up to ward off an attack to the head. Yet the clothes were intact? No tears in the fabric of the T-shirt, jumper or anorak.

'Good God,' said Hannah, now thinking about sexual assault and that the victim had been undressed then redressed. 'What the hell has happened to you?' She looked into the grey eyes. They stared back at her, something was rumbling around in there at the back of the patient's head. 'Can I take your T-shirt off?' There was no obedience, but no resistance. Hannah rolled up the T-shirt, starting at the waist. The patient winced, flinching a little so Hannah apologized and leaned forward to look over the patient's shoulder to her back.

'Shit!' She let the T-shirt fall back down and hurriedly stuck her head out the curtain to get hold of the two cops. Their seats were empty.

Anderson eventually guided George Haggerty on to the terrace, the elegant façade lit up in bright amber, two windows already showing the sprinkling lights of early Christmas trees. Anderson breathed in the cold night air, the rain had stopped.

'How long does it take you to drive up there? Up to Port MacDuff.' He looked at his watch.

'Five and a half hours? Thereabouts. The A9 is forty miles longer but six minutes quicker, if I don't get stopped for speeding. I thought the average speed cameras had put an end to that. Bastards.' Then George remembered who he was talking to. 'Sorry.'

'They are bastards. Even we can't stand them.'

'Well, look on the bright side, if I hadn't got nicked for speeding you would still think that I was involved in my wife's death, my son's death.'

'Every cloud.'

They had reached the back of the Volvo, but George Haggerty made no attempt to unlock the car. 'Have you not heard from Costello?'

'Nope, not at all.' Anderson shook his head, hands in his pockets.

'I saw her on the 8th. She called me on the 11th . . .' Haggerty rubbed his chin. 'Friday? Saturday? Definitely Saturday. Didn't say much, just told me that I wouldn't get away with it. Must have been Saturday. I was talking to the estate agent when she phoned.'

Anderson couldn't hide his curiosity. 'Did she say anything else?'

'Just the usual abuse,' Haggerty said, good-naturedly.

'Estate agent? Are you selling the house?' Anderson's shiver was nothing to do with the chill of the night air.

'Oh, there's no way I can go back and live there, not after that. I've said to Valerie to go out and see if she wants anything, but me? No.' He shook his head. He got his keys out his pocket and beeped the boot open. 'Do you think it got to your colleague in the end, the way she found the bodies? The scene was brutal.'

It was on the tip of his tongue to say, well she has seen worse. But he didn't know if that was true, but Costello felt guilty, and had ranted about the way Malcolm, according to her, had been so desperate to get away from his father he had tried to climb out the window. Anderson could see both sides. Children can cultivate anybody who will listen. Malcolm had lost his elder sister, he must have known about the attack on Valerie. His life was already unsettled and then . . . well. Then what?

Haggerty nodded. 'Well, if you see her . . .' he laughed. 'Tell her I'm innocent, OK?' The smile switched off as fast as it had switched on. 'I know she's your colleague, ex-colleague.'

'I know you have complained, but she hasn't been sacked.' Anderson nodded; the chill of the night was starting to gnaw at his bones now. 'You got your picture?' he asked, pointing to the package under Haggerty's arm.

'Yes. My dad will be thrilled. He can't believe it. A great-grandson.'

Except he isn't, thought Anderson, nodding. Good manners made him provide the expected response. 'Well, if he is ever down this way then give me a call, and we can get them together and he can see Moses for himself.'

Haggerty opened the boot of his car, the light came on and he swung his bag and the picture into the boot. The back of the car was illuminated to show it crammed full of bags and boxes, piled on top of an offcut of orange carpet, a tarp covering the back of the boot so it was kept very clean. Of course, he was clearing out his house. He reached for something packed safely at the back.

'I hope you don't mind but I came across this and I thought you might like it. Just one of those things.' He handed over a flat package wrapped in bubble wrap. Anderson unpeeled the padding and as he did, his fingers felt the regular squares, the widened border. It was a photo frame and as he unwound the wrapping, the photograph came into view. He didn't need to ask who it was. The girl in the picture looked very like Claire, lighter colouring, but the same smile, and though Anderson knew Mary Jane had been seven years older than Claire, in this picture, she looked so much younger.

Fresh faced, hair uncoloured and falling naturally round her face. The rain spotted the glass as he held it there, she became more interesting behind the pinpoints of rain water, they added an ethereal quality to her smile.

'Mary Jane, about sixteen or seventeen then.'

'Yeah, a good kid before she lost her dad,' said Haggerty. 'My good friend Oscar. And that was horrible. He sailed off, he drowned. All the coastguard found were bits of burning wreckage. The dinghy was still tied to the *Jennifer Rhu*. And if the wee boat was still tied to the yacht, he didn't get off the burning boat. You can understand the effect that had on Abby and Mary Jane, seven years of wrangling to get him declared dead, as there was no body. It was a horrible time, absolutely bloody awful. Mary Jane grew up through all that.'

It was the most animated Anderson had ever seen him.

Haggerty said, opening the door and climbing into the car, 'She didn't have a father, you know. She had three and none of us were there when it mattered.'

And with that he indicated and pulled out into the terrace.

*She didn't have a father, you know.*

What did Haggerty actually mean by that?

Oscar Duguid had died years before Anderson had any idea

that the girl had even existed so there was no way that he could have stepped into the breach. It was Haggerty who had done that. He was the one who had married Mary Jane's mother, Abigail, and then gone on to have Malcolm and make the picture of the perfect family complete. He did a quick mental calculation. They must have met, got together, married and had Malcolm very quickly.

Anderson made a note to find out how they met, exactly, out of idle curiosity as Haggerty spoke of Oscar as if he was a close friend.

Anderson couldn't imagine losing Brenda and Peter, and being able to have a conversation that only barely mentioned them. As if they were completely something of his past, talking about the horror of the scene without giving a thought as to what his loved ones had gone through.

He had never once asked, 'Did they suffer?'

Alastair Patrick closed his eyes and waited, he didn't know these men. But he sensed that they shared one thing.

A history.

After a couple of weaves left and right, the Landie came to a halt, skidding jerkily to a standstill as if the driver had suddenly realized that they had arrived at their destination. The driver and the others got out; the cold wet air snaked into the vehicle. He saw another identical vehicle, the door opened as another man, dressed exactly as the others, dark blue and black got out. That made four, the perfect sabre. There was no light except for the beams of six spotlights that shone uphill into the infinity of the night, picking up nothing but the rain slicing like tracer fire in the beam. That and a few barren stone stacks, standing like wraiths, waiting.

Then one gorilla walked briskly back to the vehicle and opened Patrick's door. He took the hint and got out.

The Gorilla and the Glaswegian climbed back in the Land Rover and drove off without a word, leaving Patrick standing in the pouring rain that bit at his neck and face, he felt its sting and recoiled, the cold air snatched at his hood, pulling it from his head, then he felt the wind tug at his hat. Watching the three other men walking around. One then walked away

and climbed into the other Landie. The other came towards
Patrick, and he felt himself stiffen, rising on the balls of his
feet, bracing himself, his fists clenching. Ready. Patrick
scanned the face behind the black mask, looking for targets.
Another old habit.

'Captain Patrick?' The voice came from somewhere behind
the wool. 'Claymore. I am your commander, and as of now
you are under my orders. Now, time to get about the night's
business.'

Patrick recognized his reactivation command, and again that
one word pushed unwelcome memories into his head, the smell
of cordite, the sound of tracer fire. Faces flashed across his
vision, bodies sprawled in bloodied heaps over the machine
gun.

He pushed the fear away. 'Your business is none of mine,
not now.' Patrick said to reassure himself.

'Shut it, Tonka, your file's about a foot thick. Don't ask,
just obey.'

'It's a long time since somebody called me Tonka. I presume
I don't know you.'

'No, but I know you by reputation.'

'Then we are not mates, so Captain Patrick to you.'

'Captain Patrick then. You are a police officer, you need to
do your job, so we can do ours.'

For a short moment they stood a metre apart. Two men
regarding each other, separated by a generation or more. One
unit bonded them and that would be with them both until the
day they died. No matter how hard Patrick tried to leave, he
would still be one of them. Their blood was his blood, their
fight his fight, even to the end.

There was a grunt, a nod. He walked away.

Patrick called after him. 'What are my orders?'

The boss turned and pointed. 'Up that gully. Fifty metres.'

The spotlights crashed off plunging him into total dark, his
eyes dazzled by kaleidoscope images on his retina. He closed
his eyes and waited, heard one vehicle depart and opened one
eye. If it wasn't for the near invisible outlines of the vehicle
that remained, he'd have thought that he was alone up here
on the Bealach. Alone with the silent sentinels of the cairns

and the ghosts howling in the wind. He saw the headlights of the departing Land Rover, the beam from the headlights consumed by the darkness, the noise of the engine eaten by the wind.

They were gone. He was alive but with no idea what he was doing here.

*Qui audet adipiscitur.*

Fifty metres. What the hell did that mean? Had they accidently killed somebody?

He was truly, completely alone. And the Land Rover was sitting, waiting, engine running. Left for him. He couldn't see anybody inside.

'But I can see that we still use Her Majesty's money to play silly buggers, always money for shite,' said Patrick into the wind, as he was bloody sure there was nobody there to hear it. Well, nearly sure. He faced uphill and now he had his night vision back and began to quarter the hillside in visual sweeps. He smiled. It had been a long, long time since he lived in a world where nobody knew your name because if you saw them as a person, then you might hesitate, and that could be fatal. He remembered the killing house, blacked out, and being told one man with a knife who kept his nerve could kill lots of people in the dark. Why? Because without hesitation he could murder every single one he met, while his enemies whispered, *'Is that you Frank?'* You were given a nickname the minute you walked in the door, the second you signed up and became one of them, one of the ten percent. The nickname meant you ceased being a person in your own right, you became one of them, one of the team. And he had been one of that team, he had been on a hillside like this many a time, cold and wet, pumped with adrenaline listening to the noise of gunfire and following the pattern of tracer fire back to its source. Four men going where an army couldn't. Small strong men, the four of them moving like an insidious, venomous little beast, working towards the heart of its prey.

And they had. Patrick closed his eyes for a moment and he was back on a hillside, clouds of smoke, the smell of cordite and burned flesh filling his nostrils, pushing on and up, climbing, running over rough ground and pushing through, going in where angels failed to fly for fear of being shot down. Slotting everyone in front of them.

He breathed deep in the air that was fresh and cooling to his lungs, air untainted by the death of those like him, born in a different belief system, in another country.

Like the past.

Valerie was hanging, swinging back and forth like a pendulum inside a clock, the tightness around her neck getting worse. She was back in the cupboard at the Blue Neptune, somebody was strangling her. She passed out, a tangle of colours appeared before her eyes, red bursting into yellow that faded to black as she lost consciousness. She waited to die.

But didn't.

She was being strangled. She reached up to her throat, clawing at the noose, her fingertips tugging at the soft fabric that was winding round and pulling ever tighter.

Then it all went dark.

She opened her eyes. It was actually dark.

Valerie was back in the cupboard, panicking. She lifted her other hand and slipped, hitting her head on the tiled floor. She could see in her mind's eye the noose tightening, constricting her throat until she couldn't breathe. She choked, rolling on the floor, her eyes closing. Then she realized she was lying down and not choking.

She was lying in the dark.

She walked her fingertips up to her neck, wondering what she would find. Unable to get her arms free, she tried to calm herself. She shuffled out the door of the bedroom, aware of something sticky under her. But she kept going, she had to get out of here. Shouldering the door open, she twisted her body and waited for her vision to clear so she knew what was on the other side of the door. She recognized this room, but had no idea where from.

She could make out movement on the opposite wall, somebody lying low and trying to stay hidden, somebody like her, tied up and kept captured.

She closed her eyes and rested her head against the wall, waiting for a noise or some clue. Her thoughts were all over the place. This was her worst nightmare all over again, he had found her and put her back in the cupboard. She needed to get out and help the other woman. Looking up she saw the woman was looking back at her. She edged her way forward as she came forward to meet her halfway.

She was looking at herself.

She was there, in the mirror of the hotel room. She stared into her own eyes for a long time wondering if she actually recognized that woman who looked back at her. She looked so much older and more tired than Valerie.

She was old. On the floor after another blackout. Time had slipped somewhere, a few minutes or hours lost, a little bit of herself had escaped. She had no idea.

Then she heard footsteps on the corridor outside. Valerie's eyes fixed on the door, willing it to open. It seemed a long time before there was a very quiet double knock.

She thought she saw a light, thinking that she might be dying now. All that bloody effort and now dying when she wasn't ready. But God smelled familiar and said something, a voice she recognized as if he was far away down a tunnel, shouting at her. She presumed that, as she knew the voice, God has been talking to her before her final breath.

She reached her hand out, ready to meet her maker.

Her mouth was dry. It hurt to move her tongue. She thought she was forming the words correctly, she hoped she could be understood, but from God's uncomprehending face, which blurred and danced in front of her, she was making no sense at all.

She tried again. 'You need to help me.'

The Bealach was a terrible place to be in winter. It was like the surface of the moon but slightly less hospitable. Bealach Na Ba the locals called it, which meant the pass of the cattle or, as it was sometimes translated, the stink of burned-out clutch. Until recently, within Patrick's memory, it had been the only road that connected Applecross with the rest of the country. Up here, two thousand feet above sea level on an exposed summit, the wind was so strong, it whipped at his jacket, almost pushing him over. Reminded him of the screeching winds on South Georgia, the Fortuna Glacier, where they had to creep about like German snipers.

He took cover behind the shelter of the Land Rover, crouching against the body on the lee side where the wind and rain came under the Landie trying to get a bite at him. Once he got his bearings, he gave in to the aching in his knees, stood up and climbed into the shelter of the vehicle, fumbling to check the keys. He set the demister at full, thinking.

He moved the vehicle, pulling it forward and repositioning it so the lights shone right down the gully, but back enough from the edge to allow him to getaway easily without reversing.

This was not a place for him, this was home for deer and sheep, this was where city folk and hill walkers died of exposure. Well, in the past that was true, but now the National Park had built access roads everywhere, the hills belonged to everybody. Now there was an invasion of mountain bikers, motorhomers, stupid people who had seen the North Coast 500 drive on the TV and thought they liked the look of it. Puffer fish looked nice too, but they were still fatal to the ignorant.

So, there was something out on that hillside that was his business, or at least what Intel thought was his business. He'd no sure idea what his monosyllabic friends had been getting at but there was only one way to find out. Coming up with the story of how he came to be here might be more of a challenge, he thought. He could always tell the truth, no bugger would ever believe that, but that truth would already be being manipulated now, by faceless men in good suits, with no blood on their hands.

He picked up the torch, turned it on, flashing it a few times to make sure the beam was strong and that it was waterproof, rolled into the rear and out the back door behind the glare of his lights. He did a quick grid search in the darkness, making sure he was alone.

Then he walked quickly across the parking area till he was in the shadow again outside the arc of the lights and began to walk uphill, rolling silently on the outside of his boots, stopping at each perspective change and checking the ground. From the dark he could see every rock bathed in stark light.

Forty metres or so up he saw it. Pale and white, out of place, waving at him in greeting. He crouched and scanned the dark above the lights. He pulled his mobile but there was a better signal on the moon than up here. He had to hurry. Throwing caution to the wind he rushed towards the movement in the heather.

It was a hand, hanging from the sleeve of a jumper caught in a whipping gorse bush, the fingers caught in the wind, waving.

Two hours after he found the body, Patrick was alone again at the top of the pass, waiting for the circus to come to town. He had rather enjoyed the drive to the north, going down the Bealach, until his phone told him he had a signal. Then he had contacted his DC, Morna Taverner, getting her out her bed at four a.m., and gave her a list of instructions, checking the local hotels for guests who hadn't returned tonight, then check the list of young men reported missing, in Scotland for starters. Then any abandoned or burnt-out vehicles within a twenty-mile radius. It might be a long list, but she was a good police officer, despite that idiot she had married and a constant lack of a reliable babysitter. As an afterthought. He called the number of Lachlan McRae, who lived next door to Morna in Constance House, one street from the seafront at Port MacDuff and got him out his bed as well.

Then he turned around and drove back up, slower than the Gorilla had driven but still bringing back an old thrill.

The body on the hill had no ID on him, Patrick was not convinced of the most obvious answer; that the young man had been a rough tourist, not an extreme runner with the jumper he was wearing. Maybe more of an extreme walker, the big knitted jumper and border collie brigade, not the Rohan Craghopper super fit lot. They were both tough, both more than a little mad according to the mountain rescue. The real answer would be more tragic, brought about by human hand.

The Bealach was isolated and high but it wasn't steep. The road up twisted and turned, gaining height over nine kilometres, meandering its way up and over the pass. Who was he? Who took his ID and why he was dressed the way he was? And

how did he end up here on a night like this when the road
had been closed for a couple of weeks now. The uncomfortable answer to that was he was either somebody who knew
the place, or he had been placed here by somebody who
knew the place and whoever did that, well, that vehicle would
be covered in blood and that vehicle would have been spotted
somewhere along the way. At this time of year, strangers stuck
out. Patrick had a slight rethink there. The North Coast 500
was far too popular. Tourists were driving it all hours of day
and night, the holiday season now lasted twelve months.
Everybody thought they knew the road because they had read
about it in a magazine in a Sunday supplement, everybody
and their uncle. Folk with 4x4s sat in pubs in the West End
of Glasgow and talked about it, boasting about how they had
driven it in a gale in October, a snowdrift in January, backwards
at midnight while whistling the theme tune from *The Great
Escape*. That was all very well until one vehicle missed a turn
and plunged down into the glen, killing everybody on board.
Then it would be his fault.

Four hours after he found the body, Patrick was watching
the circus. There was no daylight up here in the middle of the
bleak wilderness, it was all spotlights and headlights, shadows
dancing over bleak rocks and cairns.

The scenes of crime team had pegged out the stony ground,
fine puddles lying on top of the moss and grass. The vehicles
were on the hard standing at the viewing point, there had been
a decision, made by Patrick, to leave the civilian vehicles at
the bottom of the hill. The road was closed anyway and probably would remain so until early in the new year. The forestry
commission ATVs were doing the running up and down,
safe and sturdy.

Despite the weather things were going well; the lights were
on, the plates were up. The body lay there, now bathed by
light, a young man with dark hair that took a deep ebony sheen
in the neon glow, a slight burnished copper tint when caught
by the harsh glare of the spotlights.

Alastair Patrick had taken one look at the man and knew
he had been beaten to death. It looked like somebody had
danced on his head, never mind the obvious wound across the

front of the man's throat which to Patrick's expert eye was both amateurish and non-fatal. There may have been torture, but looking too closely would involve adjusting clothing, and maybe losing trace evidence, so he left it. A quick look through the pockets of the baggy jeans revealed nothing.

This was no accident.

Somebody had pulled him from a vehicle and rolled him into the gully.

No rush. The victim wasn't going anywhere.

They could wait until they had him on the slab over at the mortuary, wherever he ended up. There was talk of taking him all the way down to Glasgow, and that could take another six hours or so. Maybe he could insist on Inverness.

Patrick looked round to see the photographer in the spotlight, clicking away, the crime scene officer was helping with the video. Two CSIs were on their knees searching the ground, getting soaked and finding nothing but doing the job anyway. He had instructed that the body be taken off the hill ASAP, they would find anything they needed to find once the sun was up. He looked at his watch and that would be another three hours away.

One of the CSIs shone her or his torch in the face of the young man, eyes closed, a pink, fresh face, as if he had decided to shave when he looked in the mirror on the day he died. His face was bloodied red, the rain running over it, giving him the look of both life and perspiration. He looked at peace in this desolate place.

After dying a brutal death.

The police surgeon turned up eventually, ignoring Patrick, picking his way over the ground, dressed in a huge downy anorak, and a woollen hat pulled far over his ears. He snubbed the group as he went about his business, then he stopped. Suddenly.

The two CSIs and the photographer ceased to move, stilled exactly where they were, turned to stone.

'Who is in charge here? Is that you, Patrick?'

'Yes,' he shouted over the screaming of the wind.

'Well, you'd better get a chopper here right now. He's not dead.'

Alastair Patrick's mind swiftly moved up a few gears. Oh, so he was not dead, so why was he here? Why had they thought he was dead? Had they checked? Had he checked? Of course he had, he had placed his bare fingers over the jugular and found nothing.

Alastair Patrick walked back to the Land Rover with greater purpose than he had left it, he was ready to drive back down the pass to get a phone signal as a stretcher, aluminium blankets, an oxygen tank and mask ready, was making its way back over to the body.

The paperwork just got problematic.

He was thinking of the long drive to Inverness as Patrick watched the body being placed on a stretcher, and placed into the back of the Land Rover, resting it on the top of the seat. There was no way a normal ambulance was going to get up here. They'd take him down to the coast and the Paraffin Budgie could meet them there.

That would be safer, in this night sky, this weather, this visibility.

He called the Multi Agency Briefing.

It was someone else's decision.

# FOUR

Gareth Ahern had been volunteer ranger for as long as he could recall. He was better at it than most of the young professionals that came onto the lochside after graduation from university, all very good at the DNA of ferns and the breeding habits of otters, but not so bloody good at getting up at the crack of dawn and reading the signs of what had been going on in the wee dark hours of the night. And more recently they had had the hooligans from the city come up, making it out to the islands and killing the wildlife, most noticeably the wallabies. Last week one of the wallabies had been skinned on the beach and left in full view for the tourists on the loch cruise to see the next morning. Ahern had thought he would never see the day when there had to be security on twenty-seven square miles of water.

One of the students, a nice young bloke called Cowan who drove a VW camper, had explained it to Ahern; it was some kind of game they had, an initiation ceremony to become a fully paid up member of the gang by showing how tough you were. The aim of it seemed to be to get out to the islands of the loch unseen, then trap and kill whatever they could find. Birds, ducks, rabbits and, most recently, the wallabies. There had been signs of torture of the animals, the Wildlife Protection Unit were taking an interest now that it looked likely the attacks would affect tourism. They had asked Ahern and Cowan and others to keep watch and collect any evidence that they could.

That would be for a prosecution, Ahern knew that and knew that some defence counsel would argue some shite about the wee bastards being brought up on a council estate and deprived of the newest iPhone or designer jeans, or a job or a sense of self-respect. Aye well, self-respect came from yourself in Ahern's opinion, nobody else. You believed in yourself and others followed suit. Nobody could take your self-respect away, you had to give it away.

It made Ahern's blood boil, he had let it be known that he would do time for the wee shites. He'd take his bloody shotgun out and blow the shit they had for brains to where the sun didn't shine. The violence towards the animals angered him, the senselessness of it enraged him. But the lack of respect? That really got to him. It was everywhere in society these days.

As he walked on, in teaming rain that was caught by the gusty wind, hitting him in the face then snatching at the skin at the back of his head, he amused himself by considering how he would do it if he ever caught the perpetrators. He would take his time about it too, taking them one at a time, so they each knew what was coming. He was even thinking of some way he could get the boat away if they were on the island, so they would be stranded. And he would leave them there. He could sit on the shore and watch them as they waved for help, he'd wave back. They all had bloody mobile phones nowadays so they'd call the cruise services and get picked up and then blame the national park management or the social services when all the really needed was a loaded shotgun up their arse. And a twitchy finger on the trigger.

Ahern trudged up the hill walking south to the visit centre at Inveruglass, which had been ruined by that stupid viewing tower that folk kept setting on fire. They should ban the whole bloody lot of them; he walked on, gaining height until he saw his first full view of the loch. It was leaving eight thirty, the first hesitant flicker of dawn haloed the Ben. Every day it made his heart ache as it had done for the last fifty years, sixty years if he was honest. Bar deaths, marriages, two weeks annual holiday, he had been here every day, and even on his holidays he went north to look at Loch Maree instead.

Then he smelt it. Something bloody in the air, in the rain. And the blood was relatively fresh. His fury boiled over, he started cursing, battering the longer brown ferns with his walking stick, looking to spot the body of another animal in his torch beam. A deer from the look of it. He was furious, more death, more waste of life lost by the mindless acts of those less worthy.

He sniffed the air, thinking how unusually strong the smell

was. He stepped through the wet grass, slowly and carefully, keeping his eyes low but following the scent of the blood, and there it was. Well, there it wasn't.

A flattened area of grass, blades bent and broken, over a large area and the smell of blood hanging in the mist. Lots of blood, whatever had died here must have been a big animal. He walked around a little, the beam catching footprints in the mud. Trying to keep clear of them so he didn't mess it up for the wildlife unit and any further prosecution. He rubbed at his beard, this might be some of the evidence they were waiting for. Something had died here, but he wanted to be sure, so he looked around for the signs of an illegal snare or a trap. Finding nothing, he sighed and swallowed his anger before walking down to the café where Belinda had a mobile phone. The café wouldn't be open yet, but Belinda would be in and she'd report it for him.

Hannah was worried. The woman had come back from X-ray, there was a fracture in her occiput that had been the result of a blunt force trauma. But what worried her more was the smell of drink that had vanished when she took the clothes off her. The smell had followed the clothes to the bag. The woman's breath was clean, minty if anything, her hair smelled of shampoo – who shampooed over a huge head wound? Well, the answer to that was any Glaswegian drunk who got into a fight.

The day shift were talking about doing a rape kit. There was no chance of getting informed consent, but she could try and talk her round. Maybe get the patient to understand, talk her through it and see if she could be made to understand. But if it was true that the woman had suffered a very stressful event, been subject to physical violence, then showered, then that added up to some kind of sexual assault. Maybe from her permanent abuser. If there was any evidence it would probably have gone down the plughole.

Hannah believed there was a positive side to everything. The patient's psychotic break was doing its job, protecting the victim, keeping out the traumatic memories until psyche was strong enough to recall them. If she was a victim of a sexual attack, she was very calm, too calm. Hannah had seen that many times too, that ability to hand themselves over to a caring person but this one was more wary, far more calculating than distressed.

They were waiting for a psychiatric bed then there would be further assessments, so God alone knew how long that would be. At least she had been moved to a room rather than a cubicle with a curtain round her, dressed in a hospital gown, her head wound covered by a light dressing. Anything was better than lying on a trolley in an examination room, with everybody and their mother popping through to borrow this and that and never returning it.

She seemed to be able to hear, to understand, but did not speak or respond in any way, except . . . well, she did. Hannah couldn't pinpoint the common factor. The hospital didn't faze her at all. Was she a nurse somewhere, a cleaner, maybe a doctor? A light bulb went on in Hannah's head. Was that why the wound was cleaned? Something she maybe did by instinct, with a first aid kit or something.

Hannah found it all very confusing, but she had been told to stay here, keep monitoring her vitals, to get some form of communication going and get consent or even an ID. All hell was let loose around her as a couple came in high on all sorts of substances. She heard raised voices, swearing, then something being pushed and then a smash of something glass being broken, followed by the thump thump of security boots hurrying to the scene. Hannah felt she had had the Sunday night shift easy.

The blonde woman was lying easier now, head back, her hair swept up off her face. They had got the age wrong, Hannah thought, this woman was younger than her sixties, fifties maybe. Hannah had gone through her clothes and found nothing. Her clothes were clean apart from the bloodstains and she had good teeth, her nails were clean and cut evenly, no ingrained dirt. Two things that are rarely found on any poor bugger who is living on the street. She could have been foreign, so Hannah tried a few languages she knew hello in. The woman was fair-skinned so that cut out the Middle or the Far East, but she could be Eastern European or Scandinavian or any of those new countries that Hannah didn't really know the whereabouts of.

She nipped out to the main desk and picked up the laminated sheet with *Hello, you are in a hospital*, written on it in many languages. She showed it to the woman who looked at it, reached out a hand to take it. Hannah held her breath thinking that the woman was processing the writing and was going to point at one, or point at one and then say something.

She handed the laminated sheet back.

Hannah tried to explain that they were keeping her in for observation, to make sure she didn't have a brain bleed. 'Did somebody hit you over the head?' Hannah asked, lifting her own hand up as if she was going to hit herself. 'Did somebody punch you in the eye?' she mimed this also. The grey eyes looked right through her; they turned at the crackle of a police radio outside the room.

It looked like, to Hannah's mind, and Hannah loved mystery writing, that the woman had been assaulted. She had been caught by the shoulder, bruised and sore, hit over the head, the slashes on her back and lower arms were, well, one directional? Then she had been stabbed, but she had pulled away at the last minute. Was that possible, a sign that she had been running, a knife went out and the victim twisted as he caught her, she had put her arms up to protect herself, somebody had battered her on the head then got her on the ground and kicked her. That was what it looked like, she had worked in A & E for five years now. She had seen it all. Except why do that when they had a knife on her?

And, the woman was behaving as if she was safe in here.

Which, Hannah concluded, meant she might not feel safe outside or at home? If she had been battered by her hubby or partner then they wouldn't have listed her as missing. They would need to wait until a friend or a family member did that?

Or was this a sanctuary? Hannah turned back to look at her as the grey eyes followed her every move, not dull or dazed but alert. Hannah smiled; the woman's mouth twitched as if she had been going to smile then remembered the game she was playing.

Hannah told her they would get her a cup of something

once the doctors had cleared that, in case she needed an operation. No response. The doctor would be here in a minute – no response. In the NHS a minute can be a long time – no response.

She placed the switch for the buzzer in her hand, the patient took it. She put on a heart monitor as her pulse was fast but weak, and an oxygen tube on her top lip. All her vital signs were indicative of blood loss but there wasn't that much blood on her . . . It must be somewhere.

She left the cubicle to update the police. Her shift was over. Usually she was glad to be going home but not this time, she would like to stay to see how this panned out.

After talking to the duty doctor, Hannah tried an age-old trick, came in with a cup of tea and asked the woman if she would like it. The woman didn't respond in any language, except to hold out her hand for the tea, and proceed to drink it.

Well, that told her nothing, except the woman drank black tea and that there was nothing wrong with her vision.

Morna Taverner stood by the window staring into the rain-drenched street and tried not to make it too obvious that she was waiting. She loved her husband dearly, she loved her son and she loved her mother. She wished that some of them, any of them, or all of them, could be exactly where they were supposed to be. The child was in the bath – she could hear Finn doing his impersonation of the Death Star, so there would be more water on the bathroom floor than in the bath. Neil wasn't home from work yet, and he was supposed to be. He wasn't answering his mobile so he would be driving or out at a remote B and B to drop off luggage for those who thought it was fun to walk twenty miles a day in the freezing cold, pissing rain then go and sleep in a plastic bag in a field or in a stranger's lumpy bed. Morna thought they were bloody mad, but their madness did pay for her to go to Lanzarote once a year and it financed Neil's dream of building their forever home.

She leaned on the windowsill, peering through the glass. Should she phone her mum again? Mum had said she was just leaving the farm so she would be on her way and not able to answer if she was driving, not on these narrow country roads with their deceitful turns and hidden bends, much worse in this bloody weather and the bloody tourists doing three miles an hour on the single track road enjoying what they could see of the scenery.

Morna was needed at work and she was keen to go. She had to drive to Raigmore Hospital, two hours if she got a clear run. Somebody, or some body she corrected herself, had been attacked and left on the top of the Bealach Na Ba.

Morna fingered her mobile in her pocket. Patrick, her DCI, had phoned her twice now. She really wanted this job and if she wasn't able to respond quickly then he would call another DC. He had a mental list that he would work through and Morna was close to the top, born and living in Port MacDuff with a good local knowledge. She wanted the job and didn't want to pass it up. Something terrible had happened up on the Bealach, she was sure of it, and if DCI Patrick had contacted her . . . well, she was keen to get on and show her competencies. She wasn't going to get anywhere if she had to say to her boss again, *yes I'd like to come in and help out, I know I am late for work but there is nobody here to look after the wee guy and take him to school so on you go and I'll catch up with you when I can.*

She could imagine how well that would go down.

Why did he phone her? Was it because of something that she was already working on? Like that cut the list of possibilities down to anything. Or maybe . . . she cheered up as she saw some lights on the road, a car coming . . . then her heart sank as it went past the bottom of the road. Not her mother then. Shite, she was going to be really late.

And she didn't want to be, not after all that time off after the accident.

She looked out the window, hearing Finn splashing in the bath, all was dark outside.

Was it her pet project? Had he seen a link with that and that was why he had phoned? Patrick had warned her about becoming obsessed with the rape she was trying to link with other similar crimes. The disappearance of Jennifer Argyll in

1987 was not an isolated event. Jennifer had been the start of something, she was sure of it. Well, *she* was sure of it. And DCI Patrick had heard her out, he had looked at the file saying nothing as she spoke, voicing her thoughts and suspicions. He let her run out of steam, and then said, quietly, in that very direct way he had, that a database was only that. Ask it a stupid question and it will give you a stupid answer. Well, she could recall his exact words. All he had really said was 'Shit in equalled shit out'.

Morna had taken that to mean she was asking the wrong questions of the database, rather than 'stop wasting police time'. A few minutes here and there, she was back on it. Patrick knew she was still trawling the system, she wasn't hiding it from him, or drawing his attention to it, but she logged the minutes, and when he saw them he gave her a wry smile. He was a man of few words. That rare smile translated as 'God loves a trier'.

She turned back into the room and gave the logs on the fire another wee poke, closing the door tightly and closing the vents. She had stuck a towel over the radiator when she got the first call, but that had cooled off now. Last night Finn had been painting a wizard's outfit for a party later in the week, and had left the mask on the radiator to dry. It had a wide smile and huge ears, giving it a passing resemblance to Prince Charles at the dentist. Morna remembered she had forgotten to buy a present for whoever's birthday it was. She'd ask another mum. She looked out the window one last time, saw no car, then walked into the kitchen to write a reminder for the party on the blackboard that held her shopping list. She squirted some hand cream onto her chapped, bleeding hands and waved her fingers about drying them in the cold air.

Then Finn was shouting that he wanted out the bath so she grabbed the Darth Vader towel from the radiator and rushed down the hall. Finn was doing his impersonation of the Death Star while lying face down in the near empty bath, a snorkel covering his face.

'Up,' she said, 'out.'

He climbed out the bath, this pale-skinned creature with endless bendy limbs, red-headed and freckled. The Death Star kept pinging, the snorkel was steaming up, and Finn was waving a grey plastic X-wing above his head, keeping it to its deadly mission. He swapped it from hand to hand as he slipped his arms in his vest, then his school shirt, then his jumper. She picked him up, carrying him into the living room where his socks and wellies were warming in front of the dying fire.

She checked the clock.

'I have to go out now.'

'No mummy,' he sighed, wriggling and kicking as she tried to get socks on his feet, then the wellies on his legs.

'You will have to go next door until Granny gets here, then go to school.'

'Haribos?'

'No. That's a Thursday. You get Haribos on a Thursday.'

'What day is it today?' The X-wing executed an impressive turn.

'The day after Sunday.'

'Wednesday?'

'Nope, try again.'

'Can I get Haribos?'

'Nope.' She stood him back up, his head like an orange porcupine. She tightened the belt of his house coat then marched him, and the X-wing, out to the hall where she put an old waxed jacket over his shoulders. It was long enough to touch the floorboards. Then she plonked a flat cap on his head.

Brora looked up, but the collie judged it was too wet to be bothered about going for a walk so she promptly went back to sleep.

Morna opened the front door and shoved the boy out into the rain, frogmarching him down their short front path, through the gate then up the path of the neighbour's house. The three stories of the terraced looked gloomy and menacing in the glare of the streetlamps. The small windows looked mean; the dark closed curtains looked hostile.

Not the sort of place to run to if you were young, vulnerable and in trouble. A place where you could walk out the village and disappear. Like Jennifer Argyll.

The neighbour's front door opened immediately, Lachlan had heard her own door close no doubt and had a fair idea what was coming. He was dressed but looked as if he hadn't showered or combed his hair, the white streak in his hair was curled into a corkscrew. 'When you have to go, you have to go, Morna. Alastair has already phoned me.'

'Really?' she was annoyed that the shortcomings of her family had been so predictable to her boss.

'You want me to look after the lad.'

'Just for a couple of minutes. Mum will be here soon. Or if not, can you take him to school.'

'No problem, just watch yourself in that weather.' Lachlan placed his huge hand on Finn's head and guided both boy and X-wing into the house. 'He'll be OK here.' He looked up into the ebony sky then at her, his brown eyes creased slightly, an old cop looking at the young generation.

Morna turned to walk back down the path, pulling up her hood. 'Did Alastair say anything? Is it about Jennifer?'

'No. But I doubt it, why would it be? Take care,' and the door closed over, one final ping of the Death Star sonar.

Alone, in the street, pissing down, abandoning her son for the company of a dead body found at the top of the pass on a dark and stormy morning, thinking about a woman she had never met.


DC Wyngate drove into the car park at Inveruglass in response to a call from the Wildlife Protection Unit. Not his territory but they needed a hand and somehow the buck had stopped with him. It felt like demotion.

It had taken him an hour to drive the forty miles; much quicker once he had got out the city boundary and the rush hour traffic and he had made good time. The car park was largely empty, except a cop car, small van for the café and a Mini Clubman. It was too early in the day and too late in the year for the coaches full of old folk, on their three days' tour of the Highlands, staying in second-rate hotels but still cheaper than heating the houses at home. Nobody would go up to the viewing site. Not only was it too misty to see anything but the back of the head of the person standing in front of you, there was the small matter of the blue and white tape cordoning the area off.

He parked his car alongside the other, opened the door and looked at the sky, then opened the boot and put on his heavy duty jacket and his wellington boots.

Ahern introduced himself. He was still shaking slightly, not with nerves or shock but with finely controlled anger. Wyngate thought he looked the type, waterproof Rohans tucked into his serious Hunter wellies. The walking stick had been carved from a tree branch, the handle of it made from a horn or an antler of some kind. He was older than Wyngate had presumed; he had the air of a civil engineer or an architect out for a long country walk about him rather than a wildlife ranger. He was not far wrong as Ahern introduced himself as a volunteer ranger, now he was retired. Wyngate nodded as Ahern said he had been an architectural surveyor in his previous life, used to working with mines and underground waterways.

They walked across the car park, Ahern talking about the amount of blood, the rainfall, how much of it would have already been washed away so God knew how much the poor creature had lost at the time of the . . . He had difficulty finding the most appropriate word and ended up settling for 'event'. Wyngate struggled to walk and take notes but fortunately Ahern was clear, concise, accurate as to what he had witnessed and explained why he was there so early in the morning. As they started to walk up the hill on the path that passed the viewing point, Ahern became distressed, as he spoke of the amount of blood. He wiped his lips with the back of his hand. To his eyes it looked as though something had been chased, hunted down, he nodded to the north through the undergrowth saying there was another smaller path there that went in a long circuitous route back to the car park.

Ahern looked up at the sky, mimicking Wyngate's actions as he had left the car. 'Even with the rain washing some away. There's too much blood,' he repeated, as if the rain itself had stolen the blood, and would the guilty party like to give it back.

Wyngate looked at the ground, trusting Ahern's story rather than his own eyes. Ahern knew the area well and had got into the habit of staying away from the official car parks and laybys on the west side of the loch. He had come across a few rough sleepers and wild campers, illegal campsites littered with empty booze bottles and occasionally the odd syringe and bit of burned tinfoil. That morning he had been walking around the loch on the north-west side making his way down to the viewpoint from the north, when he had smelled the blood in the air.

'Smelled it?' asked Wyngate, panting a little with the effort of keeping up with the man old enough to be his father.

'Oh, yes, fresh and plenty. Somebody will have a deer in their freezer tonight and I hope it poisons them.'

'Any trouble up here with weird goings-on? Satanic stuff? Anything like that?'

'Nope. Just the devil that is the drugs, and that's enough.'

The two of them walked, Ahern leading the way, no sense of urgency, an easy stride of his long legs making easy of the steep hill. Wyngate was thinking about the wallaby killings, animal sacrifices? Killing animals to conjure up the spirit of Old Nick did at least make some kind of sense.

'There's no skin, no intestines, no internal tissue, just the blood? No sign that something was gralloched here?' Wyngate asked. 'Could it be human? I mean, can a human lose that amount of blood and live? I'm thinking about the drug wars that are raging in the city.'

'You are a city cop, I'm a country ranger. Both red deer and humans have eight pints of blood. One of those things you get to know doing this job.'

Wyngate realized that the prospect of a human victim had crossed Ahern's mind as well. 'The last three bodies up here were drug related, admittedly little more than kids out getting their kicks from illegal or legal highs, but they were all cold once they got to the pathologist's table.' Wyngate was already thinking that he was getting that blood tested, even if they found an antler and a copy of Bambi. He was sure the CSI team carried now an onsite blood test for that so they didn't spend too much money investigating the site of a dog fight. A two-test system, one to make sure it was blood, the second to make sure it was human. He knew it was an immunochromatic procedure and once they had that, they could then decide whether or not they needed to look for more samples for future DNA testing, but it was all time sensitive in this weather.

Ahern stopped, suddenly, putting his arm out to his side preventing them from going any further. He looked down at the grass, flattened and fractured, a main area, three-feet wide that narrowed to a tail over a space of about ten feet. There were bloodstains still easily visible, not complete, the veins of it had been washed away leaving droplets in the leaves and spikes in the channels of the grass leaves. There were traces of it, here and there all over.

By force of habit, Wyngate started looking around, half-listening to what Ahern was saying. His eyes scanning the ground for anything odd. He thought he saw a black bird, near the trunk of a sapling that was bending in the wind. It was small, jaggy and a black that was too dense to be natural.

He walked over and knelt down beside it. It hadn't been lying there for very long, the fractured plastic of the Samsung was clean. It was partially embedded into the ground.

Animals do many great things but they are not generally known for smashing brand new mobile phones. Wyngate make a quick calculation. Whoever it was had been wounded and was probably deceased. They now needed manpower to fan out and grid search the place of the attack. He turned to look out, the Ben was covered in swirling mist; the water was keeping its secrets.

This was now extremely time sensitive.

He excused himself from Ahern and started making his phone calls. Crime scene first and then hospitals.

# FIVE

There was no doubt about it. Valerie Abernethy was feeling better. Her function was improved and her brain was clearer but she had always been a high-functioning alcoholic, and she was very bright. There was a lot she could do with very little thought or effort, it all came so easy to her. She had never really learned to challenge herself. Now she was learning the hard way just how difficult it could be for her to get up in the morning. For the first time she had accepted medication for depression and her mood swings. She had admitted that to the young doctor who had appeared at the door of the surgery where Archie had dumped her. He was a hard-faced man who spoke in terms that made it perfectly clear she had two choices, do as she was told or die.

It was up to her.

He was not going to waste his time and effort if she was not going to do anything about it right here and right now.

She had looked back at him and, in a quiet voice that did not sound like her at all, said that she had lost her entire family.

'So,' he said, with a beguiling tilt of the head. She knew this meant she had walked into a trap and he was about to close it. 'You were totally sober before that? I think not.'

The doctor had repeated, 'So I'm not going to do anything about it if you are not going to do anything yourself. You need to apply yourself to getting better.' He had leaned back in the seat, talking over what she had been through in the last few years, ticking the points off on his fingers, by the time he had finished Valerie had felt that she would have felt terrible for that person, and that person was herself. She was one step removed from it all. And then the doc had said, 'I don't think that this is a good time for you to be making big decisions. You need to keep your life on the straight and narrow, you need to let your blood chemistry stabilize. You need to regain the capacity for clear thought so you can get through the day. That will be your first challenge, once you get through that then we can look at the other options. And please, don't ever do anything on impulse. Recovering alcoholics can have severe issues with impulse control. If you get an idea, even if you think it's the greatest idea in the world, write it down and think about it again the following day. It will be that lack of filter that has got you into much of the mess you are in.'

She thought about the gun she had tucked away in the back of her bag that was leaning against her leg. She opened her mouth, getting ready to say that she still had the means to kill herself, and that was still her intention, but when she spoke all that came out her mouth was, 'I have nothing to do. I don't even have a cat to look after.'

'You have plenty to do, you just don't want to do any of it. You need to work on yourself.' Those were his final words as he pressed print and the prescription slips started to churn out. She tuned out, hearing him vaguely add something, spoken to the wall, or to himself, about being a bright young woman, with a good brain and that the brain will find something to worry about unless she gave it something constructive to do, something challenging but insignificant so she could get her teeth into it but not fret if she failed at it. Then she would be OK.

'And you are going to stay with your uncle?'

'So he tells me.'

'Best thing you can do'.

And here she was . . .

At Uncle Archie's house.

Valerie looked round the room, not recognizing it but she recognized the style – it was very Pippa. Very Marks and Spencer's. But she had no real idea when she had last been in this house, or if she had ever been in this neat little bungalow with the lawn cut in precise stripes at all. She could remember the detached house out in Milngavie where Archie and Pippa had lived before they downsized. When she was a child, Archie and her dad worked together in the fiscal service, and Pippa and her mum were housewives. Valerie and Abigail had played in that house often as children. Uncle Archie and Auntie Pippa were great fun in the way that parents can never be, giving too much freedom and too many sweeties.

They had been second parents to both girls.

It was only now, as an adult herself, that she wondered if Archie and Pippa had wanted children too, in the same way that she herself had yearned for them, once she knew that she couldn't have them. Archie and Pippa seemed to have everything else.

Having a family had never really worked out for them and they had sold up and moved to this lovely, but charmless bungalow. Small, neat, easily looked after.

Archie knew Abigail almost as much as he knew her, his god-daughter. He had been Uncle Archie to them both.

She thought back to what the GP had said earlier at her emergency appointment. 'We will get these prescriptions picked up, stay well, get plenty of rest, and after a week we will see where we are. We need to survive seven days. If we can do that, if you do that, then we can all move it forward. Here's the phone and contact details of the AA and support that is available. If you get stuck. pick up the phone and speak to them. I know you don't want to hear it right now but you are a very lucky woman, you have somebody who's willing to take you in and look after you.'

She did.

Archie Walker, bless him.

Knowing her was like cuddling a serpent.


Wyngate had felt quite the king pin, in charge of the locus on the bloodstained site at the loch. There were CSIs crawling everywhere. Cops he had not been on the same shift rotation with for ages had appeared to help out, or as he was starting to see it, they were here to get in his way and he started to wish that somebody else would come along and claim responsibility for the crime scene. It was becoming a poisoned chalice.

He had been told a SIO from Balloch had been appointed, but as they had no real idea what they were investigating, he had gone back to base and had so far refused to return to a site of a 'bad nosebleed and a stolen mobile phone'.

Then a smartly dressed young man had limped out of a very clean Audi and asked the nearest uniform who was in charge. A minute later DS Viktor Mulholland had introduced

himself to Wyngate, very sarcastically. He had been seconded
back down from West End Central so the bosses said, but it
was obvious the people upstairs had been given the ideal
opportunity to get them out the way, in a two for one deal.

'Do you have a clue what's going on?' asked Mulholland.

'You are the superior officer,' said Wyngate looking around.
'And that's the site up there.' He pointed up to An Ceann Mor.

'No way am I going up there. No chance, I have a bad leg.'

'Exactly,' said Wyngate, then explained that he thought the
CID should already be here and that, if in charge of anything,
it should be traffic. Coaches kept pulling into the car park and
had to be helped to U-turn and get back out again, although
the police activity was proving a bigger tourist attraction
than the loch with its beauty hidden behind a bank of rain.

In the end, Wyngate and Mulholland had a quick resume
of the situation, they both had been dropped in the shit by
their superiors so they may as well make the best of it.

'The blood, is it human?'

'It is. They are looking for a body. So far, the nearest five
A & E's have come up with no admissions that match this
scenario. A search team is coming and I think we need traffic
out to get the road signposted right at the start of the loch turn
off.'

Mulholland nodded and looked up at the viewing point,
seeing the CSIs walking around in their protective suits,
looking rather unworldly high up in the mist. 'We'll hold the
reins until the results come in, it will go up the tree quick
enough. Where is McCaffrey? Has he gone up in the world
or something?'

'Who?' Wyngate looked at his notebook, he had kept an
inventory of names. 'No McCaffrey here.'

'Oh, he's here. I'm bloody sure that's his car in the car
park, can't be that many Mini Clubmen around with three
baby seats. He'll have sneaked in when your back was turned,
he's an ambitious wee sod that one. I'll see what's happening
over in the car park and let you know.'

He wandered off, leaving Wyngate to ponder his next move.

The search dog had been called out, they still had the chance
of finding somebody alive. The divers were more expensive and

that could wait until there was a higher presumption of death at the scene. It would be the easiest thing in the world to roll a human body down the steep hill into the loch, where it would fall down a sheer rock face into very deep cold water. The blood was human, no doubt about that. They had taken samples at four-inch intervals from the wide patch of grass that appeared to be the site of the first, and main, attack. Ahern was proving very useful as a wildlife tracker and backed up by a constable, the two of them were inching their way along a path that did not exist to the naked eye, both now wearing shoe covers in case they were right and they were walking in the footsteps of the victim. And maybe, whoever had been pursuing them. Or a killer fleeing the scene.

Wyngate felt he could leave Mulholland in charge at the car park so he too was following Ahern, knowing that the guys were on to something. Then the search dog arrived and immediately followed the path of the three men, nose in the air, rain glistening in baubles on his ebony saddleback, as he trotted along as if this wasn't difficult at all.

'A second site? What do we think?'

'Well, something happened at the peak there, then somebody ran or was chased down here.'

'Trying to get to the car park?'

'Why not go out the way they came in?'

'Because it wasn't safe to go back that way obviously. The path is really only wide enough for two side by side, not a huge amount of room to get past somebody who is trying to stop you from leaving. Or had stabbed you and was standing there with a knife? I'd run in the opposite direction.'

'Or if there was more than one of them chasing you?'

The dog was moving on, slower now, stopping every now and again to check, casting a glance at his handler to see if that was OK. Then he stopped. And did an about turn, curving his spine into the length of his own body, getting ready to come back the way he had come.

'Why is he doing that?' asked Ahern.

'The scent runs out, he'd follow it if it was there to be followed. Whoever was here retraced their steps and went back the way they came. Or was airlifted out by an alien.'

'Or,' said Wyngate, 'they caught the poor bugger here, dragged him across this grass and tossed him in the loch.'

'Then the dog would take us to the water's edge, but he hasn't. So it didn't happen like that.'

Wyngate looked at the dog, who looked back at him with eyes that seemed to be asking for a bacon sandwich. He didn't know how much to trust it. 'Yeah, thanks for that.' Wyngate's airwave crackled. He answered it, ready to point out that he wasn't a rank that got paid enough to do this job, some of those fat bastards back at Central could come out again now that this had gone up the priority list.

At the car park, Mulholland had been asking around about McCaffrey, keen to speak to the young officer who had got close to Costello during the Braithwaite case. His eyes kept gravitating towards the Clubman. The windows were condensed over. He checked the other cars that had been parked there for a couple of hours now. Light fog over the windows, McCaffrey's looked thick and dense, as if the car had been there all night.

Nobody had seen him.

He radioed in, locating the station where McCaffrey was based. And then gave them a quick call. He turned away instinctively as two other cops came close, aware of the silence in the still air and the ease with which he could be overheard.

'You still up at the lochside?' asked the desk sergeant.

'Yes.'

'Well, Isla McCaffrey has been on trying to locate her husband. He didn't appear for the start of his shift this morning and he didn't come home last night or the night before. That will be Isla McCaffrey as in . . .'

'The wife of the bloke who drives the Clubman? It's still here. I think it has been here for some time.' Mulholland read out the plate number.

'That's a match.'

'Yeah, can't be many with three kiddie seats inside.' Mulholland looked round to the deep water of the loch. He'd put an alert out for McCaffrey, talked to his senior officer, but had the sinking feeling he'd be calling out the underwater search team before darkness fell.

\*   \*   \*

When Hannah got back to her cottage flat in Govan she thought about doing the hoovering, but she was too tired, almost too tired to sleep. She was always like this after doing a string of night shifts at A & E, she became a little excitable and found it difficult to sit down and relax. The flat was cold so she sat on the edge of the settee having a couple of quick cigarettes. It was still raining outside. She watched a neighbour walk her two wee girls past the flat, the neighbour looked in, saw her and waved. Hannah waved back and then settled back into the sofa, thinking about putting a log on the fire. Then have a shower, put on her jammys, light the fire and settle down with a cuppa and toast, thickly buttered with a teaspoon of Marmite on each slice. That would normally send her to sleep, and if that didn't do it, sticking some daytime TV with its simpering banality definitely would.

She went over to the fire; it was her proudest possession, this old flat with its original fireplace and a wood-burning stove reinstated. Kneeling down she dusted the ash away and brushed it into the ash box. She pulled out some old newspaper that her neighbours upstairs kept for her, and she started the dirty process of rolling them up five sheets at a time and tying a knot in them. There was something very pleasurable in getting her fingers so dirty, before having a shower and making sure she got them clean again.

She placed a small firelighter in the grate and tossed in a few knots of newspaper and added a few more logs. Leaning back on the carpet, she thought about having a cup of tea before the shower. She squared off the pile of newspapers and put her hand down on the carpet to lever herself up onto her aching feet, then looked down at the front of the newspaper that was facing up at her, and the two faces on it, a one-word headline: MISTAKES. She looked again, picking up the paper and holding it close, reading it with tired eyes, scanning the picture, then looking at the date. The fourth of October.

She looked closer at the face, and the name. She was sure it was her. Domestic abuse took place at home, not at work, and there was the name of a colleague, a safe person. She rubbed her hands down the front of her trousers, leaving jet streams of black ash on her thighs. So this woman might be this police officer. Might be. For all Hannah knew, her husband, the abuser, might also be a police officer. But she was involved with people like pathologists. Hannah read the caption under the photograph of the grey-haired man to confirm. These people knew all about the issues of patient confidentiality and the difficulties of identification. She was dealing with people who knew the score. It was worth a shot, she reached for her iPad.

And here she was, walking around Uncle Archie and Aunt Pippa's house. He had gone to work, after making it quite clear that he was not going to hold her hand, snoop or check up on her. She had asked him, as she always did, if the investigation into Abigail's death was making any headway. The answer was always no, but he did say they were now looking at wider CCTV, the timeline and the logistics again. And that had panicked her. Alone in the kitchen, she tried to think.

She sat for a long time, staring at the tabletop, letting the coffee go cold.

She heard the phone ringing through in the hall. It would be for Archie, she let it go.

It stopped then started again. Probably a sales call, so she walked over and put her hand out. It fell quiet as soon as she lifted it from its cradle. It wasn't her house, it wasn't her phone.

The problem was, she didn't know if she could actually do it. Not again. The water she poured from the kettle kept missing the cup, spreading over the worktop. She mopped it up; wishing the tremor in her hands would stop betraying her. The need for alcohol was intense; vodka, strong black coffee and a pro plus. She was supposed to be on decaff, vitamin C, Acamprosate and Fluoxetine, never on an empty stomach. Her larynx and the muscles of her throat had been damaged when she was attacked, so she had learned to eat and drink in a certain order. She had taken the pills out the dosset box and flushed them down the toilet. She was going to have an Americano and a couple of rich tea biscuits, a habit she had learned from Abigail when she had suffered from terrible morning sickness. The pain of that thought, the easy way the memory had popped up in her mind so unexpectedly, it punched her in the stomach with more pain than any attack she had suffered in the Blue Neptune. When Abigail had got pregnant with Malcolm, it was as if her sister was rubbing her face in her own infertility. The way Abigail looked at her sometimes, as if she had it all, and Valerie deserved to have, and to be, 'lesser'. She closed the lid of the kettle, thinking how funny it was, the way life turned out. It was a true saying, it's not where you start, it's where you finish.

A fleeting memory flashed through her mind, stubble on her cheek and the impression of a scent that she couldn't identify. Maybe a perfume of Abigail's. She gripped the side of the worktop in Archie's pristine kitchen and tried to remember. There had been a man, a kiss, a cheek against hers.

Sitting amongst the Robert Annan prints on the wall, at the melamine table with its cream and light-brown striped bench seat, she sipped her caffeinated coffee, and looked out the window to a bare tree, an empty bird feeder swinging back and forth in the wind. Her Agatha Christie biography, still stuck at page fifty-six. She let the tears run. She was fed up trying to be strong. Life beyond vodka had only been a few hours old, and she had no idea what was causing the pain that gnawed and chewed at her soul. The loss of her family? The loss of herself? Mourning that her affair with the bottle might be over? She was better than that, better off than that, she had a brain and she had Archie behind her. He would treat her like a daughter.

Her future.

The lack of future?

If she ever was arrested, locked up, she really didn't care. She'd have a roof over her head at least. That wasn't the issue, at least it was something. The future that is unknown was far too awful to contemplate. She sipped at her coffee, letting the tears roll until they made little star-shaped drops on the tabletop. It was a future that was purposeless. It was a yawning great void that stretched in front of her and she could see nothing in it, nothing that was of any value to her.

Maybe she could get another cat. Yeah, she could just see Archie's face when she presented him with a litter tray. She looked out the window, there was a robin hopping around in

the garden. That wasn't something she saw when she had
Alfred.

She brushed away a tear . . .

Who killed Cock Robin? It was the sparrow, with his bow
and arrow.

It shouldn't be too bloody difficult to figure out who killed
her sister.

Surely.

That was one question that wasn't going to go away. And,
the thought struck her as another teardrop fell, that might be
the one question that she was uniquely placed to answer. Yet
she could not.

Where had she been at four o'clock that morning?

The phone rang, she jumped. Maybe she would be better
answering it and give Archie a message or swear at the person
if it was a bloody sales call. Or she could let them speak and
then say, 'Now let me tell you all about the Baby Jesus'. That
usually made them hang up. She walked, rather quickly and
with no loss of balance she noticed, into the living room and
lifted the handset. The voice on the other end said, 'Valerie?
Can you give a message to Archie? His mobile is turned off.'

'Yes,' she replied, looking round for a pen, but knowing
she used to have a very good memory. 'Yes, of course I can
take a message.'

She was so touched that somebody used her name, and
trusted her with a job that she started to cry.

The helicopter journey had been quick and uneventful, the
blades cutting their way through the dark clouds to land on
the pad at Raigmore, where an emergency medical team had
been waiting with full clinical support, right from the minute
the young man's stretcher had been clunked off its cradle on
the chopper. Ten minutes later the patient was in a cubicle,
on oxygen and plasma, platelets and four monitors, stabilizing
him to give them time to work out what the bloody problem
was. Apart from the big wide cut across his throat.

And, in amongst them all, moving between them quietly,
was Morna Taverner, a female constable, dressed in civvies
covered in a sterile gown, carrying a pile of brown paper bags

which she held open as the young man's clothes were stripped and cut from him, and then delicately dropped into a bag, to be sealed, signed and removed from the premises.

Morna Taverner had been following their conversation from the moment the trolley hit the tarmac. He looked to her like every other hiker or walker that liked to take on the challenge of the hills during the winter. An extreme hillwalker. He was an outdoorsy type anyway, as his boots were dropped into the evidence bag, she saw the dried pine needles fall from the indentations in the soles. The weather on the Bealach was too severe for trees, so he had been walking elsewhere and trans-ferred to the peak. Except if he was an experienced hillwalker, he would have been dressed more appropriately. And he would not have been out there on his own. Not in November. Not without having left notice with somebody to raise the alarm if he failed to return when expected. He wouldn't be the first to take off his jacket at the first sign of hypothermia. But there had been signs that he had been dragged to where he had been found. And the telltale cut on his throat.

He had no signs indicative of being hit by a car, no first impact abrasions on the shins, nor the impact of the bonnet and the roll off the vehicle to the road. A senior casualty officer popped his head in and looked at the chart, his vitals, and finally looked at his face.

'So throat cut and then what? He's been beaten? A crowbar? Then thrown off an elevated site?' The doctor looked a little confused.

'Agreed, he was found like this at the top of the pass, then maybe dragged to the gully. The cut throat suggests foul play. Obviously.'

'Are you the policewoman?'

'Police officers we are supposed to be called now,' Morna smiled. 'How is he doing?'

'Fair enough. We are going to wheel him down for an X-ray as soon as we get some bloods in him, get his temperature up. See if he's got any blood on the brain, we will take it from there. If he's ready, the scan will be within the next two hours but neurologically, there doesn't seem to be any panic. But right now, he's going to the high dependency unit.'

And the wheels on the trolley were clicked down, the stretcher stabilized and he was away, his dirty feet sticking out the end of the trolley, a passing nurse picking up the blanket and smoothing it down, smiling at his immobile black and swollen face. 'Any ideas who he is yet?' the nurse asked.

'Nope. Nobody has reported him missing as yet and he has no ID on him.'

'There are some bloody mad bampots out there.' She looked out the window, as if she meant Inverness itself.

Anderson was studying a printout of unsolved rapes over the last ten years, searching through it, looking for connections. The pad beside him was full of scribbles and doodles, mostly excluding those incidents from the connections he was trying to make.

He answered his phone automatically, surprised at the very quiet voice on the other end, very young, almost a girl. She pronounced his name Coleen Anderrrson, soft consonants, a Highlander, he thought. 'Yes, indeed, how can I help you?' He assumed the attitude he did when he talked to one of his daughter's friends. This sounded like a student wanting help with a dissertation. Probably passed on by Mitchum who obviously thought he didn't have enough to do and that he was only sitting at his desk, looking at a sequence of rapes for his own amusement.

'DCI Anderson, this is DC Morna Taverner. I'm up at Wester Ross, CID', she added, as if she had forgotten and had realized that he might like to know. 'I have been doing a cold case computer trawl . . .'

'Yes,' he said, and leaned back in his chair, knowing exactly where the conversation was going.

'And I came across your name more than once, about the A835 rape?'

'Not familiar with that.'

'No reason why you should be. It's the Sally Logan and Gillian Witherspoon cases you have been looking at. Our footprints over the archive keep crossing, so I thought you might be interested in Nicola Barnes, she was a twenty-three-year-old,

out on her own, taken off the road – the A835 as it comes into
Ullapool. It was the eleventh of July 2004.'

He heard her take a deep breath.

'And there was an incident in 1987? A seventeen-year-old
girl disappeared at—'

'That's a long time ago,' Anderson said quietly. 'Do you
have anything else?' Anything? He was encouraging, betting
that this was usually as far as she got in her pitch. There would
be nothing in this. She was young, trying to make connections,
seeing them where none existed. She would be on the end of
the phone sitting in a large office somewhere talking quietly,
cupping her phone with the palm of her hand. He imagined
her with a nervous tic, pulling her hair behind her ear the way
Claire had done since the day she was born if she had ever
been in trouble, or Peter's habit of biting his upper lip.

'You have been working on the Logan and Witherspoon
rapes. I think there are similarities.' She was more definite
now, fortified by his interest.

'Are you working cold case?'

'No.'

There was quiet, he could hear her breathing.

'Not exactly.'

So this was a current case she was working and had
searched the database for similarities. She sounded inexpe-
rienced. He closed his eyes and let her continue. 'There was
an injury to her left shoulder. The computer coughed that
up. And of course the rapes. The lack of DNA, the forensic
awareness and—'

'The fact he hasn't been caught,' Anderson added. 'What
does your boss say? I mean, you shouldn't be looking at this
if you are not on a cold case unit?'

'OK, but this is something I am interested in.' A pause.

He didn't respond.

'My DCI doesn't agree with me but he said I could call
you.'

'OK, OK,' said Anderson, at least she had ran it past him.
'You see, he will need something to go on, a weight of evidence
before he can justify spending time and money on taking the
investigation further. There will have been a full investigation

at the time. So if no new evidence has come to light it can be difficult to justify . . . Well, it's difficult to justify. That's all.'

Silence. He could almost hear the disappointment as if somebody had physically deflated her at the other end of the phone. No doubt this was exactly what her boss had told her.

He heard a long sigh.

'And has any other evidence come to light?' he asked.

'No.'

'And the computer system has made no other links, no other connections?'

'No. Just your name. And the method. The arm. Women . . .' All her enthusiasm had gone.

'Are you working on something else right now?'

'I'm in the hospital, minding a young man we found on the Bealach Na Ba.'

He had no idea what she was talking about. 'Do you have him handcuffed to the bed?'

She laughed lightly. 'Not that kind of minding. He was dumped up there with a bad head injury, his face has been beaten to a pulp, throat cut. We don't know if he'll pull through, we haven't confirmed an ID yet. It's so sad, but I'm sitting with him, I will be here when he wakes up. If he wakes up. There's a wee flicker every now and again, you know, so I am not risking walking away but I am bored so I was flicking through my notebook. I have been meaning to call you for a while.'

'The best thing you can do is be there. It sounds as though you have your hands full, so why don't you email me the file. And tell your boss that you have done that, make sure it's noted. He can't refuse permission retrospectively,' said Anderson. But he could kick off.

'Oh yes, yes I will.'

'I've just been given a few more days to review these cold cases so I will look at yours as well. If I find any other convergence of the cases, I will get back to you.'

As in: don't call us, we will call you.

'Thank you,' she said, 'thank you so much.'

She sounded so grateful, he felt like a right bastard.

'What was your name again?'

'Morna Taverner.'

'And your DCI?'

'Patrick, Alastair Patrick. He's from Glasgow, that was years ago, he's quite old now.'

*Aren't we all?* 'OK. Let me have a look, bye for now.'

'Thank you DCI . . . Colin, Mr Anderson, ta.' And the phone clicked off.

After the phone call, Valerie looked at the calendar, counting back and then marking the days when Costello had last been seen. Uncle Archie was concerned about her, her work colleagues didn't seem to be making much of it, so where was she? She didn't know Costello; she had seen her and heard her but had never actually met her, but she had exchanged a few words with a woman called Dali Despande – a name once heard not forgotten – who was also concerned about Costello, but was more concerned about George Haggerty. If Costello had gone off after him, well, more power to her . . .

Val had heard that more than once.

And the question: 'Had she gone rogue?'

Apart from Costello's 'close friendship' with Archie, their only connection was Malcolm. That boy had reached out to Costello, her mobile number had been on the mobile phone that had been found on his bedside table, tucked down the back of a photograph of his parents was her card with her number on it. He had called her, but Archie had said that the call was so short it looked like he had simply called then rung off, the call was not long enough for any conversation to have taken place.

And that hurt. Why did the boy not phone his Auntie Valerie? Because he knew, even at his young age, that she would be pissed?

Valerie tried to put that picture together in her mind. She had been in court more times than she cared to recall in situations like this, especially when she was working with vulnerable children. Was Malcolm vulnerable? She didn't think so. Abigail was a good mother. She could have said anything to her, but how much had her sister changed? Kids very quickly learn to trust, so had Malcolm moved on from Valerie and Abigail and realized he could only trust somebody from outside the family?

Maybe that was the point? He needed to talk to somebody who wouldn't let it get back to . . . George? To Abigail? Who had the boy been frightened of?

Her heart sank, more tears.

She had no money, no job, no carer, no family, everything had gone.

Taken from her

But this Costello had it all. A career, a flat, independence and she seemed as though she had an opinion. She had made her opinion about George quite clear. Was she right?

Had she decided to go after him? Find evidence to bring him down? Was that what was going on in her mind?

Valerie looked around the room, Pippa's style. She could either stay here or she could see what she could do. She knew George. She knew Abigail.

She got out of her bed and, moving quicker than she had for weeks, crossed the room to her handbag, opened her purse and had a good look through her credit cards. They had all been cleared when she sold the flat and there was credit, a lot of it, enough to get up and get out there.

Where would George go? She had been his sister-in-law for thirteen years, she knew him in a way that nobody else did. If Costello could do it, then why couldn't she? She needed to find the truth, whether that meant clearing George's name or not.

Something that Abigail had said that night, that last time she saw her sister at the theatre, had been playing on her mind. Abigail had moved the conversation on so quickly – she must have been wrong, it was something like *George wouldn't let me* or *George wouldn't like it*.

But he had allowed her out to go to the theatre that night. The last time she had seen her sister alive.

Malcolm in bed early as he had a cold. There had been tension in the house that night, nothing spoken but she had been aware of it. She had been wrapped up in her own misery.

Bloody hell, they had sat in that lounge, her thinking about the child that she was about to buy and her sister sitting two feet away, keeping a big secret of her own. Had she grown scared of her own husband? Abigail had mentioned that she suspected George was seeing another woman. He was working away on a new contract, he was going home to Port MacDuff more often, being away from Malcolm more often. Never inviting them to go with him. That had been months ago. She hadn't thought much about it. Abigail was bored and at home too much, she was making up all kinds of stuff about George. He was never home, he was always going back up north to his hometown where Abigail didn't want to go, or was never allowed to go. How odd that Malcolm had never gone north with his dad. He had never been asked.

She had years of expertise as a fiscal; she had investigation skills.

She had nothing, absolutely nothing left to do except drink and she needed something better than that.

But where to start? She lay down on the bed again, her hand wandering to the bedside table where she had secreted the quarter bottle behind her Agatha Christie biography. Just as Malcolm had kept Costello's card, so Valerie kept her vodka. She twisted off the cap; she adored that click of the seal breaking, like the first meeting with a new friend. Then she heard her mobile ring. She could either have a drink, then go into a long and troubled sleep. Or she could look at her phone and see who was calling.

It was a sign. She liked signs. She was beginning to trust them more than her own judgement. Her thumb was trembling as she tapped in her security number.

It was George leaving a voicemail. He wanted to meet her for lunch. Or coffee, for a chat.

Every fibre of her being wanted to refuse.

So she texted back and agreed. A quick coffee at the French Café. The coffee was a legitimate source of caffeine, and it might keep her mind off the vodka.

Valerie knew, felt, she herself had nothing to do with the murders. She knew that anything the police were doing was routine. Valerie couldn't explain where she had been that night, she had no memory she could recall. There was no evidence she had travelled to the house, she was not seen on any CCTV. So why had she felt so relieved when they had told her that?

She had no reason to kill her sister, even drunk, she was

never violent. And there had been no animosity between them. Not really.

But Abigail had opened the door to her killer, the sister who always had the bolt on the door, opening it a crack when the doorbell rang. It was a house isolated in the middle of the city, set back from the road, small windows which were always curtained and barely opened, and the huge monkey puzzle tree that grew at the side of the driveway, shielding the garage and the upper floors of the house.

Everybody looked at Valerie, as if they knew what she was thinking when she had no idea at all. She had no idea what had happened to her sister and the only person that Abigail would have opened the door to was her.

But George had a key, it was his house.

# SIX

The rain was starting to ease off, the cloud was lifting giving tantalizing glimpses of the Ben at the head of the loch. By the time the search team arrived, it was almost dry. They were going to walk a couple of metres apart in a band from the north part of the car park, the line of searchers would be following the contour line of the hill. This part of the loch side rose alarmingly, on the water's edge it wasn't very high, a couple of metres. The issue was the rock wall that descended into the water and kept going. The water was very, very deep, yet twenty or so metres south, there was a bay where little friendly waves lapped the shingle, a favourite site for wild camping.

The search team was going to walk, pulling the winter vegetation apart with sticks, looking for anything that might have some evidential value. First of all, the crime scene investigator and his team were going to gather as many blood samples as they could get. There had been pooling and spatter, not easy to see in the grass and the stony ground at the top of the rise, but as the first SOCO pulled up a blade of grass with gloved fingers, she smiled, holding out a small torch. 'There you go, seek and ye shall find. But don't let your big-footed search team stamp all over this. Give us an hour, then it's all yours. We can get it all done and over before it starts pouring again.'

Wyngate closed his own mobile, hoping his poker face was convincing. He had looked at the broken phone, sitting in its plastic evidence bag, shattered. Whoever did this knew the old adage that the way to make something untraceable was to drive a truck over it. He would pass it onto the tech team and see what they could do. But he bet Donnie McCaffrey had recently taken possession of a new Samsung 6 phone.

So Wyngate had asked, 'The owner of the car is missing, and he's a cop from Govan. Do you have a body anywhere?'

'No,' said Mulholland, 'not yet, and I hope we don't. Looks like it's going to be a long day. Hope to God this bloke's not got himself into some drug deal that's gone tits up. Hope to God I am not the one to tell his wife. She'll get no pension if he was on the take. Nothing.'

'Worse than that, we'll need to call in Complaints.'

'I've already heard from Mathieson. Her orders are that when we find what we find, we are to keep it quiet. So let the team know that there is no going home and chatting about it in the pub, otherwise they will be up in front of a disciplinary.' Mulholland thought he delivered this with an adequate sense of poise and authority, he was yielding a very big stick. He now felt like Mathieson's official contact.

A dead cop was something to be kept out of the press, but a dead cop on Loch Lomond was to be kept away from the tourist board.

But Wyngate shrugged as if he had been threatened with a trip to ASDA. 'How long do you think we will have to be here?'

'As long as it takes,' said Mulholland sounding as though he really was in charge now and he had his hands on the budget.

'Well, it's my daughter's birthday party at the soft play this afternoon, and I've been here since before dawn.'

As if on cue, there was a shout from a SOCO, who had been approaching them down the steep part of the path. He was holding something in his hand, strips of paper already in trace evidence sample bags. 'I can tell you straight away that there's a smattering of white powder here, pure cocaine on a presumptive test and a lot of alcohol. Somebody was having a party.'

Mulholland's twisted heart gave a little leap, Mathieson was going to have a field day with this. He could see himself being passed up the chain to the drugs squad. He looked to the sky and smiled. Sometimes there was a God.

Two hours later Valerie walked into the massive atrium of the Queen Elizabeth. She was still shaking slightly. The sight of George, well dressed and friendly, the way he had given her a hug and she had caught a wave of his aftershave, the side of his cheek had rubbed the skin of her face, too close, yet it felt very familiar. Too familiar. She had never enjoyed public displays of affection, but he was holding onto her as if she was all he had left in the world.

Which apart from his dad, she was.

And all the time, the recognition at the back of her mind, why was that scent of him so reminiscent of . . .? She had no idea.

The conversation was about the house and did she want anything. Any of her mother's stuff? The clock? And had she heard from the police, what were they saying?

Her brain had stopped working. She needed a drink in order to cope with any of that, so she had finished her coffee quickly and got a taxi from Byres Road to the Queen Elizabeth, stopping at an off licence on the way. She thought she was being discreet, slugging from the bottle in the back of the cab, but the look the driver gave her suggested he had seen her.

But the vodka had fortified her. Valerie was calm and in control, sucking a Polo mint as she walked into the hospital, looking for a nurse called Hannah. She had told Hannah that she would be wearing a three-quarter-length green coat and a scarf round her neck, clothes she had borrowed from Pippa's wardrobe. Similarly, a pair of Pippa's old specs perched up on her head had aged her twenty years. She hadn't told Archie. His wife's clothes were far too nunty for her, a little too big but they made her look less official, less threatening and more caring. In short, they made her look very unlike herself. She was wearing her own universal black boots, boots made for the weather. They said nothing about her as a failure. She expected the nurse to be nervous, she could get into a lot of trouble for what she had done. She had shown initiative and common sense but that kind of thing was never going to be tolerated in the NHS.

Valerie liked the nurse's thought processes about the identity of the mystery woman they had, especially the fact that the woman had been subject to some kind of violence, and Hannah wasn't going to put the victim back into a situation of jeopardy, so she had gone the circuitous route. That was the kind of thinking Valerie liked. If the woman they had was the woman who had been on the front of the *Daily Record*, then the authorities would know her circumstances. So when Hannah saw the photograph on the front page during the Kissel case, Costello looking sixty, O'Hare looking ninety, she had phoned the mortuary and got through to Jack O'Hare's office, and eventually to the pathologist himself, and he had called Archie at the house getting Valerie, and passing on the number. Valerie had put the phone down and thought this was a sign, if she could get to Costello before anybody else. If it was Costello and that was a big if. So she kept quiet about the message until she had spoken to her. Valerie was justifying it to herself; she was a familial link, her godfather was Costello's part-time boyfriend, or so the gossipmongers would have it. And Valerie would know Costello the minute she set eyes on her; she had looked her up the first time she had heard the rumour about her and Archie. And Valerie was sure Costello would recognize her straight away, depending on how bad the clonk on the head had been.

Valerie stood and looked around the vast white space, her eyes searching for a woman who looked nervous, but one who knew her way around this maze of a hospital. She felt conflicted, she wanted Costello to have resigned because she wanted her to be free to investigate the Monkey House Murders. Not lying in hospital, no use to anybody. Unless . . .

'Theresa?'

Valerie turned. 'Hannah?'

They shook hands. She was younger than Valerie had expected and well, more *common,* a toughness about the hard set of her face, the stink of cigarette smoke that surrounded her like a halo, the long cardigan that had seen better days and was probably an infection risk. After she shook her hand, Valerie covertly wiped her own hand down the outside of Pippa's coat.

'Thank you for coming out,' she said, her accent very broad, harsh to Valerie's ears. 'I didn't really know what to do, and I'd feel stupid if I was wrong. But nobody has reported her missing, we've had two false alarms already.'

'So whoever hit her doesn't want her back.' Valerie nodded

affirmatively, encouraging this chain of thought. 'You are doing the right thing. I've worked in the domestic abuse unit in Edinburgh for the last five years and what we need to avoid is this woman being returned to that environment when she is so vulnerable.'

They walked towards the lift, keeping their voices low. 'The police have nobody reported as missing that fits her description at the moment, but when I saw her, I thought I recognized her, just something about her that was familiar and some of the injuries she came in with, well they didn't make sense. She's not been living on the street, no way. I've seen enough of that in my time.'

'Me too, but what made you think it is my colleague? There must have been something.'

'Well, she has suffered a psychotic break so she couldn't tell us anything about herself but it was when I read that headline that I made the link. Well, I had been following the Kissel case, the girl who—'

'Killed her child? Yes. I think the whole country was following that.'

'And earlier today, I was lighting the fire with some old newspapers and on the front page was a picture of a police officer and a pathologist.'

'So you phoned Jack?' encouraged Valerie, knowing that the familiarity of O'Hare's name would encourage confidence. They were standing in the queue for the lift now, keeping well back, away from any prying ears.

'So I called his office, they are here in the same building but he is away, otherwise I could have gone downstairs and got him myself, but called him and, he must have called you . . .'

'Will he live?' Patrick was curt and precise.

The nurse bustled around the head of the bed, winding a flex round her hand before forcing it back in the machine, pulling over a flap and turning a lock.

'Will he live?' asked Morna, repeating the question for the benefit of the nurse.

'That's not a conversation we tend to have in front of the patient.'

'Will he live?' repeated DCI Patrick at the other end of Morna's mobile. 'I'm asking for an opinion, not the Gettysburg Address.'

'My boss wants to know what his chances are.'

'I don't get paid enough to speculate.'

'She said she—'

'Yes, I heard. Cheers.' And the phone snipped off.

Morna sat beside the young man. Not so long since she had been in hospital herself, keenly aware of the tubes and tapes. She still had flashbacks to that incident, her right cheekbone still hurt. She looked over at her patient, still intubated, his face swollen and bloody, unrecognizable. His own mum wouldn't know him.

Morna looked at his battered face, and she decided he was lovely. He was a young man, he had on very sensible clothes, stuff that his mum or granny would have bought him. They had cut the clothes from him and she had gone through them, wearing thick gloves, there was so much blood. He had been for a scan and X-rays. They had then taken him down to operate on a slow bleed on his brain. The result was, he *might* make it. He might not, but overall their attitude was a positive one. She had taken his fingerprints and a swab for his DNA; they would process that here. It was very dangerous to do an ID, DCI Patrick had a thing about that. He required proof beyond certainty, probably something to do with his background in the forces, people being blown to bits then having to be identified, she thought. They wouldn't want to get that wrong. Patrick would be insistent, he would want five markers. Both intelligence and confirmatory.

She raised the back of his hand to her nose, seeing the fine dark hair, she breathed in, deeply. Although he had been cleansed and disinfected she could still catch the scent of blood, gentle sweat, patchouli oil and something else? Petrol? She thought she had smelled that on his jumper as well. She turned his hand over and looked at the injuries on the flesh of his palms, scraps and scrapes. He had fallen on concrete at some point, recently.

As she had gone through his clothes, she had noticed there were no designer names on his clothes, all high street brand stuff. Except the Fair Isle jumper, somebody had knitted that for him, with a lot of love. The DCI's wife had made one for Finn, they took a lot of time and skill. She photographed the jumper on her phone and sent the image off to Patrick. Maybe a family member would recognize the intricate pattern and the different colours that wove and danced between themselves. Fawns and browns and creams with a single strand of deep red, well worn. The wool was balled at the armpits and almost transparent at the elbows. A jumper loved so much, it had been worn to its bare threads. She had run her gloved hand round the neck, then down the inside seams, checking there was no label, and that the stitching also looked hand sewn. This was a unique item somebody would be able to identify, unless of course he was a skint student and the jumper had been twenty pence from a charity shop.

She got out her notebook and looked over her list of the items she had photographed before she had replaced them in the brown paper bag before resealing, signing and dating the label.

Now, she was looking at the injuries, the head, the neck, the forearms, the hands, all defence wounds, or those of the attack itself, except those on the palms of his hands. Morna had recognized them, the same pattern covered Finn's knees every summer.

Gravel? So was he running along and he fell? Running along the road at the Bealach Na Ba, running to get away?

But you fall on your knees harder than you'd fall on your hands, surely?

Had he been crouching? Knocked to the ground? Or was he hunched down like he was doing the one hundred metres, down on his hunkers looking for something when he was clubbed on the back of his head, then the knife across his throat?

And why that smell of petrol or engine oil?

What had he been doing?

'I think that is his phone.' Isla McCaffrey passed the plastic bag over to the big male detective, ignoring the small nippy blonde with the bright red lipstick. 'But I can't say for sure. It's in pieces.'

'This may be totally unconnected but do you recognize this jumper?' Bannon showed her his iPad, showing an old beige Fair Isle jumper. The bloodstains down the front were obvious to anybody who had reason to recognize them.

'No, he wouldn't wear something like that.' Isla seemed to relax a little.

'Thank you, so it's quite simple,' said Mathieson through her little red mouth. 'We are trying to understand why your husband's car was up on the lochside on Saturday evening. And we are keen to ascertain his whereabouts now, as I am sure you are,' she added as an afterthought.

'You have phoned about four times asking me where Donnie is and why the car is up there, but I've told you that I don't know. He's a police officer.' Isla shrugged, confused. 'Surely you know?'

'He was off duty. There was no professional reason for him to be there.'

Isla shook her head, her dark curls, unbrushed and tangled, danced round the side of her ears. Dropping her head, she rubbed at her eyes with the palm of her hands. 'I don't know where he is.'

'When did you last see him?'

'Saturday night. He was going to work.'

'But he wasn't, Mrs McCaffrey, he wasn't going to work. He was at Loch Lomond. Can you shed any light why he might have gone there? It would help us a lot.'

'He *was* going out to work,' Isla insisted. 'He wasn't doing anything wrong. Where is he?' She folded herself up on the settee, her sobs racking her body.

Mathieson looked at Bannon, catching the odd choice of words. Isla McCaffrey was harbouring some doubts of her own about what her husband had been up to.

'I'm sorry, Isla, but we do need to know what happened when you last saw him. Do you know why he would be up at Inveruglass?'

She sat up. The precise question concentrating her mind. 'No, I don't, but he was sitting there.' She pointed to the chair that Bannon was sitting on now, a pile of children's clothes, ironed, ready for the drawer were sitting on the arm of the

chair beside him. 'Right there and his phone went, his mobile.'
She glanced at the plastic evidence bag that lay between them
like a traitor. 'And he read the message and said he was going
out. That was all that happened.'

'And what time was that?'

'About half past six? Quarter to seven?'

'Leaving his three young children to go out? Was that usual,
he got a phone call and just got up and left?'

'It had happened a few times.'

They both caught the slight falter in her tone, she knew
now in retrospect that something had gone badly wrong. It
had started with that phone call.

'The phone call or the going out?'

'Both. Have you checked the hospitals, he could have had
an accident?' She looked up and smiled, her face losing ten
years of pain with the one slight hope, somewhere her husband
might be.

'We have an alert out, if he's admitted to hospital, then we
will know. Who was this phone call from?'

'I can't work out where he might be, it's not like him not
to keep in touch.' Despite the heat, she shivered.

Bannon noticed the evasion and spoke again, now his voice
very gentle. 'I've never met your husband, Isla, but nobody
has a bad word to say about him. So anything you can tell us
will help. I look round and I see a young man with three lovely
wee children.' Bannon nodded at the photographs of the kids
on the sideboard. 'Cases involving other people's children can
really get to you when you are a father yourself.'

'Oh it did, it really did. He had been so upset by it, all that
baby stuff going on at the Blue Neptune. He had felt restricted
in what he was able to do to help. He thought he had read in
the newspaper that they had caught the people responsible.'

'That must have given him some comfort?'

She closed her eyes. 'A little, it gets confusing beyond that
as Donnie felt he couldn't say anything to me about the cases
he was working on. But he wasn't working on that case, so
he had a lot to say. The woman who survived?'

'Valerie Abernethy?' guessed Mathieson looking momentarily confused.

'So, she's another live witness to give evidence, and that made two, so that was good. They weren't going to get away with what they did to those women, to that young girl. He was pleased with that.'

'Was he talking to anybody actually involved in that case?' asked Mathieson pointedly, causing Bannon to roll his eyes at the harsh implication of the question.

'He didn't say much, but I can put two and two together. You see he talked a lot about joining the CID. Doing something that he wanted to do, to make a difference. It gave him a warm feeling in his stomach. He wanted to do what he called tough police work. Waiting and watching, ready to do something. He wanted to make a difference, that's all he wanted to do.' She started to sob again. Then sniffed loudly. 'And what kind of police are you? What did you say?'

'We investigate the police,' said Mathieson.

'Issues that the police have,' softened Bannon. 'Because your husband was a police officer we have a special protocol for cases like this.'

'So what was he doing out that night? Practising being a detective?' Mathieson was incredulous. 'Or vigilantism?'

'He wanted to join the CID, he was doing surveillance, he was learning, trying to develop more skills. He said that everybody at work was in a holding pattern waiting for vacancies, that nobody was moving anywhere. Everybody was in this holding pattern,' she repeated as if her repetition made it true, 'and he had applied for a transfer three times, been turned down for numerous training courses. We have three kids, we needed the money. He needed to get on.'

'And what was he doing to get extra money?' fired Mathieson, her mind leaping on the pure cocaine found at the scene.

The slap was quick and vicious; Isla was off the settee and over to Mathieson like a panther, the blow hit her right on the cheek. Bannon was slow to react, trying to reel in Isla's arm where the hand had connected with eye-watering impact.

'How dare you! He wasn't doing anything to get extra money,' she hissed. 'He was doing a job that you should have done, and he was helping to get evidence on somebody.'

Mathieson looked at the palm of her own hand then raised it to her cheek, then checked it for blood. Finding none, she brushed her hands together, her stare fixed on Isla with a condescending look. That was the one line bent cops gave all their dull little wives, stupid women who were kept at home and were far too trusting. But this conversation had gone too far, too quickly. She looked at Bannon.

'Isla, blood was found nearby on the loch side. He might be injured, there was cocaine present, as if he had been taking it.'

'No,' said Isla bluntly. 'Not him.'

'We have to go where the evidence takes us. Maybe Donnie had got wind of a deal and wanted to be present, to make sure before he made it official. He might have been testing the drug,' Bannon suggested.

She shook her head, and then seemed to collapse. 'He's not that stupid.'

Mathieson was losing patience. 'Isla, we need permission to look at your bank accounts, your credit cards, anything your husband—'

'His name was Donnie and you can do what you want. Look around you, we have enough, we don't have an extravagant lifestyle.'

'Some might call a cocaine habit an extravagant lifestyle?' asked Mathieson.

'Donnie doesn't even drink.'

'There was alcohol found at the scene.'

'Doesn't mean he drank it.'

'Can you think why it might be there? If not for Donnie, then who?'

'How the hell should I know?' Isla wrapped her arms round herself. 'You should be out looking for him, he could be in all kinds of trouble. Look at these poor bastards out in Yemen. Just look at the news? Why are you here? Go out and look for him? Please. I need to phone my mum, I'll need help with the kids. This is the worst nightmare, so you can do what you want, look where you want. I really don't care, but leave me and my kids alone.'

'Do you want to be here when we search the house?'

'I don't care.'

'And are you sure it was work that night? The phone call he got?'

'Yes.'

'Why?'

'Because it always was.'

'So this project he was involved in, this evidence he was gathering . . .' Bannon phrased the question carefully. It was the one question that Isla had not answered. 'Had it been happening a lot, these phone calls?'

'Recently, yes,' she sniffed.

'And how long had these calls and texts and night meetings been going on?'

Isla shrugged. 'Not before the Braithwaite case, only after that. He wouldn't, couldn't, tell me what it was about so it must have been a police matter.'

'Or he was having an affair,' suggested Mathieson.

Bannon rolled his eyes in disbelief.

'Do you want another slap?' retorted Isla. She turned to Bannon, obviously seeing him as her ally. 'It was something to do with the Braithwaite case. I've told you Donnie was first on the scene when that wee baby was found.'

'Was there anybody he was talking about, anybody whose name he started mentioning, somebody he hadn't mentioned before?'

'Like some cocaine drug overlord he had started working for on the quiet? Nipping off to Columbia on a Tuesday night to pick up God knows what. My husband is missing so can you please look for him. You are supposed to be looking after him, you . . . people.'

'And that's what we are doing, Isla. We need to know what was going through his mind. Have you heard him mention anybody he didn't speak of before, a strange name dropped in conversation?'

Isla tried to think. 'Well, Colin Anderson for one, because of the baby, Baby Moses. That entire Blue Neptune thing was on his mind, so the Braithwaite name. And then because of that he had been talking to Costello.'

Mathieson nodded. Well, that was two police officers missing.

\*  \*  \*

'Jack called me,' lied Valerie as the lift appeared with a delicate ping. 'He's one of the pathologists. We work together a lot, and he knows Costello and I are friends.'

In mutual unspoken consent they walked along a corridor past the nurses' station, the girl there looked up, smiled at Hannah, gave Valerie a quick once over and no doubt concluded that the woman with the scraped-back hair in the green coat who walked past, throwing her an officious glare, was somebody in authority and she went back to her own paperwork before the woman in the green coat gave her any more.

The unknown woman was in the last room in the corridor, by design or by chance, tucked away from the buzz of the main atrium. Hannah knocked on the door and swung it open; the woman was standing by the window looking across the giant foyer of the hospital watching visitors, nurses and patients walking past or queuing for good coffee, grabbing a takeaway that was more edible than the hospital food, She stayed looking out, taking her time to turn around, and waiting until the two sets of feet had come into her room and stopped moving. Tying her housecoat further round her waist, she slowly turned to face her visitors, her face blackened round the eyes, her expression still wary.

Hannah saw the flicker of recognition on her face when she saw the dark-haired woman beside her. Not a look that encompassed any affection, or any fear, just recognition. A work colleague, just as she had suspected. But not close friends.

'That's great, Hannah, if you can leave us for a couple of minutes,' said Valerie, in a voice that knew it would be obeyed.

'Don't stress her, she's not very strong,' said Hannah, noticing a lack of hello or any type of greeting between them.

'I think she might be a lot stronger than you think,' replied Valerie, looking at the pale face, the grey eyes and the crescent shaped scar on the hairline. It was definitely her.

'Costello?'

The face looked back at her blankly, but the eyes narrowed slightly.

'You know who I am, right?'

The thin lips moved, thinking, searching in her mind for an

answer, more recognition should come, some placement. But she knew.

And Valerie knew she knew.

The patient shook her head. 'I know I don't like you.' It was tempered with a slight smile.

'You know Archie Walker?' Valerie got out her phone and showed her a photograph, Archie looking very neat and dapper in a bow tie at some fiscal's dinner.

Costello took it and looked at the picture for a long time. 'I don't like him either.' She handed the phone back.

'Do you trust me?'

'I don't trust anybody.'

Valerie felt very calm and very in control, she was enjoying the feeling. 'Well, I am your best bet. I have to make something right. I have really fucked up, Costello, I have really fucked it up. And I need help.'

'Join the club.'

'I need your car.'

Morna took another sip of her coffee, how much caffeine could one human being take before their head exploded? Had anybody ever done any research into that? It would be much more interesting than the sex life of fruit flies or transplanting ears from a mouse's head to its bum and then back again. She had been here for nearly ten hours now, not really doing very much apart from musing on bits of information from her notebook, and running the items of clothes through her mind, seeing if there was any more information to be had there. Nothing ever stopped at her, nothing that might be of interest to her or any help in identifying the young man lying in his room. But he was breathing, being attended to, pipes and tubes being changed, readings taken. Their frequency had started at every ten minutes, then twenty, then half an hour, but not any less frequent than that. Morna presumed that any movement in that direction was positive, so she wasn't going to stop being optimistic. He had got through the difficult initial hours. Like those first few breaths of life, they were the most dangerous. As some wag had added, the last few breaths of life were pretty dodgy as well.

Along at the nurses' station the girls were busy, doing their job for their masters. All part of the important chain, but how often did they see the beginning and the middle and the end? How often did they have a good idea and the boss shot them down, even if the suggestion was sensible, they were stupid to have voiced the opinion in the first place. How much worse was it when the boss was a woman?

She was lucky to have Alastair Patrick. He might be a monosyllabic stern-faced bastard, but he was that to everybody, nobody got treated to special sarcasm or an icy glare. They all got it. Except maybe, wee Finn. Alastair and Wilma had given Finn a lovely Christmas present; a light sabre and they never forgot his birthday. The boss never mentioned any family, which always made her wonder.

The girls at the nurses' station had offered her biscuits, a grateful patient had come back with a tray of nuts and dried fruit. They had included Morna in the share-out, made her another coffee, asking if anybody knew who the young man was yet. She answered that they were working on a couple of leads. They had taken that as spiel for 'no' and gone about their business.

She had taken the coffee back to sit outside his room, then as the hours went past and anybody who could give her a row had left, she crept inside to watch him breathe.

She pulled out the brown paper bags with his clothes. It looked increasingly like she was dropping them off, rather than them being picked up. Looking through them, she stopped at the Fair Isle jumper again, thinking who had knitted it for him. His mum? She had an idea, something she had seen on the tele. She got out her mobile phone and, wearing gloves she examined the elbows of the jumper, then the cuffs under the light of her mobile phone with the magnification right up. And saw a few small orange fibres. She looked through the rest of the clothes, only finding a few more round the ankle portion of the socks. Folding the bags back up she tried to think. Then thought she wasn't paid enough to do that and tried to get through to Forensics Services, knowing the significance of cuffs and ankles, places of exposure. Places that could pick up transfer.

She could . . . The door opened. 'Fed up with you bloody cops hanging around here.' The nurse was tired and sounded more than a little angry.

'Try it from my point of view,' said Morna, restacking the brown bag.

'Do you have to be here all the time, do you ever go home? You have been here for hours.'

And she had. Once the nurse had left, Morna got on the phone and tried to explain to Neil that he'd have to get Finn tonight, she was staying at work. As usual, she only got his voicemail. So she phoned Lachlan.

# SEVEN

*Tuesday, 28th of November*

It was going to be a very long day, a very cold and wet, long, long day.

Wyngate was back on site at first light.

Mulholland had produced a missing person's report that might interest them, only because the report matched something that Ahern had said in his statement, about students coming up and monitoring the loch from the viewpoint. Ahern didn't know any specific times or dates but he recognized the name Kieran Cowan as that of a tall gangly lad who drove an old campervan. He'd seen it a few times but had no idea of the plate number.

The report said Cowan was a student of environmental biology. He was doing a project, a self-styled filming project of nocturnal activity at the loch. It was his preferred hideout that had caught the interest of the station desk staff when it was reported; the viewing site at the north-west bank of the loch.

So why was the only vehicle unaccounted for registered to a cop called Donald McCaffrey? That Mini Clubman had been there for more than thirty-six hours. Mulholland had traced the VW camper that Cowan was known to be driving. It was registered to his dad, a Mr David Cowan. But there was no sign of it around here, which suggested if he left the loch side, it was by his own vehicle. Had he taken the missing police officer with him? Cowan had no criminal record. A quick ring around his family, concerned friends and lecturers, painted a picture of a Corbynite, pint-drinking environmentalist with a passion for wild camping. The type to rant about dead wallabies.

It looked now as though he might have run into trouble himself.

Mulholland addressed the volunteers from the university, friends and colleagues of Kieran Cowan that had assembled on the loch side. They were keen to find out what had happened to him. They were young and fuelled by nervous enthusiasm, although nobody knew what they were looking for. Anything that belonged to him. They needed a much wider search than the police had already carried out and they needed it to be thorough.

Mulholland had heard the mention of a camera more than once. Cowan had not returned it to the university and that was very unlike him.

His camera? Mulholland had queried.

Most of them had seen it or borrowed it themselves. It was a special low light Macro Scub 4. Cowan had probably been wearing a photographer's waistcoat that night, pockets full of batteries and extra memory cards, wipes and brushes. In his bag would be two bars of chocolate, a flask of soup and a packet of hankies. His routine was well known to his friends, he was a young man who was known to stick to his 'routine'.


There was the usual early-morning chaos in Colin Anderson's kitchen, it resembled a café. Again.

Peter looked at his dad, then looked away. Paige even managed a half smile then slid out of her chair, taking a cup of coffee with her and disappeared upstairs. Claire and her boyfriend David had stopped talking, even Moses, still in his basket on the kitchen table, decided to stay stumm and settled for chewing his lip.

'I think you had better sit down,' said Brenda.

'Why, what's happened?'

Brenda gestured that he should sit, then she slid Claire's tablet across the table top to him, through the obstacle course of marmalade and jam jars, and dirty coffee cups. Claire, or more likely David, had a subscription to a daily newspaper. The picture on the screen was one he was familiar with. Costello, coming out of court the day she had given evidence in the Bernadette Kissel case. He read the piece hardly believing what he was reading. They had got it all, her background and who her father was, who her brother was.

'Oh my God, how the hell did they get hold of that?'

Brenda laid a hand across his shoulders, giving him some solace before she sat down and looked at the screen.

'It looks as if the knives are out for her,' consoled Brenda, with no hint of relish in her voice, though there was a time, not so long ago, when she would have taken great pride in reading this.

'It's all here. It more or less says she's responsible for . . . well, for everything but the Vietnam War. A colleague missing, a young family man, Costello forty-two-year-old spinster. And it finishes with a very nasty little line saying she isn't coming forward to defend herself.'

'Which worries me. Why isn't she?' He looked at who wrote it, not surprised at all to see that it was Karen Jones. Bloody bitch. He wondered who her sources were and, as he calmed down, why she had been so one-sided about the piece. She had given a full page spread to the lack of movement on the Monkey House Of Horror, written with the slant of Costello being first on the scene, who her brother was, and the fact that her current whereabouts were unknown.

At the bottom was a picture of George and Valerie, hugging, united in their grief and their search for the murderer. In it, Valerie looked much older, her clothes more suited to a woman twice her age.

Brenda pointed a very clean fingernail to the paragraph stating she remains in contact with a fiscal office. There was a picture of Archie Walker and a picture of George Haggerty, the caption underneath him said that he had been on the receiving end of a *personal vendetta*. And the way it was written, it sounded as if there had indeed been something personal. Especially from DI Costello. The three of them, Haggerty looking young, dark sweeping hair and very handsome. The picture of Costello looked awful, like she was a wrung-out rag.

'Jesus Christ.'

'Colin?' Brenda sat down and placed a cup of steaming black coffee in front of him. 'Calm down. This has nothing to do with you.'

'That wee shit was in this house on Sunday night and he

goes and does this! Bloody hell, it says here that "a source close to the investigation has revealed her involvement with drink and cocaine". What?'

'Did Archie know Valerie was the kind of drunk the papers are making her out to be? No, he didn't, not at the time. Costello is from a family of alcoholics, she deals with scum every day of her life. She found those bodies, who knows what effect that has had on her?'

'I don't believe you just said that,' Anderson snapped at his wife. 'You really think she would have something to do with cocaine?'

'No, but maybe she just can't cope any more. Maybe she's had enough. And when you find her, you should hug her, you owe her a lot.' She kissed him on the top of his head. 'You owe her an awful lot.'

Then his mobile started ringing following by the house phone.

Colin looked at the number on his mobile recognizing at once that it was Mathilda McQueen. Brenda watched as Colin listened. She could hear the chatter but not make out what the forensic scientist was actually saying.

'Are you sure?' he asked, his face pale. He listened again. 'Should you be telling me this? I don't want you to get into trouble. But thanks.'

There was no more chit-chat. He ended the call.

'Well, the police have a leak somewhere. You know that search going on up at the loch. They have found blood, cocaine and some alcohol. There is a mix of blood. A sample from a young police officer called Donnie McCaffrey.'

'The man who found Moses?' Brenda turned to look at the baby; recognizing the name as the man who stayed at the hospital with him when Moses had his breathing trouble.

Colin nodded. 'And another, blood from another person. Only two sources of blood, two sources of DNA. Male and female. The female sample is from Costello.'

'Oh, Colin, I am so, so sorry.'

Archie Walker was the obvious person to have on the scene. The fact that he shouldn't have been allowed due to his relationship with Costello was not mentioned. When he was determined, the chief fiscal was a man you didn't want to cross.

'We have a cop and student reported missing, and another cop we can't find. We were missing one camper van, now located. It appears undamaged. And we have the Mini Clubman also with no signs of damage. And they all have a *last seen* on Saturday night; Cowan's flat mate, McCaffrey's wife and Costello's neighbour. So, did a flying saucer come down and abduct them?'

The camper had been found three miles up the lochside road, tucked into an off-road lay-by. It had been phoned in on the non-emergency number. A van driver for a luggage transfer company, who pulled into that lay-by every day, had seen the vehicle there for three days in a row.

'I'll send Anderson out to have a look at the van, it might hold evidence.' At some point, something terrible had happened. Donnie McCaffrey had suffered some kind of injury that made him bleed and they now knew Costello had been bleeding too.

But there was an outside chance that the situation had been filmed and the camera had caught something of the events that night, witnessed it in some way. One guy, Neil, who ran HikeLite the luggage transfer company, had been out to this site before, and to the Loch Lomond campsite on a weekly basis. He had shown them where Cowan liked to be, up on the highest point of the hill. He had gestured this from the car park. He was pointing exactly to where the most blood had been found. Mulholland and Wyngate had instigated another search, this time for the camera, following all the exit routes from the monument.

Mulholland looked at the motley crew of volunteers, being told to keep in a straight line and go slowly.

They moved off as soon as the light was full although even then they still used torches, the line of twenty bodies advanced steadily and methodically.

A full hour had passed, when somebody on the high part of the land had pointed over to the water. Up until then, every shout had been a false call but the cop was dispatched to go and look anyway.

It was a volunteer. He waded into the shallows, bent over

and picked something out, holding it high above his head with a thumbs-up. A camera.

'That's bloody useful, it's been in the water for nearly two days now,' said Wyngate looking crestfallen.

'It's a marine camera,' muttered Mulholland. 'It's waterproof, you muppet.'

Valerie watched the door close in front of her. Mrs Craig, Costello's neighbour, was away to get the spare key. The old biddy was very picky about who she gave it out to. She thought Valerie was Costello's boss in some way, which Valerie supposed she was.

The little old dear was making a great play of giving Valerie a loan of the key for Costello's flat, leaving Valerie, who had introduced herself as a colleague from the fiscals' office, free rein. The old dear had glanced at the ID and twaddled off to get the keys.

As Valerie waited, she walked over to the window of the flat's hall. A nice flat right down by the riverside. It must have cost her a bob or two, this place. The hallway was carpeted; the window clean and free of bugs, there was a small wooden table under the window adorned by a couple of plants. She placed her hand over one, noting that the tremor in her fingers had gone. It came and went, she supposed as she dried out. Or at least cut her drinking down.

Who was she kidding?

If the tremor ever went away completely, she'd feel odd without it, the shake had been there for so long. The leaf of the plant stayed still as she caressed it, soft and velvety under her fingers. Somebody was making a little home here. Not Costello, not from what Valerie had heard about her; she sounded hard-nosed and career driven. But then she seemed to have a soft side too; Costello looked in on this old woman every morning, making sure she was OK. Mrs Craig had raised the alarm the minute Costello had not returned home. She was the only one who had thought to call the police.

Archie, not Costello, had said Costello's mum and gran had both been drinkers. Costello knew the signs and was very anti-drink, which might explain the disdain with which the

cop had greeted her with at the hospital yesterday. Valerie
hadn't thought much about vodka today, she felt busy and
purposeful.

She leaned forward and pressed her head against the glass,
looking over the city sky, a much flatter city than Edinburgh.
It looked more built up, she could see the cityscape for miles,
flattening away into the distance, the darkness above and the
bright lights down below, distorted into stars by the glass, it
looked like the world had turned upside down.

She felt a tap on her shoulder.

Mrs Craig was dangling a fob with a St Andrews flag on
it. 'Here's the key for you, pet.'


Morna woke, thinking the man had moved, a subtle change
she had caught out the corner of her eye. She sat and watched
him, from her seat in the corner. But now he was still once
more, as if he had been playing statues with her. Overnight
she had received an email; they had found an abandoned
vehicle down near Loch Lomond, Patrick himself was going
down there to oversee any evidence gained from the vehicle
and the local force were securing the locus until he got there.

She pulled her seat over to the bed, and rubbed her eyes,
studying him more closely.

He looked better, he seemed in less pain, as if his head felt
better and the tension had gone, allowing him to breathe a
little easier. The painkillers winning their battle against the
pain receptors in the brain.

She pulled her chair closer still; it was getting light outside.
She took his hand. His skin was warm and clammy. Her own
fingers seemed cold and podgy next to his. He had long slender
fingers covered in fine wiry dark hairs that matched those on his
chest, the little tuft of hair that peeked out from the wires that
crossed his chest and lay on the neck of his hospital gown. The
little pieces of tape on his throat looked like snowflakes.
The bandage round his head looked comical, cartoon-like almost,
wound round and round like he was a mummy.

How would she feel if this was her boy? If this was Finn
a few years on, caught like this, attacked when alone. Somebody
had cut his throat, then battered him with a blunt instrument,

stripped him of his jacket, then stripped him of his identity, only to leave him on top of the most dangerous road in Scotland. So why would somebody do that?

She rubbed the back of his hand gently.

At some point Patrick had woken her with a call and reported that there were now four young men reported missing who fitted this young man's description. Two from Glasgow, one from Aberdeen and one from Sutherland. He was getting further details. Her brief remained the same, sit tight and monitor him. Record anything and everything.

She'd need to call Neil again. Or Lachlan. It seemed DCI Patrick was determined to stop her going home.

She realized she was murmuring out loud. 'So, enough of me. What happened to you?'

He murmured something back, not to her specifically but some words came out, in the ether and to the world.

'Sorry?' she said, not sure if she had heard. 'Did you say something?'

It was quieter and more mumbled the second time. By the end of the word his breath was already tailing off, too much effort.

'You were attacked. You are in hospital, but I guess you have worked that out for yourself by now.'

The breathing changed rhythm slightly. He was waiting on the next bit, a pause between the in breath and gentle exhale.

'Well, you got a whack on the head and a few more on your face—' she left out the bit about the slit throat – 'and then somebody dumped you in the middle of nowhere but—'

He was trying to say something.

Was it Finn?

Was he trying to say Finn?

Did he know her?

Did he know her son?

She tried to halt the palpitations in her chest. Finn had been left with Lachlan, and then her mother would have arrived, and then Neil would have come home. In any case, Lachlan would make sure Finn would be OK. There would be a similar pattern today. Her son was safe, which is more than she could say for the young man lying in front of her. She had heard wrong. 'Don't get stressed. But it was so cold, you didn't bleed the way you should, so you are going to be fine.' She lifted her hand off him for a moment and crossed her fingers hoping she was telling the truth. 'All the vessels contracted, you see, so that prevents blood loss and, on top of that, you have a wee bleed on your brain but they put a wee clip to hold it until it heals properly. My gran had one of them in her head for ages and she did OK.'

'Finn . . .' The word drifted slowly on his outward breath.

'Finn?' she repeated.

'Cam . . .'

'Cam? Is your name Cam? Campbell? Cameron?'

'Cam . . . Finn.' His head rolled a little, flicking backwards and forwards in frustration. Then the hand gripped hers.

'Finn or Cameron?' She felt stupid, she could sense his frustration, see it in the way his eyes stayed closed, but the eyelids kept flickering. This was stressing him.

Then he started to breathe deeply again, fallen asleep, floating back into himself, away to get better where they couldn't chase him anymore. It was up to her now.

'It's OK. I've got that,' she told him, lying into his ear. 'Rest well.'

Morna scrolled through the list of possible matches. Two had been drunk and had left a party at the weekend and not come back yet, Morna knew that was a bit worrying in the city but out here it was a death sentence. There were two missing person reports from Edinburgh and Sutherland. If the Sutherland boy was out in this weather exposed, he'd be dead by now. It wasn't uncommon. Nor was it uncommon to have too much to drink and stagger off a harbour wall into the inky depths.

She scrolled down, looking at the other two; the Glaswegians. One was a cop missing at a crime scene. She had to read that again. Why had that not hit the newspapers? It might have but she had not seen anything other than this room for the last day and a half.

The other one was a student, from Glasgow University. She read the 'last seen', her eyes catching on the fact he had been last seen going out the door of his flat with a film camera. Having had a quick look at the description, the weight and height seemed to match. They matched those of the cop as well, she reminded herself. She closed her phone and rubbed it against her chin. 'Kieran?' She enquired of the body. 'Donnie?'

There was no response to either. He was fast asleep, drifting away in a world of his own.

If she was a betting girl, she'd go for the student. No wife would let her husband out with that ancient jumper.

DCI Patrick walked out the HQ of the Wester Ross Police and took a deep sigh. He glanced at his watch, his face creasing, annoyed at the bloody waste of his life. That was an hour he was never going to get back. ACC Blackward was clear, keep the crime local, get it solved and get it solved quickly. The tourist board marketing people had been pushing the North Coast Five Hundred as an all-year road trip. During the winter months they removed the Bealach Na Ba and sent the route the long way round, but the infamy and the beauty of the road had given it a celebrity status. It was now considered the daredevil way to go; the more weather warnings the better. Blackward had placed in front of him media clippings of the pass; classic cars, hospital beds, you name it, it had tried to go up over the road to Applecross and then to Port MacDuff beyond. And now, all that good will and hard work had gone for nothing. If there was not a quick resolution to this case then the Bealach Na Ba, that golden goose, would forever be tarnished by the memory of a young man, battered and bleeding at the summit.

Patrick had remained silent except to utter three words, 'He's not dead.'

Blackward's reply was swift. 'Yet.'

Patrick had handed over the part of the file he knew the boss liked. Solid evidence. He had a photograph of a unique jumper, and that picture was being shown to a cop's wife and a student's mother. And they were running a trace on the orange fibres, the soil from the soles of the boots. He himself was prioritising the location of the camper. Some result would come of that, even if exculpatory.

And, he closed his eyes thanking God for Morna and her

precision, he pointed to the report about the orange tri-lobar fibres. 'These could be important.'

'And where are they from?'

'Cuffs, socks on the victim. The back of the head. Areas that would have been exposed, if he was rolled in a carpet or something. It's a tough hard-wearing carpet, used in cars, caravans, boats. Not for houses or hotels. The bad news is that Nissan, Volvo and Fiat all use that same material. So do many camper vans, especially conversions.'

'Caravans? Motorhomes?' Blackward had rolled his eyes. 'The tourist board are going to love this. But if we find the vehicle, then we can match it?'

'The dye, yes, the orange dye will be unique for that run.'

Blackward had palmed his hand across his mouth. 'Sometimes I think this place is cursed.'

'It's people, it's only people.'

Blackward had nodded. 'Keep on it and keep focussed. Are we getting anywhere on the coke trail?'

'I think we might be. Too much of it is being moved around too easily. And we have left it, with the knowledge of the surrounding forces, until we get a pattern. The longer we wait, the more we know and we have more chance of getting higher than the monkeys. Would be nice to nail those who are bringing it in.'

'Are we close to doing that?' asked Blackward.

'Maybe.'

'Do you have a good idea who is moving the stuff around, locally?'

'Yes, we do. As you said the tourist board won't like it. But they don't pay my wages.'

'Who found the body?'

'I don't know. You can make that request for information further up the food chain.'

'So who contacted you?'

'No comment.'

Patrick heard gunfire, rapid, assault rifles. The noises went no further than his head. He had heard his own voice report where the body had been found but Blackward looked blank, which showed he had spent too long behind the desk.

So Patrick had excused himself before the boss could ask anything else.

Once out on the street, Patrick breathed in the salted air and watched the seagulls wheel and circle above. He was jealous of their freedom, up and around higher and higher. He phoned Morna to find out how the young man was doing. He was still alive, he was trying to say something, 'Finn' and 'Cam'. He could hear the flicking of the pages of her beloved notebook. She was in love with pens and paper, unlike her colleagues who were very keen on their iPads and electronic notebooks.

Finn? Cam? It meant nothing to him.

Colin Anderson sat down in the blue-carpeted family interview room at the old Partickhill station where Anderson had spent most of his working life. The picture of the flowers on the wall was the same, he could still see a stain on the carpet from a cup of black coffee he remembered going over. So why did he feel so unwelcome on his own turf, being questioned by these two interlopers? It was the summons that did it, the phone call from Complaints that they would like a word with him. The message was clear; get your arse down here. He had left an unusually quiet office, everybody was tiptoeing round him.

They came in, the two of them, Bannon and Mathieson. Anderson knew Bannon, not well but enough to know that he wasn't hated, not the way that some of them were from Complaints and Investigations; the cops who policed the cops. It wasn't an easy job, and Anderson doubted that it was a pleasant one, but he understood the need for the force to be policed. Mathieson, he didn't know. But he presumed she was the small blonde, blanched white, she looked as though she had seen a ghost, her nacreous face highlighted by the dark red of her lips, lips that were firmly closed at the moment, fixed in a tight, thin line. Anderson was a man who noticed women's hair, the way other men noticed curves or legs. He was quick to see that he could look right through hers. It wasn't thick and titan like Brenda's, not curled and blonde like Sally's, not long and auburn like Helena's. Mathieson was almost bald.

Maybe that was why she wasn't a barrel of laughs.

'Sorry, Colin,' she said. 'Not good of us to meet like this but I didn't think I could do this by phone.'

'Do what?' he asked, nodding, shaking hands with them both, acknowledging her apology. He knew that whatever it was; it had nothing to do with him. They were here to get him to spill the beans on a colleague, but he couldn't think who. He had mulled it over in his mind, and hoped it was about Mulholland and his leg, more a matter for HR and occupational health. He would have thought, but who knew with the state of Police Scotland these days, anything to avoid paying an ill health retrial pension.

But he knew, in his bones, it was about Costello.

Mathieson was still smiling slightly, as a look it didn't suit her. Bannon sat down, in the position of the observer. So this was important, this could be serious.

'Your partner DI Costello? Do you have any idea where she is?'

'Costello?' The question had genuinely taken Anderson by surprise.

'Yes Costello, your colleague. You have worked with her for many years. I'm sure you remember her.' The pretence of politeness was gone, now replaced by sharp sarcasm that could have come from Costello herself.

'Yes, I know who she is. I don't know where she is.'

'Nobody does. Do you know this gentleman?'

God they were treating him like a suspect. He knew the next move, to slide a photograph across the table then turn it over at the last moment, increasing the shock value.

Bannon had the grace to look a little sheepish as the 16 by 12 photograph was slid across the table towards him.

Anderson had to cough to hide a smirk.

He looked at it, a fresh-faced young man in a blue jumper – he looked like the sort of man that appears on adverts for formula milk or a new housing development. He would have two small kids and a wife who worked part time, a sandpit in the garden and every house he bought would be another step on the ladder until they started downsizing.

'I don't think I do,' he replied carefully, aware of the sweat of stress around his collar.

'Does the name Donald McCaffrey mean anything to you?'

Something sparked in his mind, but not enough to hold on to.

'Donnie McCaffrey?' offered Bannon.

'Yes.' The small memory in Anderson's mind caught the spark and came to life. 'I think he was the first officer on the scene w-when,' he stuttered realizing he wasn't about to relate an event, he was about to talk about Moses.

'Yes, when your grandson was discovered in a car, alone. A Dacia Duster that had been moved from its original parking spot.'

'In the end that case resulted in two deaths, one fatal incident and a trial in preparation, so we don't need to discuss any of that.' Anderson was acting as if he outranked them now. He did. Talking about the job was OK but they were talking about his family. 'But don't take my word for it, you can check the log.'

'We did,' said Bannon.

OK, so that wasn't what they were here for. Anderson waited, the next move was theirs.

'Colin . . .' It was Bannon's turn to speak, trying to engage him; he was going to be the matey one, inviting confidences that he wasn't entitled to. 'How well do you know Costello?'

'As well as any police officer knows another who they have worked alongside for twenty years. There have been months on an investigation when we have been in each other's pockets and other times when we hardly see each other. This is one of those times – a not seeing each other time,' he clarified for them. 'Has anything happened to her?'

'We thought you might be able to tell us that.'

'Well no, I haven't heard from her.' Archie Walker had but he wasn't going to tell them that. An unwelcome thought floated through his mind at that moment, a text identified a phone, not the person who sent it.

The two detectives passed a look between them, something that would have gone unnoticed if the person sitting opposite them hadn't been skilled and experienced in investigation techniques. They were about to change tack.

'I presume that you and Costello have had differences of opinion in the past.'

'Plenty.'

'Do you think she's gone off in the huff?'

'No.'

'So only this time.'

'Only this time, what?'

'For going AWOL. Is she in a relationship?' That was a very focussed question, and the sudden change of direction did not go unnoticed. Was it Archie they were after?

Mathieson caught the hesitation.

'The answer to that is either yes or no.'

'The answer to that question is none of my business. I am her work colleague not her big brother.'

'We are coming to her brother in a moment.'

*I bet you are.*

'Have you seen the newspaper article? That was very damming.'

'Oh, so the press are the moral guardians of the complaints? God luck with that. And you should be more concerned with finding out who in your team is taking backhanders for dealing that dirt.'

'It was bad,' sympathized Bannon. 'But it wasn't from us, it was from George Haggerty.'

'And who told him? Bloody hell,' Anderson dropped his head into his hands, all those little midnight chats with Haggerty. He'd kill the bastard.

'Anything to tell us?' asked Mathieson.

'Relationships can be very complex. Unless you see the world in black and white, most relationships are shades of grey. My reading of the situation is that she felt very responsible for the death of Malcolm Haggerty—'

'So she was responsible for the death of Malcolm Haggerty?' Mathieson was on it, her eagerness pulling her right into a trap.

'Only as much as you and I are. We should provide a safe society and we don't. Have you never been involved in a case and thought, if only I had done X or Y, they wouldn't have died.' He looked her straight in the eye, she didn't look away. 'Obviously not then. You are very fortunate.'

Bannon decided either he'd had enough, or that they were getting nowhere. He started again with his engaging approach.

'Colin we have a problem, a big problem. Costello has disappeared. So has this young man, under very suspicious circumstances.'

Anderson's eyes narrowed. 'Bloody hell.'

'This young cop was friendly with Costello.' Bannon tapped the photograph.

'I know.'

'His blood was found at the small hill to the rear of the viewing point at Loch Lomond. He may have been stabbed.'

Anderson put his hands up, palms out. 'But he is a police officer, he must have enemies? Why are you talking to me?'

'We have been in touch with the investigating officers and the case is now ours.'

'Why? Because he is a cop?'

'According to his wife, Costello invited him to a meeting somewhere, summoned him, she asked, he jumped.'

'So they were onto something?'

'Onto what?' Mathieson's eyes glinted dangerously.

'Something? I don't know. Wasn't there. Wasn't told.' But he'd bet his bottom dollar that it was to do with George Haggerty. 'Has something happened to her?'

'We have found "significant DNA" on a small sample of blood. And another DNA from a much larger sample of blood.'

'Whose?'

Mathieson hesitated so it was Bannon who spoke. 'McCaffrey and Costello. And you know how we would interpret that. The person with the bigger blood loss was the victim, the other the perp. It's a theory that we are working on.' He upended the pen on his desk letting it drop between his thumb and forefinger. 'It fits the facts as we have them, but that will and can change as the evidence comes in.' He smiled benignly. He didn't believe it either. 'It's just a theory.'

'You think that Costello attacked and wounded McCaffrey? Why the hell would she do that?'

'That is how we would interpret the evidence if there weren't two police officers involved. The problem is that we have no evidence that anybody else was there.'

'Barking, wrong tree and up. Put that in any order you want.' Anderson was scathing in his lack of respect.

'We need to go where the evidence takes us, Colin, and it makes no sense to me,' said Bannon. 'Can you shed any light on it?'

'As I said, it's a theory and being who she is, her family . . .' said Mathieson, staring directly at Anderson. 'Maybe with a little bit of mental instability . . .'

'Hers or yours?' asked Anderson, staring straight at Mathieson.

'We'll see.' She closed the file. 'I presume this interview is over.'

'You presume right.'

# EIGHT

The landing of Costello's flat smelled of fried liver and onions, making Valerie feel vaguely homesick yet comforted. She could remember that far back with no problem at all.

'Did you see the newspaper this morning?' The old woman smiled. 'It's terrible what they print nowadays.'

'Don't worry about it, they are just trying to stir up some evidence from the Monkey House of Horror. Costello was very involved in that.'

'And is she all right?'

'Yes, she's fine but we are keeping her out the road, not quite witness protection but that kind of thing.' Valerie was amazed at how easily she lied. Mrs Craig looked like the kind of old dear who would watch *Law and Order*, she'd believe in witness protection.

'Here's my number, you can call me if somebody else wants to borrow the key and you are not sure.' Valerie swapped the key for a small piece of card with the number of her new untraceable mobile number. 'Don't give it to anybody else, please.' Valerie smiled her sweetest smile. 'We need to keep her safe.'

Valerie slipped the key in the lock, opened the door and walked into Costello's life. Costello could not tell the whole story because she didn't know what exactly had happened, but she knew how it had felt when it had happened. And that was far more telling.

Valerie walked into the living room; the huge glass wall that looked over the river was covered by a closed curtain, bathing the room in a dull half-light that suited her purpose and her mood. The subject of her visit was lying on the glass table beside a cup of half-drunk tea, a cold deflated teabag still hanging over the side of the mug. Valerie picked up the laptop and unplugged the power cable. Whatever Costello's brain had forgotten, this laptop would recall perfectly.

She looked around, finding a credit card in the kitchen cupboard above the kettle, as Costello had said. The spare car key in a drawer in the bedroom, her passport in a small case at the bottom of her wardrobe. She looked at the picture, sitting down in front of the mirror, holding her hair up, imaging it blonde.

She didn't look like Costello at all. But she didn't need to.

Walking into the bathroom, she stopped in her tracks. Rivers of red ran down the tiles of the shower cubicle; Costello had been bleeding badly in here. Valerie held onto the wall, looking at the bloodstained towels, the red pooling on the shower tray. She carefully picked up a red piece of cloth, then realized it was the back of a white blouse, bloodstained and cut, slashed through by a very sharp blade. It took Valerie's breath away. Evidence should be bagged, tagged, sterile and contained. It was shocking so close, like Abigail's lilac blouse. She should call somebody, she could call Archie, but that would unravel the whole story and where would that get them?

It could get Costello into a lot of trouble.

No, she had to be a little cleverer than that.

She nipped out to the kitchen and rooted around until she found a pair of marigolds, then went back and bundled up the rest of the bloodstained clothes, grey trousers and a dark cardigan, and stuffed them at the bottom of the washing basket. If they searched the place they would find them. She rinsed out the shower cubicle with bleach and found and wrapped the bloodstained blouse in a roll of cling film, gathered the rest of the stuff on her list and left quickly, locking the door behind her and then giving the key back to Mrs Craig.

Morna had been snoozing in the corner, prodded to wakefulness by a quiet ping. She opened the email, forwarded by DCI Patrick. The attachment showed the student matriculation card of Kieran Cowan, aged twenty-three, student at the College of Sciences where he was studying environmental science, zoology and biology. His classmates said he had left that night to film at the loch as part of a wildlife preservation project. *Film*. And he had his camera with him. There had been an incident, blood had been found. Alastair Patrick was trying to find out details. She'd let him know, but if a DS from Glasgow called Vik Mulholland phoned it was because Patrick had passed on the number.

The jumper had been recognized by Kieran's mother who thought she had knitted it. Patrick wanted more to confirm ID, commenting that when he had shown the picture of the jumper to Wilma, she had given it one glance and said, 'Oh probably,' in reply to his query, 'Did you knit that?' Thus proving to himself that Fair Isle was not singular. Lots of women knitted it, the jumper was years old and no woman would recall that individual colour scheme. The item in question could have been bought in a charity shop last week. It was not an identifying jumper and DCI Patrick was not bringing a woman over two hundred miles only for her to say, 'That's not my boy.'

So Morna phoned Mulholland and left a message, asking him if he could obtain a DNA swab from the parents. But she knew, she just knew, that it was Kieran in the bed in front of her. Then she emailed Patrick with an update on the boy's condition. She held back the fact that they had said he would have sustained brain damage, being so cold for so long with a slow bleed adding to the loss of vital oxygen.

It was a waiting game now. And she didn't want to mention it in case it got back to the mum. Let them enjoy their good news. Their son had been found alive. She read the email again.

*Cam finn? Cam ra?*

Camera.

She patted him on the back of his hand. 'I have it now.' Before pulling out a notebook and scribbling it down. She'd call Mulholland.

Lachlan and Patrick sat in the corner of the pub, each sipping a whisky, keeping their thoughts to themselves.

'How did it go with Blackward?'

'Usual shite.'

'Ruby McDonald turned up eventually to take wee Finn for the duration, so the boy is over at the farm.' Lachlan shook his head. 'That Neil is a tosser. I knew that Morna would let down her parents one day, such a good wee girl, good at school, good career, then she goes and marries that useless muppet.'

'He might be a useless bastard. He's working a lot of hours though.'

'So I noticed. But then so is she. We need to get Finn back here.'

'You can make that happen, Lachlan. Morna trusts you.'

'He'll be back. Ruby's too busy to deal with the boy. How is Morna getting on? Is she OK? I heard she was at Raigmore babysitting the victim from the Bealach?'

'You heard right,' said Patrick.

'You got any idea who he is yet?'

Patrick shook his head. 'Somebody went to a lot of trouble to kill him, remove him and dump him. I think he's safer where he is. There's more to come.'

Lachlan nodded, settling back in his seat. 'And Abigail Haggerty?'

Patrick nodded. 'Oscar's wife. George's wife.'

'Aye, her. You think that George is going to come back up here for good.'

'I do.'

'Interesting.' Lachlan closed his eyes and took a sip of Talisker. 'And do you think that he will be going up to the lodge? That's what he usually does.'

'I think that will be first place he will be going.' Patrick licked the whisky from his lips. 'But will he go alone?'

'Following his ghosts? Somebody has been phoning the harbour authority asking about the *Jennifer Rhu*, asking about Oscar's drowning. It's the talk of the town.'

'People talk. Let them. I have a smart little DC asking about Jennifer Argyll. And that DC is going to talk the very clever Colin Anderson into having a look around at the Jennifer Argyll case and all that will lead to Sharon Sixsmith and Nicola Barnes. Colin Anderson is not a man who knows when to stop.'

Lachlan let out a long slow breath. 'Are we happy about that?'

'Not bothered, let them find what they can find.'

'What's that line from the film, "fasten your seatbelts. It's going to be a bumpy night".'

They raised a glass to each other, with a sense of closure and contentment.

Anderson was sitting on the settee, waiting for Isla to calm down. He was glad her parents had come to take the children away; one three years old, one two years, the other little more than a baby. Isla's parents were obviously very fond of their son-in-law, a good sign in Anderson's book; dads want good husbands for their daughters. Isla herself was red-eyed and worn out. Her dark hair looked as if she hadn't combed it for a week. She still had some fight in her though.

'So, who are you? Just another bloody cop to talk shite about my husband because he's not here to defend himself? How dare you!'

He had heard about the treatment Isla McCaffrey had given Diane Mathieson, so he retreated into the seat, but she didn't move. She started crying again.

'It's quite simple, Mrs McCaffrey. Your husband is missing, my DI is missing. It's unlikely to be a coincidence given they know each other so well.'

'They were *not* having an affair!' she sobbed.

Anderson couldn't help the smile that curled onto his lips. 'No, I very much doubt they were. The thought had never crossed my mind. And I'm bloody sure the thought had never crossed Donnie's mind either.' That got her interest. She looked up and sniffed, smoothing her curls down around her face, giving her the appearance of a distressed Jane Austin heroine. 'I am not here in any official capacity, but my friend is missing and I am worried about her . . .'

She tilted her head. 'Who are you again?'

'Another bloody cop.'

'Sorry.'

'No offence taken, but we do need to talk.'

'I'm so worried,'

'So am I. Costello knew your husband and thought a lot of him professionally. She thought he was a man of high moral standards and good police instinct.' He felt he was writing

Donnie's obituary. 'They worked together in the case of the baby that went missing.'

Isla's mouth formed a perfect 'O' as the facts fell into place. 'Moses.'

He nodded.

She narrowed her eyes slightly. 'Your son? It was in the paper. You are *that* Anderson.'

'Indeed, my wee grandson.' He felt himself smile; she smiled back.

'With regard to Donnie and Costello, I don't know and am not allowed to know any more than you do, but please don't take any of that shite from Mathieson and Bannon. I think she's a bit power hungry and he's under the point of her stiletto.'

'I guessed that.'

'Costello is out there somewhere, and she's alive. We think. We hope. They might be together. It's a big thing for anybody to kill two police officers. It wouldn't happen in this country, not without what we call "noise" on the intelligence. Somebody would know and somebody would talk. People can't keep their mouths shut.' He looked at her reassuringly. 'When Costello was a new recruit, about two weeks out of Tulliallan, she was called to an incident in a multi-story. A young woman had been run over by a car, deliberately. She was eight months pregnant.'

'Bloody hell.' Isla's hands flew to her chest, still sensitive to feel another's pain. 'That's awful.'

'It was. The baby survived but the mother didn't. Costello was first on the scene. She sat on the concrete, holding that woman's hand until the ambulance came. That baby has grown up to be a powerful lady in . . . well, certain circles of Glasgow society. She's no angel but I think if she heard of anybody killing DI Costello, there would be a shockwave in the Glasgow underworld, and we'd feel it. There has been no such thing. What I'm saying is, you can't kill two cops quietly. Not in this city.' He kept the nagging voice to himself. He was talking about regular police work, and he doubted Costello and McCaffrey were doing something regular, otherwise it would all be logged. It was under the radar of Police Scotland, it might have been under Libby's radar too.

'And you know for definite that nothing bad has happened to him?' she sniffled.

'I'm sorry but I think something very bad has happened. That blood is too much to be, well . . . insignificant. But your husband and my colleague were on the side of the gods. There's no way they were up to criminal activity themselves . . .'

'She was in the paper. Her brother was a murderer. That's what it said.'

'Yes I know. The daggers are out for her and that worries me even more. If there's one thing Costello can't come back from, it's idle gossip. You need to tell me everything you can remember about what Donnie was talking about, thinking about. Anything you can . . . He must have said something to you.'

She seemed to consider this for a moment then sighed. 'He was talking a lot about the Abigail Haggerty case. The one where the boy was killed.'

Anderson felt a little stab of ice in his heart. 'Most of the country was talking about that.'

'He seemed to like Costello, you know, early on when they were working together on the Braithwaite case. She was going to help him get his competencies and get into the CID. That's what he really wanted. He was fed up of being on the outside of where he wanted to be. He had watched Costello, getting things done and making decisions, putting pieces of the puzzle together and being able to think about what was missing, he was doing all that alongside her.'

'She told me that herself, he had a good nose for it.' Anderson hoped that she wouldn't notice his use of the past tense. 'Would he have told you if Costello had asked him to help out unofficially?'

She thought about the question. 'I wouldn't have been keen. It could have damaged his future career. I didn't ask and he didn't tell me. I had some faith that Costello would keep him on the right side of the law.'

'What do you think he was doing up at Loch Lomond on a Saturday night? Or why might his car be there?'

'No idea.'

'And you have no idea where Costello is?'

She shook her head.

'And no idea where her car is. They could have both got into her car and gone somewhere else?'

'Why was there drink? And cocaine? Was she, well, into that kind of thing?'

'No. And that tells me more than anything that the scene was staged. Whoever did this didn't know Costello at all. There was somebody else there, trying to discredit them, hurt them professionally. I'm not sure who that might be?' He left the question hanging, trying not to suggest anything to her.

But Isla looked confused.

'We will get to the bottom of it.'

'It's been three days now, are they going to drag the loch?' she voiced an uncomfortable association of ideas. 'Do you think my husband is at the bottom of the loch?'

'I have no idea. It's not my call to search. They won't tell me but if I find out anything I will call you.'

Anderson walked down the slabbed path of McCaffrey's house. A sandpit in the front garden was closed and tarped against the weather. He guessed the bulky upright was a trampoline. He got in the car and checked his messages. He had missed a call from Mitchum. He called back straight away.

'Anderson, I'll be quick. After they found blood at the lochside I've been under pressure from the fiscals' office to put a trace on Costello's mobile.'

'Good.'

'Well, its battery was put in again this morning and a text message was sent, to Archie as usual. Its activity was very brief.'

'But you got it?'

'We did, bounced off Fearnmore and Skye, vaguely.'

'At the top of the North Coast 500, up north, up near Port MacDuff?'

'And why do you say that? Specifically that?'

Anderson was quiet.

'I need some transparency here, Colin. There's been a young man left for dead at the top of the Bealach Na Ba.'

'Again North Coast 500 to Port MacDuff. George Haggerty grew up there. That's where he went the night of the murders.'

Anderson pulled the phone away from his ear as Mitchum erupted, thinking again about whose fingers were tapping out those texts.

Valerie closed Costello's laptop, lay down and closed her eyes, trying to think she didn't trust herself to remember what she had seen with her own eyes, or more importantly what she had not seen.

She needed to be careful.

Costello and she had both walked round the house in Balcarres Avenue in the same way, following each other's footsteps through that house of murder and bloodshed.

The smell of it being cleaned recently. Costello's instinct had led her upstairs where . . . where somebody had left the CD player repeating that song. 'The Clapping Song'.

That song reminded Valerie of Malcolm.

She ran through the words in her mind, the words about them all going to heaven.

That was a sick joke.

Then George had clapped at Costello at the funeral, Valerie had been too drunk to go. She had intended to go, of course, but had fallen asleep instead of getting dressed, waking up on the sofa with her good black suit crumpled underneath her, still on its hanger.

She could recall times in the garden at Balcarres though; she was sure, happy memories. Could she remember though, her and Malcolm, maybe Mary Jane had been there too, at the bottom of the garden? George at the back door telling them the kettle had boiled, standing in a gap at the back door, the white muslin sheet swirling around him. Then him clapping his hands together to get their attention.

*Clap clap.*

Did she actually remember that? Or did she think she did simply because it fitted her version of events.

Archie had told her that Costello had already voiced her concerns about Malcolm's safety in the house to some of her colleagues, telling them that he had tried to climb out his own bedroom window to get to her, his dad had interrupted that by appearing at the front door. The single foot, in his trainer, poking out the first-floor window had been quickly retracted. Costello had said the boy had been out, hiding behind the bins, shivering, sick with the cold, dressed only in a Celtic top and leggings. Malcolm had even left a message on Costello's phone, and to give her due, Valerie thought, Costello had brought the matter to the attention of the child protection services.

But Malcolm had slipped through.

There was no evidence that he was a child at risk.

Valerie thought about the minute she had stepped into George's bedroom. Her sister's bedroom. She wanted to see where her sister had fought for her life. The carpet was the same, except for the large hole cut out at the bottom of the bed. The mirrored doors were sparkling and spotless, the duvet was folded up at the bottom of the stripped bed.

She had been quiet, not wanting to interrupt the silence of the ghosts.

These people shouldn't be ghosts, her sister, her little nephew.

The big question was: who had killed them?

The fascist with the lipstick had been murmuring something, 'Yes, of course. Mr Haggerty is devastated at his loss. He has been very helpful.'

Motive? The fascist had shrugged, standing in the doorway watching her every move.

Valerie had shaken her head thinking that maybe her sister had misdiagnosed a patient and they, or their family, had got angry? But folk don't kill over that. They complain to the BMA or the papers, or Facebook.

But Costello had a good theory.

Money.

The life insurance Abigail carried. The life insurance Oscar had carried. The mortgage on the Balcarres Avenue house paid off. That made Valerie stop and think.

Oscar presumed dead. The *Jennifer Rhu* on fire, sinking. No sign of Oscar.

She checked her watch. She was having Costello moved at

that moment. Nobody would know she was there, the strict rules on patient confidentiality would see to that. She had a fractured skull and she was scared, very scared.

Costello had two other questions on her notes.

One comment. Who would Abigail open the door to? What had been said in that phone call?

Valerie tried to recall what she had been told. There had been a fight, verbal, voices raised. The nosey neighbour had called the police three times in the previous eighteen months. Each time Abigail had sent the police away, saying it was nothing. So another episode of shouting had provoked no alarm. It seems George had left, Abigail had texted him while he was on the road then George had called back. They only had George's word for what was said on that call. Or whose finger had pressed send on the text from Abigail's phone. He could have been talking to anybody. It wasn't proof that Abigail was still alive. The estimated time of death was much later, more like five or six a.m. Dead for ten hours when found. Valerie knew how easy it was to confuse a jury about time of death; the musculature of the body, the fat content, the temperature of the room, all that was a movable feast, one that she had dined on in court for the clients of the Crown.

Back at the house Bannon had spoken, standing behind Mathieson, looking over her shoulder. 'Valerie, your sister was very cautious; she had opened her door after one a.m. The time of death was three a.m. Cold night but the heating was on.'

George liked the house to be cool. He didn't like spending money on the heating. And it annoyed his chest. Abigail liked to sneak it on when he was away up north. Was there hell to pay when he came back? She closed her eyes to get her mind back on track. Was Abigail expecting somebody and she had started an argument to get him to leave? Nope, George had a call that summoned him north. So had George told her to expect somebody?

Was that why they were both dressed? No risking going to bed because somebody was going to call.

And who would that be? She had no faith in Mathieson getting anywhere.

Valerie thought back to the house. She had asked to see the
boy's bedroom. The minute she stepped onto that grey carpet,
she had spotted the gap on his bookcase, where his Millennium
Falcon usually sat. She had asked if George had mentioned
it. He hadn't.

But it was gone.

Mathieson had dismissed her with a scathing look. Even
Archie had shaken his head a little, worrying about a toy at
a time like this. It was a big toy, nearly two-feet long. And
Costello had been Googling the street map of the area, looking
as if she was timing routes in and out.

By foot.

And every route she picked went over the Kelvindale Bridge
to the footpath. Valerie shook her head, closed her eyes and
tried to concentrate. She could figure this out; she had the
skills to do this. That was far behind the house, streets away,
a long walk from the front of the house in Balcarres Avenue
and Valerie knew from her professional experience how closely
that CCTV had been examined. So what was Costello doing,
looking at the bridge? A footbridge behind the house, at the
far end of the estate.

Looking at the internet history on the laptop and a document
Costello had called 'The Sideman', she started tracing the
detective's thoughts. The Sideman?

Valerie picked her phone up and Googled that. The feeling
of her fingertip on the screen, familiar and comforting. It
reminded her of doing her job. The Urban Dictionary said
sideman meant an irrelevant and powerless guy. She swiped
down reading the more formal definition; an instrumentalist
supporting a soloist or a principal performer.

Costello had called this whole file The Sideman. Had she
known, or suspected, the presence of another man there? She
read on, her brain starting to spark with unanswered questions.
Costello's theory was that the sideman had been in the car
when George drove in to the garage. George had gone into
the house, the sideman had stayed in the garage. George got
a phone call to go north, which gave him an unbreakable alibi.
The sideman had come out the garage and entered the house.
Did he have a key? Or had Abigail been called and told to

expect him? Was that what the phone call was about? Valerie thought what that call might sound like. The house was close to the hospital. *So X's mum has been admitted to Gartnavel. I've told X he can pop in and get some kip. He'll be exhausted after the drive down from Port MacDuff.* Was that what the phone call had said? Then he killed them. According to Costello's route, he had exited via the back garden, a long walk through the streets then over the river. And away.

Had it been that simple?

Had it all really been that simple?

So who was he?

The brown and cream Volkswagen camper was parked in the innermost corner of the long lay-by, hidden by bushes, keeping its secrets to itself. It sat a little out from the verge of wet grass as if somebody in good shoes was going to be getting out the passenger door maybe to stretch their legs or to photograph a lovely sunset over the treetops in the wood behind.

DCI Alastair Patrick paused for a moment looking at the sky, then at his feet, as if there might be some answers there. The younger uniformed cop stood back and left him to it. It had taken him two minutes to judge that the DCI from Port MacDuff was a quiet man and that he was not one to be provoked to idle conversation. He watched as Patrick leaned against the front of the VW and checked the number plate.

'Definitely his car.' Patrick nodded and gestured that whatever silent machinations he had been turning over in his head were now over. He turned as a BMW pulled into the lay-by. The uniformed officer stood, arm out telling the driver that there was nothing to see here and would he kindly drive on. A tall fair-haired man got out the car, already showing his warrant card.

He approached the camper, passing a wry smile to the junior officer. He pulled on a pair of gloves as he passed.

The quiet man turned to greet him, lifting his cap. 'It's Colin Anderson, isn't it?'

'Indeed.' Anderson was at a loss.

'DCI Patrick. Port MacDuff. My DC thinks you are the best thing since sliced bread.'

'He doesn't know me then?' Anderson was finding it hard to read this small, wiry man with his cold stare and purposeful posture. Just looking at him made Anderson feel like a slob.

'She. DC Morna Taverner. She is looking after a young man in Raigmore Hospital. We think he was the driver of this vehicle. We are covering the same ground here.'

'Really.' Anderson wished he had had some more sleep, he wasn't catching on.

'A man with his throat cut and his first words are "camera" and "film". We phoned that in and were told that you already have recovered a Scub from the loch. This man witnessed what went on at the lochside. I'm sure of it.'

'Who is he?'

'Kieran Cowan, student, lives in the west end of Glasgow. No criminal record, nothing untoward about him. Except why did he stop? Why here? To answer his phone? Mechanical failure? To meet somebody? Who slit his throat? How did he get to the summit of the Bealach? It's about 160 miles from here. I asked for an abandoned vehicle check of a twenty-mile radius, it should have been two hundred.'

Anderson looked through the driver's window. 'And who?'

'Whoever.'

'Meeting somebody he knew?' Anderson stood back, trying to find an innocent explanation for the camper being here, abandoned. Why had Cowan walked away? What happened to McCaffrey? And Costello? He couldn't bear to think they were looking for another body. Two bodies. The thought made him chill.

'Family reported him missing. He had been away filming so they left it twenty-four hours plus, thinking he'd got carried away.' Patrick's gloved fingers rattled on the roof of the vehicle.

'Did he tell his friends or family what he was doing?' asked Anderson.

'They said he was looking for criminal activity against the wallabies, he was headed for the car park at Inveruglass. Where McCaffrey's car was found.'

Where their blood had been found.

Patrick's bright blue eyes looked straight through Anderson. *This is nothing to do with wallabies.*

'Your DC?' asked Anderson.

'Morna Taverner? Very good, she was talking about booking you a room at the Exciseman. She suspects you will be coming north, I think she's right.'

'News to me.' Anderson tapped on the window.

'It'll be worth your while.'

'Was Morna the one who called me about the Logan and Witherspoon rapes?'

'She would have phoned you about the Barnes and Sixsmith attacks,' Patrick answered, making his point. 'You two should get together and feed your obsessions. And while you are at it, see if you can cure her of her terminal clumsiness. A car smash and two nasty falls.'

Anderson looked at him puzzled, then went back to looking through the window, holding his hand up against the glass on the back passenger window to protect the glass from the rain to afford him a better view. 'He locked the vehicle before he left it.'

Patrick looked around at the hills, the darkening sky. 'What happened? Did the three of them go away in the missing Fiat?'

'Costello wouldn't drive two bleeding bodies around, and she was injured too. So where is the Fiat and who brought the camper here?'

'Good question. We got hold of the mum, she's bringing spare keys up here, but that will take time. And we need to talk to her about the identity of our young victim.' Patrick hitched up his trouser legs then got down on the ground to look under the car.

The power pendulum had swung again; Anderson was back in charge now. 'And how long does it take to drive from here to the Applecross pass?'

'The Bealach Na Ba?' Patrick wiped his palm over his eyes, trying to see something, then got out his mobile as he was wriggling in the ground, pulling his gloves from his fingers with his teeth. 'Three hours, three and a half from here? Can be five from the city. The roads are good until the last thirty miles or so. Somebody forced him to stop. And abducted him.' The blue eyes narrowed, looking back along the road to the turn off for the loch. 'Agreed?'

'Agreed. So, what do you think? There are no skid marks on the road. It looks like he left the vehicle of his own free will? Did he run out of petrol? Was he flagged down by somebody in trouble?'

'No, he would have pulled the camper in behind the other vehicle. This is parked up at the corner. And why would he take his bag out for that? Why did he leave his camera at the locus? Was he filming and somebody thought he had caught something incriminating on film? So then he got to his car and drove away . . . but then what? Why get out again?' He looked around him, over to the trees. 'He had pine needles on the shoes, his knees and his hair. And gravel in the palms of his hands.'

Anderson looked to the left and the right, and to the forestry commission woods. Then down.

'Morna said his cuffs smelled of oil or something. Was he crouching, feeling under the car? Then what, he ran away? Was chased away?'

'Should we wait for crime scene?' Anderson was looking around the tarmac of the lay-by, which told him nothing, no skid marks, no stains, no tyre marks. But Patrick was now studying it like he was reading the small print of a contract.

'It'll take time for them to get here. It's our force who is dealing with it and Inverness aren't going to stick this on their budget. There's no CCTV cameras out here, are there? I tried to order the footage from the four nearest for the four hours after eight p.m. on Saturday night but you lot have them.'

'There's none at the loch either, the cameras were trained on the shore after the issue with the wallabies but I'll hurry it up for you and see if anybody was giving him aggro on the road,' said Anderson.

'They made him stop. I know how I would do it. If you know beforehand that you want to disable a car. It's a bit like hobbling a donkey. It'll go but it won't get far,' said Patrick with something that resembled a shrug. 'I'm presuming no access to the engine, so it has to be covert.' He walked back to the vehicle and put the torch on his mobile phone back on, then knelt on the ground, swinging the light, making a square of it tracking the outer border of the vehicle's body. 'Over there, the front wheel arch, above that.'

Anderson walked round the car and knelt down, putting his arm up, feeling along the wheel arch, as Patrick told him to move his hand towards the front of the car.

'You're on it.'

'It feels like part of the car.' He tried to pull off the metal box he could feel but it didn't move.

'Try sliding it,' suggested Patrick.

The box gave way with familiar release and repel of a magnet.

It was a small tin, an old tobacco tin. Anderson held it up to Patrick who merely nodded as if it was no more than he would have expected.

'And how does that stop a car?'

'A few heavy ball bearings, fill it with warm candle wax, then stick a magnet on the top, close it and attach that to the bare metal on the inside of the engine casing.' He looked at Anderson, raising an eyebrow. 'Then the heat of the engine melts the wax and the ball bearings start to clatter around, the person stops. It's a much loved old vehicle, he would have stopped. And I think somebody was following. Hector will tell us.'

'Who's Hector, your great crime scene guy? We have a great forensic scientist here, Mathilda McQueen, nothing gets past her.'

Patrick walked back towards the Land Rover. 'Not much gets past Hector, well, not anything edible. He's a very fat spaniel,' said Patrick and Anderson was left to take of that what he could. 'I'll see you at the pub later.'

# NINE

Anderson was so tired his headache now would not go away, it pounded incessantly behind his right ear. His eyes were dry, he was hungry but he had no appetite. All because of that wee bundle of peachy loveliness that cried in this basket. Moses had been quiet for an hour between three and four o'clock but apart from that, all Anderson could remember was noise. He had stayed in the kitchen, but he hadn't got as far as sleep when Moses started crying. Claire, her boyfriend David, and the ever-present Paige, had stayed in the front room, watching a documentary about Charles Manson, and eating a Chinese takeaway and Doritos. He had heard Claire and David arguing the toss about why people had followed Manson so blindly. And would it all fade to memory now that he was dead? Unlikely. He might have gone but the memories live on. The horror of it.

As he passed the door, sometime after midnight, on his way to the downstairs toilet, he heard Paige ask, 'So who is Charles Manson anyway?'

Now it was about half four. He walked into the kitchen where Brenda was preparing some milk formula. She was muttering over her shoulder to Moses who was in his basket on the big kitchen table, kicking his legs, wanting his covers away. They had a brief conversation, a weird conversation, like all their engagements nowadays. They now lived together in the same house because of Moses. They couldn't stay together for their own children but they could for a step-grandchild. Brenda was seeing another man, Anderson had met him twice in the passing. He was an accountant called Roger who, being wary kept out of Anderson's way, but he seemed to make Brenda happy – which is more than he himself had managed to do for the last few years.

Brenda turned and smiled. 'I can handle this, I think he has wind.'

'So do I after eating that Chinese. I can't sleep.'

'Well, go and do some work then, that's what you always used to do.'

It was a pointed jab, but mildly delivered. He smiled. 'I'll try to get some sleep before I need to go,' and he went back to his bed and lay there, listening to the noises of people in his house. Like when Claire and Peter were young. Day turns into night and back into day.

He picked up an old Henning Mankell he kept starting but he couldn't get in to it. He took out his tablet and flicked through a few emails, seeing the one from Morna Taverner, with its attachment. The files of a rape – had she said rapes or attacks? – that she wanted him to look at, an enthusiastic rookie. He read on, thinking about them as he looked at his watch; he'd had two hours sleep. She had included Sally Logan in her list, he pondered on the one fact that had always bothered him about her attack. Who would know she was there? On a Scottish hill at six on a summer morning, not somewhere you'd be – unless you had a reason to be there. Or prior knowledge that your victim was going to be there. Anderson decided he'd go into work early. He had a few things of his own he wanted to look up, starting with the employment and human resource history of one Morna Ann Taverner nee MacDonald.


Valerie looked at the red and white brick building, an old house, a big house that had once had a child and a family, kids played in that garden and the trees at the back had swings attached to them in a previous life. But for as long as Valerie could recall, it had been a GPs surgery. Abigail used to say, as they waited in their dad's car at the traffic lights on Crookston Road, that she would work there one day and heal the sick. That was Abigail, she always had grand ideas. Valerie really only ever wanted to go into law and make money. She didn't want to be all holistic, healing people and getting complete strangers to feel better about themselves.

That was Abigail all over; she had worked all during her marriage to Oscar. The bold but unlucky Oscar. Then Abigail had married George and it had all gone a bit . . . well, she had to think of the word. Quiet? Abigail had ceased to be Abigail. She had become George's wife. Valerie had thought at first that it was her sister treading lightly in a new marriage after the tragic loss of her first husband at sea.

Oscar was only presumed dead. Only presumed. The unwelcome thought had been pointed out to her with crystal clarity by Costello and her blackened eyes. They had never found the body, just the *Jennifer Rhu* burning, the painter attaching the dinghy half undone as if Oscar nearly managed to detach it but had failed to escape the flames. What was left of the yacht had still been burning when the coastguard had arrived.

Another one who had gone to heaven in a little rowing boat.

Abigail had been shattered by losing Oscar but had seemed keen to get married again. She wanted a father for Mary Jane. And then she had met George who, like Oscar, came from Port MacDuff. In fact, it might have been at the memorial service for Oscar that Abigail first met George. Valerie had searched for a memory. She must have been there but she could only recall swigging back a good white wine and then doing her teeth in the loo after she had been sick, filling the toilet bowl with sausage rolls and mushroom vol-au-vents. She had a very clear memory of that.

Abigail and George had bonded over the loss of a husband and a friend. At first Valerie thought it was the thrill of the new husband, *George does this* and *George thinks that,* then Valerie came to realize that Abigail had simply changed. She had challenged her about it, of course, and Abigail had said in that way of hers, that in retrospect was slightly nervous, that she was, for the first time in her life, relaxing. George made good money, and there would be a payout from Oscar's life insurance once seven years had passed and he could legally be declared dead. So there was no pressure on her to work, she had loved her adopted daughter, of course, but now she had a son of her own with George and that was special. And that sounded like all the roses in the garden were lovely, with no thorns at all. So why was George disappearing up to Port MacDuff at the slightest opportunity?

Costello wanted to know how much insurance Abigail

carried. The house had already been valued. George was quick to think about getting it on the market.

Was it all about money?

She glanced at her watch now, unfamiliar on her wrist. She had been invited to a meeting at the cop shop tomorrow morning but she was not prepared to face that fascist wee bitch again. Time to dance to a different tune now.

She walked up to the door and opened it; a receptionist looked up, a universal smile. 'Have you got an appointment? We are not actually open yet.'

'Dr Irene Marshall. She is expecting me for a chat, I am not a patient.'

'Oh?'

'I am Abigail's sister, Dr Haggerty's sister.'

'Oh.' The professional face immediately collapsed into one of concern, her eyes began to well up, a manicured hand went up to her mouth. 'I am so, so sorry, you must be Valerie.'

She nodded, thinking that this was the first person who had shown any real emotion about Abigail's death.

'Yes. I can't tell you how bad it has been.'

Then the expression changed slightly as the receptionist recalled the newspaper reports about the alcoholic sister, Valerie, the one who tried to buy a murdered woman's baby.

'Can I get you a cup of tea?' The receptionist waved her hands vaguely over her desk to a door marked 'offices'. 'You have a wee sit down in there and I'll tell her you are here, she's on the phone right now.'

Five minutes later the door opened and Irene Marshall came in, carrying two cups of hot tea. Valerie felt her stomach tighten. She needed a vodka, ProPlus and caffeine. She had a small bottle in her bag, next to the gun still wrapped in a hotel towel. The drink was talking to her, whistling at her for her attention. She pushed the temptation away, she had to try to stay focussed on this. Abigail might have said something. It's impossible to work alongside somebody and not get an idea of their lives no matter how much remained unsaid.

Did she allude to him being abusive? Were they in financial trouble?

'Hi, so sorry to keep you waiting.' Irene smiled an

empathetic smile and handed Val the tea. 'How are you keeping? I saw you at the funeral, but well . . . not the time or the place.' She sat down on the free office chair and she wheeled it towards the table, a ridiculous scurrying motion like a child in primary one. That left Valerie standing where the patients waited. She wasn't being invited into the inner sanctum. She was being politely tolerated. How much had Abigail said about her troubled sister? It had all been in the papers anyway.

'How are you doing?' she said, accompanied by a professional, distant smile.

'I'm fine.'

The next question would be, *have the police got any further forward with their enquiries.* She was close.

'Have they found anything yet? Do they know who did it?' She leaned forward, trying to engage.

Valerie sat down, feeling five years old and somebody was trying to explain to her about the birds and the bees. 'They won't tell me anything, they say that I am too close. It's about George,' said Valerie, the name came out hard, like a ricochet off a cliff face. It stung the silence between them.

'George?' Irene was confused. A phone rang in the distance. They heard the receptionist answer it, a quiet muffled conversation.

'The police never asked us about George. They asked about patients that might have mental health issues, anybody who might have wished her harm.' Irene shook her head. 'But she was doing so few hours, she was really only seeing her own list of patients. Working alongside us, but not part of the team. Which was her choice.'

'Why was that, do you think? Why was she only working those few hours? Was she not happy here?' Valerie looked at her own fingers tapping at the side of the doctor's desk, the skin red and flaking, her nails bitten to the stumps.

Irene Marshall was looking as well, making up her own diagnosis. 'Oh yes, but she wanted to be at home.'

'And that was why she cut her hours down?'

'Yes, Valerie.' Irene had a terrible condescension in her voice. 'She really wanted to be at home, be a housewife. After Oscar died, she threw herself into her work but she wasn't really cut out for it. She wanted a home, and to be at home, and when she married George she took her chance. I don't blame her. This job can be incredibly stressful.'

'But she loved her patients.'

'She did, she did. But the job isn't what it was. Cuts, patients knowing all their rights and none of their responsibilities. It's a highly stressful job, we were glad when she cut her hours, it saved us money. And when your sister got stressed, she wasn't the easiest person to work with.'

'No?'

Irene shook her head. 'I am only trying to help you, Valerie. Your sister could be a little overbearing at times, and I know I shouldn't speak ill of the dead, but she was a different person after Oscar died.'

'After Oscar died or after she married George?'

'One and the same.' Irene avoided the question.

'How is George coping? I've only seen him a few times since it all.' Irene raised an eyebrow, questioning. Was this not in keeping with her happy family internal monologue? Or the photo that had been in the papers.

'At first I was in hospital.' Valerie's fingers went up to the soft wool of the cowl neck of her jumper. 'He was grieving. He comes from Wester Ross, Port MacDuff, so he has been up there mostly. There is nothing down here to keep him.'

'Abigail always spoke as if you were a close family.'

Could she sense a note of sarcasm there? Or was she being oversensitive? 'We are.'

*Were.* Past tense.

Irene moved to get up, the chat was over.

'Did the police ask anything about Abigail, anything personal?'

Irene gave her a sidelong glance. 'That would be a confidential conversation.'

'I'm desperate, they tell me nothing. She was my sister.'

Irene sighed. 'The police were asking me if Abigail was having an affair but the answer to that is no.' She nodded as if that was the end of it, looking right at Valerie as if she could hear the internal monologue of every justification for every drink she had ever had.

'Did they also ask if Abigail thought George was having an affair?'

'They did, and Abigail did think that George had been unfaithful to her. She had said that to me. She thought she was being betrayed, lied to.'

Valerie took a deep breath, the waft of Ralph Lauren after-shave coming back to her, familiar and sweet, a brush on the cheek. 'Really? Did she ever tell you who it was he was seeing?'

Irene nodded. 'I'm surprised you had to ask. It was you.'

Anderson was having a good think about what Patrick had said. Not a man to waste words, his obsession, her obsession. Morna's, what had he said, 'clumsiness'? A car crash and two nasty falls? Not so much a light bulb moment as a blind man doing a jigsaw with no picture to go on. And no corners to start with. Whatever injuries Morna was sustaining, her boss did not think they were due to clumsiness.

Bannon, though, had been very approachable in a 'if Mathieson asks me I'll deny I ever said it' kind of way.

Anderson had seen the brief phone call as a trade-off. 'I'll tell you what I know of Costello as a human being, and you tell me what you know about Haggerty.' Bannon had been quick to jump on that, repeated the alibi. 'He's innocent, yes. I don't want to know that, I want to know what he does for a living.'

'Something unintelligible with numbers. Project manage-ment with accounts. He's contracted all over the place.'

'Does he have a degree?'

'Yes, business and accounts, computing or something.'

'What university?'

'Is this relevant?'

'Which one?'

'Errr, Strathclyde, I think.' He heard the tap tap on a keyboard.

That made sense. Glasgow was academic but Strathclyde was known for its business school.

'No, I tell a lie.' Anderson could hear Bannon typing. The movement of a mouse being lifted up and put back down again. 'He was at Glasgow.'

'Do you know when?' Anderson was doing a quick calculation of Haggerty's age.

'Nope, they would know though. Why?'

'I'll tell you when I'm sure of something. And you can tell Mathieson that you worked it all out for yourself if it becomes pertinent to the current investigation. How old is Haggerty?'

'Born 7th June 1972.'

'Forty-five. OK thanks.'

Now that wasn't a something, but it also wasn't a nothing. He had a little further down the investigative road to go. Had George Haggerty been at uni at the same time as Sally Logan? The same time as he himself had? So were thousands of other people. Especially as Sally lost that year when she hurt her knee. She was around the uni for five years not four . . . that made an overlap more likely. But how many men are on the outskirts of two rapes?

Himself? Braithwaite? Haggerty?

How much commonality was there really?

As he himself said, it's not a big ocean when the fish swim in the same small circles.

By eleven a.m., Anderson was on his third coffee and had filled three sides of an A4 pad with frenetic scribbling. Despite the serious subject matter, he was totally absorbed in his work this morning, to the extent he was even enjoying it.

Morna was conscientious and methodical, not one to leave any stone unturned. He had logged in to the system to view her access record to the files. She had been off early in the year after suffering injuries after a road traffic incident. Before that she had suffered a head injury after a bad fall. Another fall had left her unconscious for two hours. So she was a good detective with little spacial awareness, guessed Anderson. Apparently it was an ongoing joke in her station although he didn't see Patrick as a comedian. That comment was barbed. Was she a victim of abuse?

It seemed as though Morna had been looking at these cases for four or five years. Before then she seemed to have been on a career break, he checked with HR. That would have been to have her son, Finn. Then she seemed to have gone back to work and started looking up cold case rapes, searching the Police Scotland combined database for anything that might match. But match what?

The top of her list of matches? The cold cases he was working on were Sally Logan and Gillian Witherspoon, but the occupant of her number spot was an unknown name to him but one Patrick had mentioned.

Sharon Sixsmith.

There was no indication that she had been raped, only that she had been found dead after falling down a crag near Tornapress. Then he saw it: a badly injured left shoulder. So what? He could imagine falling down between two sheer rock faces, you were bound to hit a few bones, injure a few joints on the way.

But it was the damage to the left glenohumeral joint Morna had focussed in on, judging by the fact that it was the only similarity. Then he thought, Sally had been out hillwalking early morning on her own. This girl had been found, at the bottom of a crag, her VW camper van . . . Anderson's heart gave an exited little extra beat and he told himself to calm down. Retro VW camper vans were a lifestyle choice. It told you about the person as a consumer, not about them as a victim. He looked back up. Sharon Sixsmith, twenty-two. The photograph showed a slim, dark-haired girl, she looked very fit, very bright, she didn't look the sort that would get into trouble easily. Her eyes glowed with quiet confidence, she looked very capable. He scrolled around, found the notes on the camper. It looked as though she had been abducted from it, but it had taken three months to find the body. Three months? The criminal connection was not made until afterwards. At the time, she was just another missing hillwalker. And it would have been too late for a rape kit.

The boys had a map of Scotland up at the far end of the office, but Googling was easier, especially as the deposition site had been so remote. There was no name, just a map reference and that was too sparsely populated for Google to show him anything more than a screen of bright green. The satellite image looked like the face of an evil giant, a black gash for a smile, wicked in its contortions. The theory was that she had gone for a walk and got lost, or had been abducted from her VW with no sign of a struggle, or got drunk and was driven away. And she ended up falling down a crag; the investigation at the time went nowhere. A few local troublemakers had been brought in but easily dismissed. This was in April of 1987. Sally had been raped in 1992.

The second on her list was Nicola Barnes. Another rape, although she was still alive. Her car had started to make an odd noise. She had stopped, a good Samaritan had stopped. Anderson's stomach flipped at the name.

George Haggerty.

Anderson let out a long slow breath.

He'd had a quick look at the car then said he'd call a garage. There was no mobile signal, such as the range was in those days. He had driven away and called the garage once he was in range. He had been charming with his lovely smile and big brown eyes. It was while she had been waiting that Nicola had been attacked from the back. Her left shoulder dislocated. No forensics. She had been gagged and blindfolded but had said two things of interest. Her attacker had been wearing something like a boiler suit, and there was a noise that distracted her. Like a slapping sound.

A clapping sound?

George had an alibi, drinking cappuccino in a coffee house where he had told the waitress about the girl he had left with her broken down car.

Another perfect alibi, for him.

Anderson was impressed with Morna.

The third one the electronic intelligence path took him to was much older. This case was a woman called Jennifer Argyll who had vanished into thin air in 1987 on the coast near Port MacDuff. So that was what had sparked Morna's interest, she would have grown up with the case. Anderson knew how these cases became legends in the local stations, everybody would have an opinion. That was as far as Anderson got as Jennifer's file had been transferred to cold case, which he couldn't easily access. But Anderson knew Morna could pluck those connections from thin air just as easily as Jennifer had disappeared into it.

Anderson picked up the phone to call Mitchum, he wanted a meeting to tell him he was going up north. He wanted Morna to book him a room in the Exciseman. There was the added bonus that he couldn't hear Moses crying from up there.

# TEN

Erin and Rachel had left Lomondside campsite after a hearty breakfast, cooked outdoors on a single burner Calor gas stove, starting with a knob of butter melting and finishing with the full English swirling in a golden gravy of animal fat and rainwater. It tasted delicious. Then they packed up the tent and repacked their day rucksacks, leaving the bigger rucksacks to be picked up by HikeLite and taken up to the next stop at Bridge Of Orchy.

It was a three-hour walk, to be completed that morning. They hadn't made good progress, the rain and wind had been in their faces every single step of the way.

At half eleven, there was a brief cessation in the onslaught of rain, so they decided to rest before they reached Tyndrum. They were walking cold and tight-legged. The stony path underfoot was puddle after puddle, their waterproof boots had held out for the first thirty miles of the West Highland Way and had then become absorbent. Now it was a question of keeping the water swilling around their feet warm, and keeping out the ice-cold water that lay in wait in the deeper puddles. They walked in silence, the two of them in single file. Changing every so often with one in the lead being battered by the elements, the other sheltering behind. The rain seemed to be changing direction exactly as the path changed, so it was always hitting them in the face. The weather and the conditions underfoot were challenging as the guidebook said it often was when doing winter walking on the west coast. This wasn't pleasant hiking, this was a trial of endurance and character. The beautiful, stunning scenery was clouded, often they were walking through the clouds themselves. And it wasn't quiet, always the splish thud of their boots on the path, the pitter-patter of rain and the squeak of their waterproofs against each other.

They were walking up to Tyndrum to the 'By The Way'

hostel, a hot shower and a cooked meal that was devoid of rainwater. They could dry off their socks, get a rest and, hopefully, a good night's sleep that wouldn't be interrupted by the wind clawing and baying at the door of the tent and the constant irregular flap-flap of battered canvas.

They walked past the River Fillan, flowing high and angry, its grey waters tumbling and rushed. Two gold panners, covered in waders that reached to their armpits, and gloves that melted into a hat showing not one single flash of skin, stood on the calmer parts of the river, ever hopeful of finding a tiny nugget of a darkly glistening stone.

They turned away from the path to the river, heading north towards the hostel. They would be there in half an hour, maybe a little less if the path started to decline, a little more if the wind blew up again. They knew from the map that the lochan was ahead of them and they both wanted to see it. They had hoped the rain would clear, so they could get some photographs taken. They had been discussing it in the pub last night, warm and cosy, and more than a little drunk, looking at the map and trying to get a signal on their mobiles. As was usual in these parts, the barman proved better than Google and was happy to supply the two students of English Literature with the colourful history of the area, despite the fact that he was from the Ukraine. He told the story of Robert the Bruce throwing his sword into the lochan, a fine claymore it had been, about five-feet long and it 'weighed a ton'. The king was being pursued at the time by a couple of armed horseman, probably English, but the details were sketchy. After a few more drams, the defenceless king single-handedly brought down the entire English army before legging it.

They were going to ask if the sword in the lochan was protected by a lady of the lake but they thought the locals might not find that funny and kept their counsel.

Sure enough at the side of the footpath, they came across the stone, a large rectangular rock with the outline of a sword carved into it. 'They used to swing a claymore around their heads you know,' the barman had said, 'hacking bits off anything or anybody too close.'

The lochan nestled in the hills, mist drifting right and left, low on the dark, black surface of the loch. There didn't seem to be any clear border between land and water, no clear line at all, greens and reds and blues, muted black and browns all melting into each other. They stood, looking in silence, catching their breath, before both of them shrugged off their rucksacks, a signal that they were going to rest a while, at least the stone gave them something to sit on.

In silence they sat, the two of them, staring out over the water. Being mesmerized by the mist drifting from left to right, right to left, slowly revealing something on the far bank. Something with legs that floated out in the black water, something with arms up on the grassy bank, somebody with fingers grasping, as if he had reached out and nearly, very nearly, made it.


Anderson closed his eyes and cursed inwardly, his exhilaration of the early morning evaporated in an instant.

They had found Donnie McCaffrey.

There was no doubt it was him. His DNA was on file. They had swabbed the body at the site and the sample had been brought down to Glasgow and processed immediately.

As Anderson was in Mitchum's office, the boss had taken the phone call, his face had turned ashen as he had put the phone down.

Then Mitchum had warned Anderson in no uncertain terms that he was to cooperate with Mathieson and Bannon's investigation. Totally nothing was to override this, no sense of personal loyalty, nothing.

It has to be investigated and it has to look transparent. And where the hell was Costello?

Anderson said he had no idea, as politely as he could, sitting there trying to be calm but thinking where, and when, Costello's body was going to appear.

'Do you think I might do better if I went north? There's a link to my cold case rape enquiry.' He explained about Morna's invite, Patrick had given his consent. The look of relief on Mitchum's face was so joyous, it was as if Santa had existed after all. 'Go, with my blessing. It'll keep you out of Mathieson's claws.'

Anderson excused himself. He went to the toilet where he threw up all the coffee he had drunk that morning, burning acrid in his throat as he wretched again and again. His phone was beeping, as a wave of text messages came in. He leant against the wall of the toilets and took out his mobile, scrolling through, messages from Wyngate, Mulholland, Bannon, another couple of colleagues all wanting to know what was going on. Plus, DCI Mathieson requesting another meeting sooner rather than later. Anderson had been hoping that one would be from Costello saying something, anything. Any kind of explanation for the death of a young man.

Sometimes there is nothing scarier than silence.

Isla McCaffrey sat down on the settee, not speaking, unable to speak.

Mathieson gestured to Bannon that he should put the kettle on. They would have to get on with the investigation and the family liaison officer could do all the handholding she needed to do once they had left.

But PC Donald McCaffrey's wife was sniffling a lot, Mathieson thought she might get further if there were some reinforcements present. 'Do you want a friend with you? Is there somebody we can get for you?'

Isla nodded. 'Can you get Pari, she lives next door?' She shook her head, already worn out and wishing everybody would go away. Maybe she could go back to sleep and wake up again or go back out to Lidl and do her shopping, somehow she needed to rewind the day, rewind the last few days and get back to the point when his phone had beeped and he had looked at it and smiled. He had got up, and left. He had told her not to order too much from the Argos catalogue, don't spend too much on the boys.

Now he was dead.

Gone. Not coming back. Ever.

The female detective was sitting in front of her now, her small pale face all bony and full of contrition. The man had gone out to get her neighbour, her friend. Pari was one of life's calm people. She had been good when Nathan had choked, that was a midnight rush to the hospital. And when she had gone into labour with the youngest and Donnie had been at work.

A policewoman arrived, a beautiful coloured girl and she had muttered a few condolences and then gone into the kitchen to join the tall bloke who had been in the kitchen clattering cutlery. Isla could hear drawers being opened and closed now; they were looking for teaspoons and coffee.

That was one of the last things he had done before he left that night, he had loaded the dishwasher, all the dishes left from that Saturday where her mother had talked about the arrangements for Christmas dinner and he had pulled faces at her over the chicken casserole.

Now he had been killed. She couldn't believe what they were saying now, she put her hands over her ears and kept them there, watching whose stupid red lips that never seemed to stop moving.

When she stopped talking, Isla let her hands fall, she wiped the tears from her eyes, tears of anger not sadness. All of it would hit her later, she was sure of it, but now, here in her own living room, she had a fight on her hands. Somebody had taken her husband's life. And now the police, his colleagues, were ready to attack his reputation.

'I am really sorry to have to go through this with you,' said the torn-faced blonde.

Isla McCaffrey looked at her face and doubted it very much, she looked like a kid who was waiting for the gingerbread to come out the oven.

'Sorry, can you tell me again what happened, I don't think I'm getting this at all.'

'I was saying that we have found Donnie's body at a lochan up near Tyndrum,' said Mathieson. 'Do you know Tyndrum, thirty miles north of here, a few miles further on from Inveruglass?'

'Why? Why was he there?' Isla's face was blank, the news hadn't quite sunk in.

'I'm really sorry, but as yet we do not know, but we are very suspicious of foul play and we are trying to ascertain—'

'Do you think he was murdered? Donnie? My Donnie.'

'Yes, I do. PC McCaffrey had sustained fatal injuries.'

'What injuries? How did he die?' asked Isla giving herself a comforting rub on the arm.

Mathieson bit the side of her lip, ignoring the warning sign from Bannon. 'We are waiting for the post-mortem results. Do you feel you can tell us what he was doing at Inveruglass? What he was doing there that got him killed?'

Bannon had driven Mathieson from Isla's house back to their divisional headquarters at Govan. He had tried to drive legally, with Mathieson snapping at him and swearing at other drivers who had done no wrong other than being in the vehicle in front of Mathieson. They had left Isla with speed that bordered on rudeness the minute Mathieson's tablet had binged and she had glanced at the comments of the email attachment of five photographs. There was one nod to Isla, a brief 'We'll be back' and she had stood up and was out the door, leaving Bannon to apologize, and cast a look at Pari, who caught the meaning and nodded.

'Archie, you know we have found Donnie McCaffrey's body earlier today.' Mathieson sounded tired. 'We are bringing the body down here for a post-mortem, of course, but nobody is telling me bloody anything.'

'Yes, I know. I don't get it. All this is connected somehow, I can't see it. But I'm not going to stop trying. You still think that Costello has got something to do with it? And now these photographs have come to light.' Archie Walker flicked through the photographs feeling sick to his stomach, how a whole life was about to come tumbling down. 'Do you ever think that you never know anybody as well as you think you know them?'

'In my job, all the time,' said Mathieson.

Walker felt sick. He'd been sympathetic and stuck by Valerie during all the chaos that she'd brought upon herself, but there was no way he could help her get over this, indeed he wasn't sure he wanted to. She was having her private life drama. A young police officer had lost his life. No contest. 'I'm struggling to understand these.'

The photographs were so incriminating that even Mathieson was quietly empathetic. 'I'm sorry, Archie, but these put a totally different spin on the situation.' She took the photographs from the procurator fiscal's shaking hand and flicked through them looking for one in particular. The one that showed George Haggerty and Valerie Abernethy in a tight embrace. He had his hands cupping her jaw. It was obvious to anybody that this was not a brother-in-law/sister-in-law saying goodbye. 'Has she ever hinted that she was having an affair with George?'

Archie snorted. 'With George? She always said she couldn't stand the man but I can see it leads you to the conclusion that this was an old-fashioned love triangle, maybe sparked by . . .? Oh, I don't know – how do you justify something like that? Or was she playing at hating him. For Abigail's sake, for my sake?'

'A psychologist would say that Valerie was robbed of one kind of family so she was ready to take on another, one that happened to be her sister's. If you look at what she'd been through, what she was about to go through, the humiliation of the court case. She'd know a decent defence counsel was going to rip her apart. "Miss Abernethy, did you seriously think that you could buy a baby and get away with it?" How emotionally crippled was she going to sound when she answered that? "You were turned down for adoption, Miss Abernethy, would you like to tell the court why, because you were too drunk." Considered too drunk to be a mother . . . and there's Abigail, all sweetness, light and loveliness.'

'So why would she kill the boy?'

'Maybe she didn't mean to, maybe he came in and saw her, maybe that's what sparked the intense rage. Malcolm standing up for his mother. Nobody had ever stood up for her, had they? In her eyes, I mean, addicts always think that everybody is against them.'

Archie shook his head again. 'I really don't believe this.'

'Which is why we are telling you before we put out a warrant for her arrest. That arrest may take place at your house. You need to be prepared for that.'

Archie was speechless for a moment, then said, 'But playing devil's advocate, it does explain what happened to that Star Wars Lego thing she was going on about. That some kind of emotional hook or trophy or whatever you want to call it.'

'We are, of course, going to question George again as he

has lied to us about their relationship, but he has an alibi. It's likely he was trying to protect her – and himself. But we both know that knife was not in his hand.' Bannon had the pictures now, three of them were taken of the couple walking up Great Western Road past the petrol station. He was studying them carefully.

'Can I ask how you got hold of these? The obvious question to me is who took them and why?' said Walker.

It was Mathieson who answered. 'They were sent to me directly from a private detective. He hinted that Abigail had employed him as she didn't trust Valerie and has been waiting for Abigail's lawyer to say it was OK to send these images to me. Believe that if you want. He refused to give his name and we will send the photographs away for forensic examination to make sure they have not been doctored, although they look genuine to me.'

'Is that it?'

'We'll trace who sent them, don't worry.'

They both looked at Bannon, who had coughed meaningfully after swiping through his phone. 'The headlines on that day were . . . yip . . . So this petrol station looks like the one on Great Western Road. You can see the newspapers on the display rack outside. The firestorms in California were front page news, and that corresponds with the date. I think, you could get that enhanced and that would confirm what day it was. The *Evening Times* is there and it's dark so this must be late and I suspect this guy has sent you these photographs and this one in particular because it shows George and Valerie together on the evening Abigail and Malcolm were killed.'

'Which is useful,' understated Mathieson, after a minute of shocked silence.

'Which is very convenient. I'd get them checked out,' said Walker, not able to keep his eyes off them. 'Far too convenient. You have the murder of a young police officer to solve; I suggest you get on with that.'

'And it hasn't gone past me that she's wearing heels in this picture. She's five seven, plus those heels five feet eleven. I don't need to tell you the significance of that,' said Mathieson. 'The height of the spatter shadow at the crime scene. The person who had that knife was five feet ten or eleven, or smaller with heels. I know it's all circumstantial but it's all starting to point the same way.'

Bannon nodded. 'Whatever way it blows, be prepared for the shitstorm.'

Valerie walked out of Judy Plum heading down Mitchell Street. She felt better than she had felt for ages. Liberated, that was the word. She had a plan, something to do with her life. She had bought a blond shoulder-length wig.

Susan, as the woman in the shop had introduced herself, had been empathetic but very matter of fact. It was easy for Val to say what she was looking for. A short blond wig, slightly longer at the back, with a fringe, a longish fringe if possible. She looked around, picking out two she thought would do. Susan held her fixed smile and looked at Valerie's naturally dark hair, such a dark brown it was almost black.

'It might not suit your colouring,' Susan counselled.

'I want something totally different. A totally different look,' said Valerie looking in the mirror and feeling rather joyous.

She walked down the road, thinking about buying a warm jacket and some outdoor boots. She was more than a little fed up with Valerie Abernethy. She didn't know DI Winifred Prudence Costello but she intended to get right under her skin. She knew a bit from what she'd read in the paper. And had guessed that Uncle Archie had a thing going with her and Archie might be old but he was nobody's fool. He didn't like stupid women, so DI Costello was not stupid.

And Costello was going nowhere, she had much more use as a smokescreen, a confusion, an obfuscation. One of Archie's favourite words. That seemed fitting.

She had left the hospital and made a few phone calls, mostly to the Freigate Clinic, a small private hospital that was best known for treating rich people with substance abuse issues, and as such they had three very good psychologists on the staff and two psychiatrists, none of whom had ever set eyes on Winifred Costello.

Valerie had hired a car to take Costello, under an assumed name, from the Queen Elizabeth to the private facility where she would have her own room. And the pay as you go phone that Valerie had just bought for her would be waiting there for her.

She had been lucky that Hannah had been convinced by her story, by her fiscal's ID with her finger covering the name but not the picture. She had told enough lies over the truth to be convincing, and there was the obvious evidence of Costello who had been subject to an attack, and Hannah had to help in their efforts to protect her. Hannah had nodded, but not before asking a few questions about Costello's medical care that proved she was not as gullible as she might appear.

Valerie caught a taxi, directing the driver to Archie's house, checking her phone in the back seat. She saw the breaking newsfeed flash across the screen, the body of the missing police officer had been found. It pulled her up short. She must have squealed as the driver asked her if she was OK. She nodded and examined her phone. Two missed calls from Archie, one from DCI Mathieson. Her mind started to race. She sensed, knew, that she was about to be hauled in to help with enquiries and she knew where that would lead. She adjusted her position in the seat, her mind racing. As she leaned forward she caught sight of the *Daily Record*, lying on the passenger seat. The heads on the picture were tucked under but she knew by the position, Pippa's coat sitting in the window of the French Café. Her and George. He had set her up for the media. Bastard.

As they turned the corner she saw a police car pull into the same street two cars ahead of them. She asked the driver to pull in feigning that she had just remembered she needed to see a neighbour. Did she need anything? She put her hand in her bag; the gun was there, that was all she needed. She paid the driver and walked the rest of the way, staying on the opposite side of the road until she could see, out the corner of her eye, the two cop cars at Archie's house. Without missing a step, she turned right and walked down the side street back into the city. The steps she was taking felt familiar, the gardens she passed, the streets signs, as if she had walked this way before.

\*   \*   \*

Archie was keeping away from his own house. There was a warrant out for Valerie's arrest, there wasn't much more he could do before he could be justifiably accused of perverting the course of justice. Mathieson had decided that Valerie should be brought in and left to stew, and had acquiesced that Walker would supply her with a very good defence brief, Archie had already called Kerr, he was on standby. Walker and Mathieson were both now on very different sides of the fence, but both being experienced they were politely going by the book. Transparency above all else.

Costello? Now Valerie?

Was his life going to get any worse?

So he was now standing watching Mathieson and Bannon search Costello's living room. They had done everything but ask him the question they really wanted to know the answer to, some vestige of professional respect had kicked in. But Walker had no doubt of the arsenal of ammunition Mathieson could bring to bear down on him.

He couldn't appear as concerned about Costello as he really felt; she was a colleague, but over the years she had become so much more. He thought a lot of her, he had total respect for her, but he wasn't in love with her. She was far too annoying for that. It was just . . . he was desperately worried about her.

In response to their indirect question, he had told them he had been in the house a few times, and as far as he knew nothing had been moved or changed. Nothing looked out of place.

'So you don't know where Valerie is and you have no idea where Costello is?' asked Mathieson, her purple Nitrile gloves clashing with the bright red lipstick.

'Or the Holy Grail, or Glenn Miller.'

It was Mathieson that got to him. She was a shady little creature who pouted as she spoke. Was she really so hard and brutal as she looked? Or was it the insecurity of her position, the fact that Bannon would always get a better response from a witness than she ever would. But then maybe that made them an effective team, like Anderson and Costello, the ying and yang.

Her thin blonde hair was sculpted in a wave that kicked out

to rest on her shoulders, a fringe that sat two inches too high was fixed on her forehead with hairspray, the overall effect was that of a blonde helmet on a Stepford wife. She kept talking to Bannon out the corner of her mouth, quietly as if he, as the chief fiscal, was not worthy to hear it, his opinion not worthy to be sought. Bannon, give him his due, was younger and believed more in engagement to get results. Whatever Costello had got herself involved in, it was directly related to what she had seen that October morning six weeks before.

Walker couldn't shake the news about Donnie from his head. 'You don't really suspect her of killing another police officer?' His tone of voice was testimony to just how stupid he thought that idea was.

'At this point I don't really know what to think. I can see her getting angry and lashing out at him, nothing pre-planned, but provoked. Don't you? I've read a fair bit about her. Listened when you and the others are talking about her, I think she'd lash out when she thought she was on the moral high ground.'

Archie could only give a little nod while admitting to himself that Mathieson wasn't too far off the mark.

'And there was the incident when she broke Viktor Mulholland's nose. One single punch. Hardly the act of a professional police officer.' She sighed, looking round the living room, her gloved hand sitting on her hip, a stance that reminded Walker of Costello herself. 'But you know her better. Tell me what you think happened.'

'All this is complicated enough without people starting on hypotheticals.'

'Where would she go, though? Any relatives? She must have somebody.'

'None that I know of, but you might be better asking Colin Anderson.'

Bannon had his hand down the back of the sofa, pulling out a few coins, a remote control, and a crumpled paperback. He looked up and raised an eyebrow, having heard the gossip and possessing enough sensitivity not to point out that it was him here, not Colin Anderson. And his presence spoke volumes.

'What about intimacy?' asked Mathieson.

'Excuse me?'

'Had she mentioned McCaffrey to you or any of the gang of four, in an intimate way?'

'The gang of four?'

'We will be talking to Costello's colleagues, Anderson, Wyngate and Mulholland so we will know if she has mentioned something that maybe you have forgotten.' It was Mathieson's turn to raise an eyebrow, questioning.

Walker answered carefully, 'Not that she told me, but she did know McCaffrey, as a police officer.'

'Off the record, do you have any ideas where she is?'

'And if it's off the record, you shouldn't be asking. But I will answer *on the record*. I do not know where she is.'

'But you know her and we know how well you know her. She has a good police record, mostly,' she added, 'she herself, but when you look back at her family, it's all there. All there for us all to see. So you are here to make sure that we do our job properly, but that is all. Do I think she'd kill a colleague? No. But when I read about her family, about her brother? Then I can think that she has a cop's sense of moral outrage at what happened to Abigail and Malcolm that fits in with her personality. I can see that she might have pulled a young cop like Donnie into her way of thinking . . . and maybe when he realized how far she was prepared to go and he said that he wasn't . . . Then I can picture a scenario that fits what we have here. There could have been a fight, he might have come off worse.'

'I can think as far as that. But she would not be running away. She'd be standing here shouting. And her blood was there.'

'A trickle of her blood, and she is nowhere to be seen, and she has been texting you so she's about somewhere,' said Mathieson.

'But she has gone on the run. She certainly hasn't been back here. That's what I'm thinking. And Donnie McCaffrey is very dead,' added Bannon.

Archie nodded, giving the idea some thought. It wasn't that far away from what he was thinking himself. It was a logical chain of thought that could explain everything and nothing. It would fit the way she had handed in her notice, and left

Mitchum in no doubt about what she had thought of the lack of investigative progress into the deaths of Abigail Haggerty and her son Malcolm. But if she had injured Donnie, she would have taken him to the hospital, not up to Tyndrum to die.

He watched them in silence. Costello's living room was still dark, they hadn't opened the big white curtains that covered the picture window and hid the beautiful view of the Clyde. He lifted his mobile from his pocket, checking it for a message from her, nothing.

He read a few emails from work, looking busy. He didn't want to appear that he was watching them but he couldn't help himself, thinking like a prosecutor. He followed them, seeing what they were seeing and trying to interpret the facts in a different way.

Her car was missing. Her laptop was nowhere to be seen. There was an abandoned cup of tea. Had she left in a hurry?

They went through everything and every room. He followed them out to the linen cupboards, Bannon opened the door allowing Mathieson to look in, have a good search round. Archie could see the white laundry basket on the floor, Mathieson in her haste had missed it and she nodded to Bannon to close the door which he was about to do when Bannon said, 'What's that?' and picked up the bag that was lying in the laundry basket.

'Interesting,' he said as he looked in, avoiding Archie's eyes. 'Bloodstains. On a bath towel. Get all that bagged.'

Mathieson picked it up, suspending it between a gloved finger and thumb, explained it to him as if he was a child. 'Covered in McCaffrey's blood.'

'Somebody's blood. She was bleeding too, remember?'

'There's a pair of trousers and . . . oh no.' She pulled out a jacket and showed them the large slash at the back. 'That looks superficial, that didn't go through. She was well enough to come back here. He lost his blood, and his life at the scene.'

'Well, get it tested and we will find out,' Archie said. 'I can put a rush on it through Matilda McQueen.'

'No, I don't think so. I think, as we basically have the budget from Complaints, then we will get a private lab to run the tests. Not that I suspect McQueen would be underhand in any way but we are going to aim for transparency here. It's time for the truth, whatever that is.'

'Of course. The fiscal's office will support you in any way we can,' Archie said. 'And in my role of chief fiscal, my office is formally requesting a copy of that email, with the photographs attached, of course.'

Mathieson stood up, looking straight at him, trying to figure out what he was thinking. 'Of course, transparency in all things, Mr Walker.'

'Thank you.' This time he gave way to the relief he felt.

Whatever mess Costello was in, she was going to have to get out of it herself.

Walker was wound as tight as a rattlesnake. Brenda had given him a cup of coffee and he was making half-hearted attempts to amuse baby Moses, who was gurgling when he was the centre of attention and scowling when he was not.

Anderson took a long time looking through printouts of the photographs; he placed them on the coffee table in something that approached chronological order. 'You know, Archie, if I was the defence council, I would be asking myself exactly what these photographs show.'

'They show my god-daughter is a lying little piece of shit.'

'Do they? Look at the clothes, three different occasions from the look of them. Valerie is not dressed up, she has no make-up on.'

'She has heels on?'

'She has the shoes on that she was wearing when she was taken to the hospital, that night. She was Valerie Abernethy, the suited, Porsche driving fiscal, on her way to the Blue Neptune; she'd have been in high-heel mode.'

'A woman can borrow clothes, but nobody can wear someone else's shoes,' added Brenda, thinking she had to give some female input.

'And look, she's never kissing him, he is kissing her. Look at this one.' He held one out for Walker to have a better look at. 'In that one, she has her hands up; her palms are on his chest like she is ready to push him away. And it's all a little convenient, isn't it, that these suddenly appear on Mathieson's desk from an anonymous source? So maybe not a little lying piece of shit, maybe she's being manipulated by somebody who is very good at it.'

'Haggerty?'

'I think so, you know what effect those pictures will have on a jury. And Mathieson has moved on them. These pics will get Valerie arrested.'

'I have Kerr booked for her defence, I think she might need somebody good. I will make sure he interviews whoever took the photographs. It's a bit too convenient that it shows Valerie left the hospital and walked in the direction of Balcarres Avenue on the night of the murders. And she has no memory of it.'

'I think Mathieson is too quick. You need to get her to look at that CCTV again, further afield. Find out where Valerie and George went. Don't accept all this at face value.'

Archie Walker looked defeated, he looked crumpled; a sad sight in a man who took great pride in his appearance.

'I've always said the crime was far too controlled for an addict like Valerie.'

'So get hold of Valerie, get her together with the best legal representation and get Mathieson on the back foot. There's holes in her case a bus could get through. You are a lawyer after all. Play the game the way Mathieson plays it.'

'Just one problem.'

'What?'

'I have no idea where Valerie is. Her stuff is in the room at my house, but her handbag has gone.'

'God, it's like that Agatha Christie book when they all disappear one by one.'


Mathieson was cold and wet by the time she got hold of Colin Anderson in the interview room at West End Central at half six at night.

'Right,' she said banging a cup of coffee on the table in front of him. 'Just so you know, we have found bloodstained clothing at Costello's residence.'

'With a slash in it,' added Bannon.

Anderson kept his face straight. 'So a serving police officer who has worked in major cases leaves that kind of forensic evidence lying around her flat? Where did you find it?'

'In her washing basket,' answered Bannon, helpfully before Mathieson could stop him.

'Her washing basket.' Anderson threw his hands up in the air. 'Well, you probably got her right there. I'd say that was the act of a guilty person, putting dirty washing in the washing basket. Jesus, if she had anything to do with this you'd find no evidence at all. She'd have walked down to the river and chucked it in there. It would be floating past Ireland now.'

'People do things by force of habit. Even cops who should know better.'

'I'll give you that,' agreed Anderson sweetly.

His acquiescence unnerved Mathieson slightly, for one single beat she was put off her stride.

'They knew each other; McCaffrey and Costello, so what happened to him? His wife says that Costello texted him, he went out to Inveruglass to meet her. And there was an incident that involved blood, cocaine and alcohol.'

'Crap,' said Anderson.

Mathieson wrote that down.

'Costello wouldn't touch alcohol if you paid her.'

'So he did the drinking and she drove her car, we haven't found it yet.'

'No. Let me put that another way. All evidence is open to interpretation, so I think you are mistaken in your interpretation of the evidence that has been put before you. Do you want to write that down?'

'I know that, Colin.' Bannon was back to first-name terms. His voice was soft and sympathetic which unnerved Anderson more than if he had been scathing and threatening. 'But you can see the uncomfortable position we are in. We have no sign anybody else was there.'

'You didn't know Kieran was there, did you? You don't know who put the tobacco tin in the wing of the camper. No, you don't. Stop bowing to pressure and do your fucking jobs properly. I'd never jump to the conclusions that you have. Unless she was standing there with a smoking gun, covered in an obscene amount of gunshot residue, while standing next to a bleeding McCaffrey who was screaming, "Oh Costello, please don't shoot me again".'

'She was there when the bodies were found at the house, the Haggerty house,' said Mathieson briskly.

'So was Archie Walker. They found the bodies together, full stop.'

'How did she know to go there? There was no inclination, no pointers, she just decided to go round there and hey ho, a twelve-year-old boy and his mother had been stabbed to death.'

'You saying that doesn't change the facts of the case. She went round there in the company of Archie to inform the deceased about the state of her sister, a fiscal called Valerie Abernethy who is—'

'Mr Walker's god-daughter, yes we know. Who is having an affair with George Haggerty? And who we are now looking for in connection with that crime.'

'Again, that's your interpretation.'

'Why did Costello go with him? With Archie to that house? Why?'

'He's a friend, and it was a police matter. Costello had derived the plan to catch the person who had killed Mary Jane Duguid, remember.'

'Your daughter?'

'So it subsequently turned out. And Valerie was nearly killed by Braithwaite. Why shouldn't Costello go?'

'But why with Archie, then, if it was not a family affair.'

'She went because it was a family affair and she's not family. She's a serving police officer.'

'Was, Colin, she *was* a serving police officer.'

'She was at the time and was keeping it all above board.'

'Does she do what Archie suggests? Does she go out with him? Are they having an affair?'

'Well, he took me out for a pint last week, are we having an affair too?' he snapped back.

Bannon was doing his softly, softly thing again.

'I've seen the pictures of that scene, they were pretty horrific. Do you think that could have pushed her over the edge and she might now be planning to take some investigation into her own hands?'

'By killing a fellow police officer? No, I don't think so.'
But that was exactly what he thought, Costello and McCaffrey,
a two-man tag team. Just like Anderson and Costello had been
but Anderson could always rein in Costello, he doubted
McCaffrey would attempt to do that.

'What do you think then, Colin? We need some help here.'

It was a textbook ploy to get him to talk but he could see
how it might be for them and, he acknowledged to himself,
there was the possibility that with pressure from above they
might be forced to close the case on the most obvious evidence
available in the absence of Costello to give her version of events.

'Well, if you don't hear it from me you would hear it from
others. It's a popular theory but I don't think so. She'd be here
kicking and punching. I think it broke her and she has gone
off to lick her wounds. I think she felt very responsible for
the death of Malcolm, the boy had called her on his phone.
She had alerted Children's Services. A woman called Dali
Despande had placed it on a priority list of some sort but there
was no real evidence that the child was in danger. Until somebody stabbed him twelve times, of course.'

'But that person was not a member of the family, so why
bring Family Services into it? Surely the tragic outcome of
that situation shows that Costello got it wrong, it wasn't his
dad that the boy was afraid of. Maybe it was Valerie.'

Of course it was his dad, thought Anderson, of course it
was. Whatever else had gone on in there, Malcolm Haggerty
had been scared of his own dad. Colin recalled the conversation at Mary Jane's funeral. 'She was very suspicious of
George, and wherever she is, I think she still will be.'

'And this?' Mathieson pointed to a picture of the young
police officer, a death forgotten in the internecine arguments
about a woman who wasn't there.

'I don't know about that. Or him. I haven't heard. I've
worked with Costello for years and all I get is titbits of a lot
of blood, a bit of cocaine, a lot of alcohol. If you want to give
me all the relevant details, I will certainly give you my opinion.
If you value it, knowing her as I do.'

'We feel you might be guilty by association, if you assisted
her in some way.'

Anderson nearly laughed. 'You have got to be kidding, look at my service record, look at hers . . .'

'Yes, we know,' said Bannon. 'We know that, you and I both know that, but if this goes to court they will argue that if anybody helped Costello, it would have been you.'

'You do know about Costello's family past?' If Mathieson was supposed to edge that question in carefully, she hadn't made a good job of it.

'Yes I do. I know her brother nearly killed her, which is how she got that scar on her forehead. And obviously I know about her brother and father. It's all over the bloody papers.'

'It's in the public domain.'

'The timing is rank.'

'That doesn't change the facts. You do see our problem,'

'If you think she did that—' he tapped his finger on the photograph – 'then I think you are barking well up the wrong tree, she might lash out in anger but not that.'

'So where is she?'

'I have no idea, has there been any movement on her credit cards? Her bank cards? Trace her phone, you're the police you can do what you want.'

'She's taken money out from her account. The transactions started again this morning. And she brought a pay-as-you-go mobile using her credit card. She knows we've been tracing her calls. We will trace the CCTV cameras and then we will bring her in. And we have a White Fiat on CCTV on the A9. Just waiting confirmation.'

Anderson knew that wasn't true, Mathieson was playing him. They'd have confirmation on the car owner immediately, but it made him sit up. 'Really? She's up and moving? She bought another mobile?'

'And headed north. Do you know of any friends or relatives up there?'

Anderson smiled. 'If she turns west off the A9, and joins the North Coast 500 route then you have a connection. She has no relatives up north, she has no relatives at all. But George Haggerty is from that part of the world.'

Mathieson nodded. 'We had worked that out. And you can see how it looks. I'm sorry but Costello is a suspect in this, so as with any suspect, her life, her friends her career, all of it, is under scrutiny. Until we know what happened to McCaffrey, Costello remains a person of interest.'

'And the boy, the one in Raigmore? Cowan?' Anderson directed the question to Bannon who flicked open his folder and ran a finger down an index, then flicked over a few pages. He could hear Mathieson's fingernails tapping in impatience and got the feeling Bannon was winding her up. He would have the information Anderson wanted at the forefront of his mind.

'So preliminary report from the scene of crime, and the tracker dog. Basically, the tyre treads of the camper are at the viewing point car park and he left there at speed.'

'Suggesting that he had done or seen something that he wanted away from?'

'Maybe he drove north for a couple of miles and ended up in a lay-by.' He looked up. 'I think you know about the waxed ball bearings?'

'Two miles, was that enough to melt the wax if they had been put in at Inveruglass, at the viewing site? Or would it have to be warmed by miles of driving?'

'The engine would be hot anyway, he'd driven up from Glasgow remember. And what an easy vehicle to follow. There was no phone or camera in the car, the camera was at the bottom of the loch and the keys were found in a field thirty feet from the lay-by.'

'So he was chased?'

'He stops the van because of the clatter, his assailant comes up behind him, probably friendly as Kieran takes the keys out the engine. There is an incident that involves Kieran being on the ground, then the dogs pick up a scent running towards the trees, over the wire fence, thick trees, running deeper into the forest, he was veering as he ran . . .' He cocked his head. 'That time of night it was dark, keeping in the cover of the tree trunks. Then the dogs found the main site about a hundred yards in. Blood. Disturbance, and then he was dragged out.'

'Why?'

'No idea why. There are signs of blood loss and two things of interest. He seems to have lost his waistcoat, loose, lots of

pockets, like a photographer's but the best thing is the few
fibres found on a branch, that looks hopeful of something. As
if somebody put their hand on a branch and they've left a
trace. The lab at Inverness has been sent the sample, so they
can be processed alongside the sample from Kieran.'

'So Costello did that, then pulled the body back to a small
Fiat and drove 300 miles north to drop it on a remote mountain
pass?'

'Something happened. She has not come forward, but she's
up and about. You have been on this side of the desk long
enough to know what it is like and that there are, very rarely,
any surprises,' said Mathieson.

'And if she has gone rogue—' Bannon took a look at the
picture of the young cop – 'I can understand her logic. She
has a very developed sense of morality and justice which
sometimes the police service cannot deliver. And I think she's
keeping you and Archie out the loop because she doesn't want
to make trouble for you. She is a very loyal friend, she doesn't
want to involve you in her . . . well, whatever it is she has
planned.' Bannon shrugged. 'That's my thoughts.'

'But she wouldn't do this.' Anderson pointed to the picture
of Donnie. 'This guy was one of us.'

The other two sat and did nothing, forcing him to speak.
He studied the photograph of the dead young police officer.
'Who has done the forensics on this?'

'Your usual team.'

Anderson nodded slowly. 'OK so O'Hare, McQueen?'

'Yes. Costello's DNA is all over his dead body,' said Bannon.

Mathieson argued, 'I'm a simpler soul. I'm going for the
obvious. She killed him. Maybe not intentionally, maybe it
was something that got out of hand but . . . Well, you can't
argue with the science. Their bloods are mingled. Bloods.
Both of them were bleeding. We have one body and the
other one is missing. They met in that car park after Costello
had summoned him, and something kicked off. There was
a fight.'

'Could they have been attacked and she got away?' Anderson
asked.

'Away to where? And from what? If that was the case then

why wouldn't she run here so we can help her? Why keep below the radar?'

'Well, you can't have it both ways. If she was keeping below the radar there's no way she'd use her bank card. She's too clever for that, she knows the way we work.' He thought for a moment. 'Was it an auto bank?'

Bannon looked down. 'Yes and a visa card.'

'So you don't know for sure that somebody else isn't using it instead of her? You need to look at the cameras.' He got up to leave.

'It was a female fitting Costello's description that bought the phone. The film does look like her, short blonde hair, anorak.' Mathieson stood up, small and insignificant between the other two detectives. 'And if you hear from her in any way, shape or form, you will tell us.'

He paused. 'I will tell her to get in touch with you, of course.'

'Not quite the same thing, DCI Anderson.'

'It's the best I can do.'

And he left.

# ELEVEN

Isla had been told to go to bed. Her mum and dad were staying over, and the kids were in the spare bedroom with them. The GP had come out and given her a sleeping tablet, well, five, to get through the next few days.

So she lay alone in the bed she had shared with her husband, as the world went on as normal outside. They had been married seven years, he was her husband, her best friend, dad to her children.

She wondered where Costello was right now. No one seemed to know.

She couldn't get her head round that.

She stared at the ceiling, lying with the light on, her mind not really keeping up with the issues that everybody had brought up, how are you going to cope? She had no option but to cope. Her children would grow up, they would remember their dad. She'd make sure they knew him and the man he was.

And why he had died.

She stared at the ceiling again. There was a spider's web up there, dancing.

She lay in the darkness and then cried her eyes out.

All that did was give her a headache and make her eyes sore. She had no emotion left, except anger. She could hear her mum and dad next door, talking quietly. They still had each other, in their sixties they could still lie in bed entwined in each other's arms.

The pain of that stopped her breathing.

She felt she had nothing to say. She wanted to look after the kids but couldn't look at them with their huge trusting brown eyes, ready to ask where Daddy was. When was Daddy coming home? The questions were bound to start coming and she didn't have the heart to answer them. She didn't have the heart, full stop.

It had been ripped out of her.

Her mum and dad were now settled in the youngest's room and the kids were all piled in together.

Why not use the fourth bedroom? Her mum had asked, and got a dig in the ribs from her father. It was Donnie's room, just for Donnie.

She got up, pulled on her dressing gown, a big fluffy white one that Donnie had bought her when Nathan had been born. He had wrapped it all up in paper, when she opened it in the hospital he'd had to take it back home as it was too bulky to go in any of the cupboards. And she was scared it might get lifted.

She brought it up to her face, smelling the scent of Donnie's aftershave, the times she had lain on the sofa, on a Saturday night; her lying in his arms sipping a Prosecco, him sipping a beer and watching the football while she flicked through a magazine.

Little things, he was never one for the big gestures, but he was always there, always thoughtful.

She went to the next room, the small room that sat next to the box room. She undid the little hook at the top, a simple plain hook sitting in a brass ring. She twisted it round, lifting it off, the door swung open and she closed it behind her very quietly. She turned on the light switch, the tiny room lit up like Wembley Stadium. Books, a laptop, a sound system and one lazy boy easy chair, with a blanket and a pillow on it.

Donnie's den.

He would come in here when he was on night shift and he needed a kip during the day. He'd lie there with his headphones and watch a film on the laptop or listen to his music, a whole wall of his favourite CDs, keeping them away from small sticky hands. And then his vinyl collection, his greatest love: Hotel California, Dark Side of the Moon, Going For The One and every one of David Bowie's thirty-five albums. His adoration of the sidemen, the unsung heroes.

She sat on the arm of the recliner, and reached over to put on the sidelight, then got up to put the overhead light off. The room changed character totally, calming now, relaxing. Lying down on the chair, she pressed the button to drop the back, the footrest coming up under her legs and she pulled the blanket round her.

This was his favourite place, her eyes scanned round at the picture of her and the boys pinned to the corkboard, a list of stuff she wanted him to pick up at Argos for Christmas, before they sold out or it got too busy.

Christmas. How the hell was she supposed to cope with Christmas?

Without Donnie? Two words she could never imagine saying together.

She closed her eyes, she had to be strong. Or she'd fall apart, she didn't really have to do anything, her husband had been killed. She could see herself in the car, him driving the kids squealing in the back, him winding them up and her trying to get them to calm down. They had driven up to Inveruglass many times. The last time the boys had climbed to the viewing point with the Gaelic name.

*How do you say that, Daddy?*

*No bloody idea.*

The youngest had climbed up on Donnie's shoulders for a lift, she had taken the eldest by the hand, then had walked up to the top step of the viewing platform where they had a clear view right down the loch. They had sat together. Their hands intertwining automatically, she had had her gloves on, it had been cold. The boys had climbed up and down the steps, the big boy helping the wee boy, punting him up, helping him down. Near the bottom, Donnie had set off to retrieve them.

Donnie had loved the place. Why would he go there, why did he take Costello?

He had liked her, she was still missing. There was still a chance that she would be found alive. At that moment Isla hated her, she was single with no kids: she could die and nobody would notice.

Was she on the run after killing Donnie? She doubted it.

So he had gone there, met her and been murdered. His body taken up the road to Tyndrum, thirty miles north, dumped in a lochan. Thrown away like trash.

By whom? And why?

He wasn't doing anything official, it was something he'd had an idea about. He would have written something down or noted something on his computer. He had a brown notepad somewhere, he was always scribbling here and there.

There would be something in this room.

She was wide awake now.

She looked over at his desk, she could start up his computer, and find nothing. She would do that later. Closing her eyes, she thought of him sitting in his boxers, on the recliner, his mobile in his hand. They had been phoning each other, Donnie and Costello. How often, she had no idea. He had taken the phone out the room, when she had been present, nothing unusual in that, she had no interest in his work, apart from how it affected him.

So he would be in here, on his phone, making notes, even something he typed up on his computer, he would do that while he was on the phone. She glanced over at the bin, it was empty, of course. She had emptied it when things were normal and Donnie was going to walk back in the door.

She closed her eyes and asked Donnie for help. If he was out there in the ether, she needed his help right now. His name was being dragged through the shite and she wasn't going to let that happen. She thought about the last time she saw him, she was going through the Argos catalogue making a list. Why was she thinking of that? She had a nice notebook with flowers on it, that was her Christmas notebook. Donnie had a simple reporter's notebook with a spiral of wire across the top, usually with a blue biro rammed through it.

He had been using it to get the measurements for the new tiles for the bathroom floor, well, that wasn't going to happen now. But he did use that notebook a lot, she had seen him here, on this recliner, phone jammed in between his ear and shoulder, notebook on his thigh, his foot up on the chair, scribbling. She had been telling him that his dinner was ready, he had nodded. It was cold by the time he had come through. When had that been? Last week? The week before?

She didn't know why but she knew now that he had been talking to Costello.

She scanned the small bookcase in the room, and there it was, lying on top of The Godfather DVD collection she had bought him for Christmas last year. She reached over and picked it up. He had written his name on the front page, like a school kid, he had even underlined it and added a doodle of a motorbike.

She flicked it open feeling like a spy, intruding on his life. There was nothing in it. Of course he had torn out the pages with the notes for the bathroom tiles and stuck them on the tiler's business card. There were little fragments of paper at the top, where he had pulled pages out, recently from the fact that the tiny pieces were still trapped in the spiral. Even as she had moved it from the bookcase back to the seat, some had fallen on the carpet, she picked them up carefully and laid them out on top of his keyboard, wary to lose anything that might have been part of him.

Then she looked back at the pad, flicked the top page over, letting it fall in behind the rest. He had been using it, she could see the indents of his writing, the circular doodles that he did when he was bored, or thinking, circles that would pair up and morph into motorbikes.

They had been watching that forensics programme together where the farmer had placed a bomb under his own car, then slashed himself and then shot his neighbour dead making out his neighbour had been targeting him. Donnie had pondered why the farmer didn't move house. But Isla could remember the CSI had held the notepad to an oblique light source and read the indents of the threatening letter that the neighbour was supposed to have written. She went over to the desk and switched on Donnie's desk lamp. She could make out a few letters, see the individual pen grooves of the doodles.

She turned the light out and went back, so the only source of light in the room was the small Ikea desk lamp. She moved the pad back and forth, seeing numbers and cms, that was him making the measurements for the tiles, but there was something else.

A name. It looked as though Donnie had written it and then gone over it again and again, doodling over the letters as he was on the phone. She could make it out, more than a few letters. She fired up the computer, feeling better now that she was doing something, she Googled the name, variations of the same, the search engine brought back a few possibles. Nothing that matched exactly what she had thought she had read. But one entry caught her eye, not the bar at the top but in the two lines of small print underneath.

And then, at the bottom a name she was more familiar with, that was scribbled all over this page. It was just Donnie, being Donnie.

*Oscar Duguid, believed drowned, search called off. Leaving a wife Abigail and a daughter Mary Jane.* Isla, read that again; Abigail and Mary Jane, Kelvindale Bridge, NC 500, phone land registry, harbour master and Jennifer. Jennifer was common enough but not Abigail or Mary Jane. Neither were particularly common names. Donnie had been ranting about that, the name of the girl Braithwaite had killed though Donnie thought they would have a tough time proving it. Braithwaite, who was arguing it was all his wife's fault, the wife who had conveniently fallen from the top of a high building. Not enough to be not guilty but enough for there to be reasonable doubt in the mind of the jury, he would be a good witness, he might get off.

She couldn't sit here and do nothing.

Anderson sat at his kitchen table, the house was quiet for once, just a steady beat of music from upstairs somewhere and the rasp of Nesbit's snoring. The blank page of his iPad was staring at him. His head was hurting just thinking about what Costello had got herself caught up in. He was concerned about her safety, more concerned than he dared to voice, even to himself. He had seen the worried look on Walker's face, even the fiscal had stopped fooling himself that the texts had been coming from her. They could have been sent by anyone who had got her phone off her. And nobody knew who that was.

But now she had come out of hiding and was back on the road, having purchased a new phone.

He wished he could feel a sense of relief in that, but, and there was a but, it wasn't her.

He called up the map of Loch Lomond, tracing the route

to Tyndrum which followed the West Highland Way. Just as the Bealach followed the 500? Anybody who wanted to be there, had a reason to be there, hiding amongst the tourist traffic.

He thought about the others, the pile of paperwork on the rapes. Mitchum had given him a week. He was so fucked up over this he hadn't given a thought to Sally and to Gillian. Was there a connection as Morna thought?

He tried to put that to the back of his mind, making himself think about the An Ceann Mor viewing point. Somebody had chased the student down. Told him his car was leaking fluid? Maybe Cowan had already stopped due to the noise made by the tin of ball bearings. There must have been some kind of chase, the boy trying to get away and he was pursued through the trees. His attacker caught up with him, battered him in the face then slit his throat. Then what? Why take him so many miles away? A journey that would take over three, maybe four hours and then dump him on a remote mountain pass?

Was it because he was going there anyway? Not out of convenience, but for ease of explanation if their vehicle was spotted en route. Years ago the body should have lain at the pass until the road reopened in the spring but now there was no presumption of isolation. Why roll the body out the car and into a gully? Were they too weak to take it any further? Yet they took the body from the woods to the lay-by two hundred miles north? Tired? Injured? A different person? Or a lack of time? A woman?

Anderson pushed that thought away and looked again at the screen. Or was he pushed for time? Would his tardiness be noticed, and remembered by a third party? There had been many places, better places, to leave the body on the way up. Places where it would not have been found.

It had taken them three months to find Sharon Sixsmith.

So why there?

And found by who?

It was reported a body was found.

He swiped to read the report on the finding of Kieran Cowan, confirming there was a huge part of the story missing. Who had called DCI Patrick? The report said nothing and Patrick said even less. The ones that shall not be spoken of. Small men of few words, short hair and wide necks. Anderson knew who trained in places like the Bealach. Those who needed the bleakest, toughest landscape the British Isles could offer. He knew who and what they were, and he guessed that Alastair Patrick had been one of them. A small lithe Glasgow man with a chip of ice in his eyes, that man would blow your head off and would feel no compunction about doing it.

And that took a certain kind of moral toughness.

Anderson needed Cowan to pull through for him and tell him what happened on that hill, with the blood and the heroin and the alcohol. He had very nearly escaped.

But what of Costello?

He closed his eyes. The music stopped, Nesbitt woke up. A deathly silence fell on the house, just as he had made the decision to go north for some peace. Morna had been pleased of course, Brenda slightly less so.

He opened his eyes wide, startled by the sudden thought that he was leaving his family here, while George Haggerty was still on the loose. At least Mathieson was not taking those photographs at face value and was finding difficulty in tracking the private detective agency who had any records of that assignment. Anderson wondered if it was all an elaborate set-up for George's alibi. He was the only person who really benefitted. Valerie Abernethy was ignoring Mathieson's calls to a meeting, which was a stupid thing to do. Archie thought she was lying drunk in a hotel room somewhere, he was torn between trying to help her, and risking being kicked in the teeth again.

George, of course, had used his charm. Over the phone he admitted he had gone out for a walk the evening before he went up to see his dad in Port MacDuff. He had indeed popped in to see Valerie at the hospital and it was true that she had left the hospital at that time with him. The hospital was less than a mile from the house, so what was so odd about that? The other pictures did not show what they looked like. Just innocent hellos and goodbyes.

Valerie had disappeared now.

George said he had no idea about that.

Anderson thought that George Haggerty was a liar. The wee shitty liar that Archie Walker had been talking about.

His phone rang. He answered it immediately. At first he didn't recognize the voice.

'I need to show you something.' Whoever she was sounded upset.

'Sorry?' He was slow to catch on.

'It's Isla McCaffrey. I need to show you something.'

'Oh Isla, I'm so sorry about Donnie.' He tried to think. 'I was about to go up north tomorrow so I could pop—'

'Were you? Why?'

'On business. I heard about your husband.' To his own ears it sounded beyond futile. He hadn't known the young man. He had hardly given him a thought since he knew that Costello might have broken cover.

'Can you call in here, please?' she interrupted.

'Do you still have your parents there, are you alone?'

'They think I've lost the plot but there's something here I need to show you. Now.'

'There's a name here.' It was three o'clock in the morning and he was studying a single piece of paper under a light, holding it at an angle so he could read the shadows and indentations. He was also trying to ignore the footsteps of Isla's parents in the hall. Three times they had knocked on the door, asking if everything was OK. 'Earl somebody?'

'Earl Slick, he was one of Donnie's heroes. That has nothing to do with it, it's that bit at the top we need to look at. I think he was on the phone to Costello and making those notes at the same time. It must have been important, the way it's scribbled down.'

Anderson sat down on the office chair, the exhausted young woman with red, puffy eyes sat in front of him. She explained where she got the paper from, her grief momentarily lost in her enthusiasm.

'He was on the tail of these guys or something.'

'On the trail of Earl Slick? Who is this Earl Slick? He has underlined that more than once.' He could see himself taking notes on the phone, receiving a lot of information, writing it down then, as the connections were made, his pen would come back to the important point, identifying it so it did not get lost in the page of scribbles. So who was Earl Slick?'

'Well, he's most famous for being David Bowie's sideman but—'

Something jolted in Anderson's mind. 'A sideman? Define a sideman for me, Isla?'

Her tired face creased, thinking. 'Well, it's a guy, a musician who always plays with another guy, usually more famous. The sideman is never a celebrity, but they are always there. Slick has been Bowie's sideman for over twenty years and . . . Roger Pope with Elton and . . .'

'A partnership that last years, one in the open, the other staying well in the shadows?'

'Yes, but they are really good session musicians in their own right. They prefer to be in the background making money and making music, but never in the limelight. They just don't want the fame.' She stopped talking, looking at a signed picture of a spikey haired Earl Slick on the wall. 'That was Donnie's prized possession.'

Anderson let her talk, thinking that George Haggerty had stopped for Nicola Barnes when her car broke down. Somebody had come back to rape her. Had Haggerty called him and told him there was a tasty wee morsel waiting for him. And settled back to give himself a good alibi, while the other man took what pleasure he wanted. And that begged the question, what did George Haggerty get in return? The murder of his wife and child?

He blinked, confused. For some reason Oscar Duguid crossed his mind; the friend of George's who had drowned. No body ever found.

Anderson looked back at the paper in his hand, gratified to see what was in front of him; Donnie and Costello, two police officers had, in some way, got to the same conclusion. 'Interesting. We need every bit of information on this. Jennifer. Jennifer? Somebody has asked me about a Jennifer but not a *Jennifer Rhu.*'

Isla pointed to the computer screen. 'That is, or was, the *Jennifer Rhu.*'

'A yacht? Isla, Donnie would be so proud of you.'

How far had Donnie and Costello got? Definitely suspicious of the main man and the sideman. George and A N Other. Strangers On A Train for the modern age.

But did they have any proof? Or was Costello trying to make sense of all this. He scanned over the indented shadows on the document. NC 500 was an obvious one so his brain latched onto that; the North Coast 500. Where the victims on Morna's list were clustered? Clustered was the wrong word. The victims had been using the same roads, because they were the only roads there. Not the evidence it appeared to be, unless it was written there for another reason that only Costello and McCaffrey knew.

He asked Isla to find Kelvindale Bridge on Google maps.

'Interesting,' said Anderson, looking at the image.

'Is that not near where the woman and the boy were killed?'

'It depends what you mean by near? But yes, within twenty minutes' walk.'

The only people that might know how far these leads went, well, one of them was dead and the other one was missing.

He hoped.

And he needed Mathilda McQueen. He had to get Mathieson on board. He picked up his phone and called Bannon, asking him what CCTV they had requested from Balcarres Avenue and then told him it might be better to get the cameras around Kelvindale Bridge, out of interest. Bannon swore at him for waking him up. Then asked why.

'I'd just do it if I was you.'

'If you are holding back information, Anderson, Mathieson will hit and not miss.'

'I've been mauled by worse than her. Get the CCTV and let me know if you get anything. You can keep the Brownie points.'

By nine a.m. Anderson was packed and keen to start his journey north to meet the clumsy Morna and renew his acquaintance with the quiet man. The weather forecast warned of foul driving conditions but so far his plans for an early start were being thwarted at every turn. He had been summoned to McCaffrey's post-mortem. A copper at Govan had called in to say that he might have a lead on the missing female detective. Anderson dismissed it as he had all the others. Until he saw the contents of the link: an admission report of an unidentified female, taken into the QE 2 hospital early on Monday morning.

Over the next hour, he tried to get hold of a PC Turner, eventually tracking him down in the canteen at Govan. Turner had picked her up while on the night shift after being contacted by the Sally Army. He related the story of her injuries, her location, her lack of ID and lack of memory.

'Really? No memory.'

'Nope.'

'Age?'

'Like in the report, about 60, I'd say. Stinking with drink.'

Anderson's heart fell.

'She has no idea who she is but drinks black tea.'

Anderson spent the next forty minutes on the phone to the hospital, thirty-nine of them on hold, thinking. How injured she had been. Lucky to be alive.

Was it Costello?

The music stopped. 'A friend had come to collect her.'

'What friend? To where?'

The hospital had no idea. She had signed herself out on the basis there would be a private package of care requested by her new consultant, as yet no request had been received.

Anderson wondered if he was getting the runaround. 'Do you have a name?'

'Well, it was a woman.'

'A name?'

'No, try your luck with the ward but you'll get nowhere if you are not a relative.'

'Cheers.'

Costello had no relatives. So who had it been? Another twenty minutes on the phone to the ward and he got a nurse called Hannah. And Hannah had a name, Theresa Neele. He doubted that. Anderson asked Turner to look at a picture he was about attach to a text.

He heard the phone beep. 'No, not her.'

Anderson's heart fell again.

'It could be her mother?'

Anderson put down the phone. And dropped his face into his hands, he had no idea how stressed he had been. He let out a long slow breath. She was out there somewhere, under medical care. Now they knew where to look. She'd lost her memory.

Silly cow. He wiped a tear away.

Thank God. He needed to call Archie but the phone rang instead. He swiped it thinking it would be Turner, or Hannah, with some detail remembered.

It was Morna returning his earlier call. He said he was stuck in Glasgow but would set off as soon as he could, and he'd like to meet straightaway. She told him to come round to the house now that she had been liberated from Kieran's bedside. He was on the mend and would be available for interview soon.

'It looks like he's going to be OK in the long run. His parents are with him now but don't hurry to interview him as he has retrograde amnesia.'

Anderson smiled. 'That's OK.' He then asked exactly where Port MacDuff was. The answer didn't exactly fill him with wonder.

'Port MacDuff? Think Ullapool but with slightly less charm. And more rain.'

That was hard to imagine. He had once heard Ullapool described, with infinite sarcasm, as the entertainment capital of Western Europe.

She had asked if he knew where Fearnmore was. 'Where Loch Torridon meets the Sound. It looks out onto Rona.'

The relief at knowing Costello was around somewhere had lightened his mood, tempting him to say, 'Rona? Never met the woman,' but held his tongue. Morna sounded very earnest, she might not have a sense of humour. 'Port MacDuff, right on the coast. You know Applecross.'

'Well, I know the road by reputation.'

'Yeah, you'd better come the long way round.' she cautioned, 'unless you have a 4 x 4 and even then, we have snow up here already and there's more forecast.'

'Was that not where your young man was found, up on the Bealach . . .?' He made a mess of saying it.

'Bealach? Yes indeed.'

Anderson saw an opportunity, 'Who found him then? If it's inaccessible at this time of year.'

'DCI Patrick.'

'Why was he there?'

'You need to ask him,' was the confusing reply, and she offered to book him a room at the Exciseman for that night. He said that would be very nice and she gave him the address. Then the line went quiet. Then she asked, well stated, 'You've looked at my list, haven't you? Do you think there's something there? That's why you want to come up here.'

'Yes,' he thought, but my reasons are not yours. Then he asked her slowly, what she thought had happened to Sharon Sixsmith.

Her reply startled him. 'You should start with Jennifer Argyll, then Nicola Barnes then think what happened to Gillian Witherspoon. They had the same injuries to their shoulders, and the other one, now that she's dead. Patient confidentiality dies with them. They told me about the shoulder reconstruction she had.'

'What dead one? Gillian?'

'No, Sally Logan. Braithwaite. The one who dived off the top of the building, or was pushed, you know the one who—'

Out of the mouths of babes. Anderson felt his throat go dry, this girl had no idea she was talking about the grandmother of Anderson's grandchild. But she was doing what a good detective would do. He thanked her for the information, he'd explain the rest when he met her. Then he said, for curiosity, testing her, 'Just one more question. Who was Jennifer Rhu?'

'Not a who, a what. That was the boat that went on fire, killed Oscar Duguid.' She said it with the ease of familiarity. Of course she would know, it was a small place. 'He was a pal of George, but you'll know that.'

'Yes. I do, George Haggerty. Do you know him well?'

'Friend of my husband. Why?'

'Just that the name Jennifer Rhu came up, but you solved that mystery. I'll see you later.' He swiped his phone off.

Morna Taverner was on the ball, he'd have to watch himself with that one. She reminded him of Costello.

But now, he had a post-mortem to go to.

Anderson stayed outside of the post-mortem suite, he had been late anyway. On his way into the hospital, he had flashed his card about and eventually tracked down 'Hannah' who was terrified she had done something wrong. It took all of Anderson's charm to get the whole story from her. She had been trying to track down anybody who might know her patient, then she had traced a friend of Jack O'Hare. And she had been called Theresa, Theresa Neele.

The name was vaguely familiar.

Anderson had Googled Theresa Neele, and got Theresa Neale, the name of Agatha Christie's husband's mistress and the name Agatha had used when she had disappeared in 1926, claiming loss of memory.

Sweet.

Hannah gave a brief description, tall, long dark hair tied in a bun, well spoken. From the procurator's fiscal office, she'd had a card.

It was close enough for Anderson; Valerie Abernethy had taken Costello away.

Abernethy had spun a good story, giving Hannah the impression they were going to a private clinic, but had no idea where and Anderson knew that Costello was now behind a big iron curtain called patient confidentiality. She had effectively disappeared again.

And now so had Valerie Abernethy.

By the time he went into the mortuary itself, the post-mortem of Donnie McCaffrey was over.

'I am not repeating it all just for you,' said O'Hare. 'He died of a single stab wound, having suffered five but only one was fatal. Everything else was staged. The cocaine – none in his system. The alcohol – none in his system. He was a clean young man who clearly got involved in a situation. And Mathilda wants you to call her. George Haggerty was stopped for another traffic violation, speeding again.'

'You working for Traffic now?'

'No, but good news travels,' said the pathologist, ticking off boxes on a very long piece of paper. 'She called as she knew you would be here. There was blood found in the boot of his car, it was deer blood so don't get excited. But the sample picked up some orange tri-lobar fibres and that pinged with something the lab in Inverness has found. I hear you are going up there. And if you weren't, you bloody well are now. Fibres in Haggerty's boot match the fibres on the Bealach boy's clothes. Not often Mathilda gets to pass on good news so I thought I'd steal her thunder.'

'He had an offcut of carpet on the floor of his boot,' Anderson remembered. 'Orange.'

'And it will be universally available, I bet. He's giving us the runabout, Colin.'

'They are giving us the runabout.'

O'Hare's pen paused. 'Are you onto something?'

'As you would say, a tentative yes.'

'Did you call Valerie Abernethy about a woman in the QE?'

The pathologist shook his head. 'No, I called Archie's house and she answered the phone. Did she not pass the message on?'

'It's fine,' said Anderson thinking how marvellous it must be to work with the dead, whose capacity to think and be devious was extinct. Just how easy was that?

# TWELVE

Anderson made good time, four hours twenty-seven minutes to Port MacDuff. He'd taken the longer but quicker route, up the A9 then across country at Inverness. The air was getting steadily fresher and colder so by the time he was eating a late lunch in Ballinluig it was freezing. By the time he drove past the police station at Port MacDuff, it was freezing and blowing a gale. He thought he might have frostbite. Despite the weather, he decided to stretch his legs after the drive and walk to Morna's house.

He left the car in a public space and got out, making sure his case and laptop were locked in the boot. Pulling on a thick jacket and a woollen hat, he set off along the seafront, letting the sea spray, lifted by the wind, sting his face. Morna lived in Constance House, which was set one street back from the front on Castle Terrace. He stopped to watch the ferry go out, feeling the sea air in his lungs, getting the sense of freedom and of being at one with nature, in all its power. Port MacDuff had a winter population of about two thousand, double that in the summer. The sun took that moment to come out from behind thick cloud to warm his skin. The view over the Inner Sound, the water, the low hills in the distance, dark clouds chasing after the sun, was incredible. And it was so very, very quiet. He could see the attraction of living here, why people came here to escape. No questions asked. Every second person had an English accent, most of the rest were Europeans who had reasons of their own to escape to the arse end of nowhere. Beautiful though it was.

He watched a gang of bikers line up to get on the ferry, their engines roaring. The noise rolled across the bay, at odds with the beauty of the scenery. He turned round, chilled by the wind and keen to keep moving. He saw a thin grey-haired man leaning against the rail further along the harbour. Anderson was sure it was DCI Patrick. Accompanying him was a tall,

leanly built man, dark-haired with, from this distance, some
grey at the front, maybe even a Mallen streak. They had both
been watching him, Anderson was sure of that, but there was
no wave of welcome. Nor did they turn and walk away. They
just watched. So Anderson waved at them both, then set off
towards Castle Terrace, the map memorized from his phone.
There were only a few streets in Port MacDuff, it was a small
port surrounded by hills on three sides and the very deep water
of the Inner Sound on the other.

He kept walking, knowing that Patrick and his friend were
still watching. Anderson knew that Patrick might see his being
here as a right royal pain in the arse. Patrick could do nothing
but acquiesce to his presence; Police Scotland working together
and all that crap. But he enjoyed the walk up to the impressive
terrace of three-story houses, all painted in different bright
colours. His heart was lighter, Costello was alive. He could
cope with anything.

Number twelve was bright blue. The five houses in the block
had a clear view over the Sound, the buildings in front
had been demolished, leaving a flattened area, obviously now
used as a temporary car park, a weird assortment of vehicles
parked in a very haphazard fashion with no white lines to
guide them. He noticed two matching vans parked, a tall young
man standing at the open back door of one, clipboard in hand.
On the ground were a couple of large bags, easily five-feet
long. As Anderson passed, the man read the label on a small
rucksack and then placed it in the bigger bag, repeating the
process with the next bag, a small holdall; he was moving
awkwardly, as if he had a sore neck or a sore shoulder. As he
lifted the zippered flap on the long bag, Anderson caught a
flash of the orange lining. The man saw him looking and
straightened his posture, adjusted the collar of his boiler suit
and stared directly back. To his left was another man dressed
in a white coat doing something very noisy with white fish
boxes, stacking them to left and right then stacking them back
the other way. The rear door of his van was open, the refrig-
erator unit on the top was quiet. He too looked up at Anderson
as if they both possessed some sixth sense that had alerted
them to his scrutiny. More likely he was a stranger here and

they were curious about him. Strangers here should walk along the front, take photographs, buy coffee and get on the ferry, not walk the backstreets looking for number twelve.

Better people than them had tried to psyche out Colin Anderson, so he opened the front gate of the blue house, casually looking over his shoulder to read the side of the van; HikeLite, and a mobile phone number. Anderson tried to gauge the man's height; tall and slim, this was a young man. The fish guy was older, stockier, but was still looking over as Anderson turned to walk up Morna's pathway.

Noted.

Morna opened the door, her face brimming as if he was a long-lost friend. If he had been twenty years younger Anderson thought he would have fallen in love with her there and then. Her red hair streamed down her back, her smile as wide and fresh as a Bavarian milkmaid.

He followed her down the hall listening to her incessant chatter, then into a cold living room. The old blue sofa was covered with a brightly coloured patchwork blanket from the middle of which a crumpled face looked out at him. The blanket was wrapped round a young boy, too obsessed by his X-wing to even look up. From the two posters on the wall, Anderson judged the creased face on the blanket was Hans Solo.

'Somebody a *Star Wars* fan then?' he asked.

'My other half. I think it's genetic.' She nodded at the boy on the sofa. 'Neil's very good on *Star Wars*, *Alien* and *Bladerunner* but can't remember to pick his son up from school. Sorry,' she said, as if he was too important to be interested in her life outside of work. 'I'm DC Morna Taverner. As you might have guessed.'

'Glad to meet you, DC Morna Taverner. DCI Colin Anderson, call me Colin, I work a closed unit so we don't need to be formal.'

'Yes, sir,' she replied, then laughed.

He noticed the swing of her hair, a russet mane.

'And this is Finn, he's a very rude wee boy. I'll put the kettle on.'

Anderson said hello to the boy and got a flicker of a smile

in response. Anderson walked round the back of the settee, taking in the thin carpet, the cold chill in the air, the peeling paint.

Somebody was short of cash here, yet Morna would be on a good salary surely. There was a sense of this house being temporary, nothing in the way of homeliness, a few pictures of Finn on the wall, two years of primary school, proud in a uniform that didn't really fit him. And one wedding photograph, the bride easily recognizable as Morna, the groom just as easily recognized as the man outside with the two vans. HikeLite? Those vans were expensive, Anderson wondered who ran the company. It would be too obvious if he walked back to the window and looked out to see if both vans were still there. Morna was chattering away from the kitchen, asking about his drive up, the roadworks, the weather. All the things you need to know about if you live this far from a good supermarket.

'Is that you then?' he asked Finn, pointing at the school photograph.

'Aye,' said the boy, showing Anderson his X-wing.

'Lovely. The Millennium Falcon is my favourite. Do you have one of them?'

The boy shook his head. 'Death Star, and Imperial Stormtrooper.'

Anderson moved slightly round the back of the sofa, stepping over a dog basket, smiling awkwardly at the boy but the curtains precluded him from seeing the vans in the makeshift car park. All he could see was a fat woman walking past with two Scotties on the same lead. Even she seemed to take a good look at the house as she strolled, oblivious to the weather. He looked beyond her, something trickling into his head, in the car park, in his line of sight, a vehicle pulling away, a small white Fiat car driven by a blonde with a hat on.

He turned back into the room, trying to keep the grin from his face, looking round his eyes saw the picture. It hung on the wall over the fireplace and was a huge photographic print of a beautiful house standing high on a cliff, old and grand. A glassed terrace ran along the front so that anybody sitting there in a comfy Chesterfield enjoying a good malt, could see the waves at low tide and on a clear day, Raasay, Rona and Skye beyond. They were easily recognizable, even to Anderson.

The gold engraving on the bottom of the frame said Le Adare Lodge.

'Is that your house?' Anderson asked the boy, getting a cheery, ridiculous laugh in return.

'Nooooo.'

'Are you sure?'

A huge nod.

'Would you like it to be your house?'

Another big nod.

'Is it your mum's house?' asked Anderson.

Finn shook his head. 'No, my dad's. Chewbacca lives there.'

'Don't you start him going on about that again,' mocked Morna, appearing at the kitchen door with two steaming mugs of coffee and a box of Viennese Whirls in the crook of her elbow. 'Everybody does.'

'Sorry, I didn't mean to stare. It's very impressive. Is it French? The name?'

'The name? It's a corruption of the Gaelic for Dolphin Point. It's the highest point on the coast, over there.' She indicated to the front door, so he presumed, she was talking about the clifftops to the west. She placed the cups on the narrow table on the back wall, a bit rickety.

It dipped when Anderson sat down and leaned on it, spilling a little coffee from both mugs. 'Sorry.'

'No worries, there's normally a bit of paper in there to keep it level.'

They sat facing each other. The table was so small, he could have easily reached out and touched her fingertips, her blue, cracked fingertips he noticed. And he did want to reach out and warm her tiny hand in his. He was glad she had placed a large box between them.

She put the Viennese Whirls right in front of him, still in their box. 'Have you looked at Jennifer Argyll's file yet?'

He was thrown a little at her directness. 'No, not yet.'

'That was where she disappeared.' She pointed up at the picture. 'Last seen walking up to the lodge.'

'Oh right.' It was not that the lodge itself was unimpressive, it was the size of the picture in such a small house. Anderson couldn't think he knew anybody under the age of thirty who would have a picture in their house bigger than their TV screen. 'You son seems to think you own it.'

'He thinks Chewbacca lives up there and he believes Santa lives at Fearnmore Cragg farm and that he snogs Betty Alexander from the post office.'

'The innocence of youth. Are you planning to buy the house when you win the lottery?'

'Aye, that'll be right. I would have to buy a ticket though to give myself a chance, Neil does think of the lodge as his ancestral home. Only because his mum used to clean the floors there and he hung around it a lot as a child. If you are here for a while, you should take a drive up to Dolphin Point, the views are amazing.'

He looked out the window, the view of the car park opposite had been obliterated by a squall of rain. 'And do you see dolphins?'

'That's what we tell the tourists.'

'And what is it now?'

'What's what?'

'The house, is it a hotel or something?'

'Nope,' Morna said, 'it's a heap of bricks. Thank god.' She leaned closer to him, he could see the individual freckles on her nose. 'Bad karma, as if the spirit of Jennifer was making sure it was never going to be a success. Her ghost walks the cliffs, you know. I thought that was why you were looking at it, because of Jennifer.' She sounded disappointed. 'I thought you had read the file.'

'I will, believe me.' He sipped his coffee, breaking that chain of conversation. 'So who looks after the wee guy while you are doing all this? His dad?'

'No, Finn gets the runabout. Neil runs HikeLite, and he is so busy at the moment as he's self-employed and you don't want to turn away any business, do you? He's outside I think, loading up the vans.'

'Neil Taverner?'

'Yes, do you know him?' She smiled, proud of her husband.

'I think he came forward about an abandoned old Dormobile a few days ago.'

Morna didn't flinch. 'Sounds like him, he loves all that old crap. If the owner hadn't claimed it, he'd have tried to buy it.' She shook her head, indulging the vagaries of the man she loved.

'Works all hours, does he? Nights? The 500 is busy.'

'You guessed it.' She was oblivious of the seismic leap Anderson's heart had just made, and the struggle he had not to interrogate her right there and then. 'And for people doing the West Highland Way. Well, that was how it started. He's now getting a lot of business out the 500 as well, it used to be summer-only trade but now the season is all year and he has two assistants, three vans and a larger minivan.'

'What does it entail?' He kept his voice casual, merely making easy chit-chat after a long drive.

Morna looked at Anderson and waved her hands, expansively pulling ideas from thin air. 'Say you want to cycle the 500 on the sixth of December. Well, you would email Neil your route, the hotels you have booked, where your overnight camp is going to be or an agreed pick-up point if you are wild camping,' she warmed to her subject, 'and he will take the heavy bag. That means you only have to carry it from the post office to the camping site. If you leave your bag packed in the morning, Neil picks it up, and when you get to where you are going, your bag will be there for you. It's fifty quid for the West Highland Way, hundred quid for the 500, due to the distance involved. But it's easier now as we can make the vans rendez-vous and swap bags and the vans then go off north, south or west. So, Neil is away less. We also do more remote places off the way, there's a small extra charge to do that but it's worth it, it's getting so busy. Folk are having to take B and Bs and hotels further from the route, in the summer at least. It's so popular, there are mad winter walkers out now. In that!' She nodded at the window.

'I prefer the comfort of the internal combustion engine.' Anderson smiled at her. 'Does he employ anybody?'

'He's very busy.' She evaded the question.

'Just that he has three vans, can't drive them all at the same time so I presume business is booming as the 500 becomes more famous. There must be lots of work, I'm not from the revenue, I don't care if he's moonlighting.'

All Morna said was, 'He works lots of hours,' then she looked at Finn. She spoke like a woman whose husband was having an affair; never there, never with their son. A fractured family.

So,' said Anderson, 'maybe you can you tell me about Jennifer?'

'Jennifer Argyll?'

'And,' said Anderson, 'the *Jennifer Rhu*. Tell me what happened there.'

A look of slight shock passed over her face. 'OK,' she said. 'Oh, but you'd be better talking to Lachlan. He was a cop at the time, he was in charge of it. It was big news. At the time.' She looked disappointed.

'OK, I'll speak to him. Is this file for me?'

She brightened immediately and opened the lid of the box. Anderson took out his notebook glancing at his watch. This could take some time.


Lachlan McRae was indeed the man Patrick had been with, he was exactly what Anderson had always imagined the inhabitants of Wester Ross should be. He was tall and solid without carrying an extra ounce of fat although he must have been in his late sixties, maybe even edging into his seventies. He seemed to absorb the weather and walked at a speed that had Anderson struggling for breath trying to keep up with him at, or maybe that was the wind snatching the breath from him. Anderson was relieved when they stopped at a set of traffic lights that had no traffic to control and Lachlan gave him very scant details of the disappearance of Jennifer Argyll thirty years before, in November 1987. The older man didn't want to say very much about it and Anderson didn't ask any more. It was a debrief. Anderson felt he had the measure of these two, Lachlan was ex-military and Anderson knew he was being told enough of the story to tantalize him. The girl had gone out on a date with an untraced man and had never come home.

'So where was her "last seen"?'

It was then that Lachlan turned and looked at him. 'Up on Dolphin Point, up at the Lodge,' he said, with a shrug that seemed to say, *so what would you expect?*

They walked across the deserted street, a gust of wind blew a sudden squall of rain over the tarmac in front of them, the raindrops bounced up to soak their trousers. Anderson put his hand up to keep the water from his eyes. Once it had passed he turned to Lachlan, who was laughing 'don't worry you get used to it'. But Anderson's eyes fell into the further distance where he caught sight of a woman with her hand also on top of her hood, fighting the force of the weather – but not before he caught a glimpse of short blonde hair. As soon as the woman saw him she turned and walked away, vanishing round the nearest corner.

Anderson stopped walking, causing Lachlan to turn and make sure he was alright. 'Sorry, I thought I saw someone that I used to know.'

'Who?'

'Just a cop I used to work with?'

Lachlan patted him on the back, pushing him on slightly, not letting Anderson entertain any thought of following her. 'Don't worry about it, this place isn't only home to the ghosts of the past, ghosts of the future hang about here as well. She's been around for a few hours. Do you know her?'

'I think I do?'

'Do you have a name?'

'Does she need one?' asked Anderson, feeling a sense of relief, but it was his relief nobody else's. 'Do you know where she's staying?'

'Not without a name.'

'It's OK, I'll track her down.'

The he realized Lachlan had stopped walking.

'The Exciseman's that way.' He indicated down the street and left Anderson to his own thoughts.

'OK,' he said to himself, ignoring the image of Edward Woodward being burned to death.

Checking into the pub was a matter of showing ID and getting a key. His host was curt to the point of being surly. Anderson could cope with that.

He climbed the narrow stairs, his rucksack over his back, laptop in his arms, the wooden tagged key hanging from his finger. Once in the clean, but tiny room, he checked his phone. No signal. Sure that he had seen Costello, he didn't know if he was relieved that she was up and about, or disappointed that she'd felt she couldn't let him in on what she was up to. Or maybe, as Brenda had said to him, it was simply none of his business. He could ask around the hotels but she'd have booked under an assumed name. Any official search would be flagged up immediately and he'd find his remit up here changed to tracking down and bringing in his friend 'to help with enquiries'.

He needed to be careful.

He also tried to ignore the black rolling clouds coming in from the Inner Sound. He was hoping to go out and phone Archie, to tell him that Costello was up and about and that he would try to meet her, and then phone the office for access to the cold case file of Jennifer Argyll. He'd like to see that for himself, not be influenced by the agenda of who was telling him what.

So, he put his phone on charge. The information file tucked under the lamp on his bedside table said the best signal was down at the ferry terminal. He looked out the small window, along the water. The clouds, like his mood, seemed to be getting darker.

On the seafront, his jacket collar rolled up to keep the draft from his neck, his gloved fingers struggled to get Archie's contact on the mobile. The call was answered immediately, Anderson told him that he thought he had seen Costello twice, up in Port MacDuff, sniffing around George Haggerty, or more likely, somebody called Neil Taverner.

All Archie said was 'oh'. Anderson knew there was something else Archie had to tell him, something more important.

'What's happening at your end?'

'I backtracked the CCTV on the night of the murders.' Archie's voice had that clipped quality, he was not happy.

'Should Mathieson's team not have done that?'

'She was checking it for around the time of death, and is

now doing six a.m. through to twelve, and on a wider range of cameras. They have somebody carrying an object that looks like the Millennium Falcon in a bin bag, going across the footbridge. Mathieson missed the exit route, the time, the lot.'

'She's used to investigating cops, this murderer is much cleverer than the average cop.'

'What's that noise?'

'It's a wind tunnel called Port MacDuff. It'd be lovely when, and if, the sun ever shines.'

'Colin? Between you and I, I backtracked the footage from the time George met Valerie at the garage.'

'Did Mathieson not?'

'No, I was more interested in what Valerie was doing.'

'What does she do?' He was trying not to snap at the fiscal but he was beginning to understand the true meaning of the words wind chill factor.

'Nothing. But I go back. You know the off-licence? George was carrying a bag. Easily seen on the footage but not on the images that appeared in the paper. It's a bottle.'

'Alcohol.'

'George had been in earlier that day. He'd bought vodka.'

'OK.' Anderson was trying to piece this together. 'I presume George doesn't drink vodka. Or Abigail?'

'Neither. I think he bought it for Valerie, gave her it, took her somewhere, and left her . . . Last thing on film is them walking into a crowd down near your place.'

'Leaving her with no alibi? You can sanction a request for more footage, but I don't think you need to bother. We have them, Archie, it's a matter of time.'

'He set her up, Colin. He set her up.'

'There's a lot of it about. Don't worry about her, Archie. We are nearly there.'


Anderson sat in the corner of the pub with a coffee and the biggest fruit scone he had ever seen. It was warm, a small tub of fresh butter sat on the side with a small ramekin of strawberry jam, he could see lumps of fruit. He basically enjoyed his work but sometimes it was truly a pleasure. If only the locals would stop looking at him as if they were sizing him up for a wicker cage.

They had all looked round when he had walked in, the seven or eight men, regulars he presumed, from the way they looked fixed onto their seats, the shape of their bodies moulded into the leather.

He gave his order at the bar, the sign clearly said coffee and scones served. If they wanted to think of him as a namby southerner so be it. He hoped they didn't have him pegged as a Christian for his lack of alcohol. He'd know if Britt Eckland put in an appearance. He placed the box file on the table and got out his notebook. They would know why he was here, it would be useful for him to be seen working. As he made himself comfortable, two men got up within a couple of minutes of each other. The taller, younger left by the door that pointed towards the gents and returned a couple of minutes later. The other man, bald, older with a couple of days' stubble on his face went out that same door leaving a trail of Eau De dead fish in his wake, but he failed to return.

Anderson turned back to the file.

Jennifer Argyll had been a truly beautiful seventeen-year-old. She had grown up in Inverness and moved to the port with her parents when she was fifteen. She had worked as a junior clerk in the port authority and on 20th November 1987, she walked up to Dolphin Point and was never seen again. It was that simple.

Nothing else, but he could see how that smile, that face, might have haunted a generation. She had the look of a young Claudia Cardinale. Jennifer had, for some reason, gone off the cliff, or so it was presumed. Her body had never been found despite sea searches, leaving her to walk the clifftops forever in her ghostly form, so the rumours went.

He had Googled the Le Adare Lodge and apart from the many reports of the fire that had flattened the place on 13th of January 1995, there was not much. He looked at a few photographer's shots of Dolphin Point itself, the pictures mostly populated with dolphins. Then he came across a website for Historic Scotland, where people had put their old cine films on line, and he found a treasure trove. He had only been looking for about ten minutes when he struck real gold. There was a film taken in mid-1950s, maybe a bit later, of Le Adare Lodge, a corruption of the old Gaelic of Leumadair, as Morna had said. The scene flickered to life to show the picture of the water, the sea, the waves, then it panned unsteadily round to reveal a man standing on the veranda of the lodge. A set scene Anderson had seen in many of the old postcards of the lodge. The man was dressed in full highland regalia, the kilt, the tartan Glengarry, the sporran, the lot and he was laughing at the camera, saying something a little self-consciously before two ladies appeared, both dressed in their best for the holidays in neat box jackets, high heels and skirts that floated round their knees. They both had hats on, handbags matching their suits dangled over their arms. The man in the kilt greeted them, and two young men also in kilts appeared carrying leather suitcases, one in each hand, and a couple of hat boxes under their arms.

The staff, no doubt.

He Googled the name. Interesting. All the names were interesting.

Were these the wives of the sort of men who would be out shooting anything in sight over the next few days? Anderson nibbled at his scone, it melted in his mouth and he watched the film, enjoying it rather than analyzing what he was seeing. It went on for seven or eight minutes, bits of film tagged together from here and there around the lodge, jaunty figures flickering in black and white, stag heads, the huge open log fire, guns hanging everywhere. He was looking at this when the convivial host turned back to the garden, the camera panned back to the grass that swept down to the cliff steps. He watched with interest as the camera turned indoors to catch a couple of kids running across the terrazzo dance floor. Anderson smiled, that was a piece of history right there. He was still munching his scone, taking a mouthful of coffee when the camera panned back out again, the kilted man stood on the veranda, summoning some other member of staff.

*Clap clap.*

*Clap clap.*

\*    \*    \*

Oscar Duguid. Certainly not a common name. A few threats and a quick visit to DCI Patrick had confirmed what Anderson suspected. The kilted man in the cine film was Donal Duguid, the father of Abigail's first husband.

Presumed dead.

His boat had been called the *Jennifer Rhu*.

Rhu was a village in Argyll.

And Jennifer Argyll was also presumed dead.

Anderson was being played, again.

So he did what his instinct told him to, he finished his coffee, nodded goodbye to his watchful companions, left the pub. He drove the Beamer the three miles to Dolphin Point.

In the very last of the light, Anderson stood in the breeze, fresh but no longer howling the way it had been earlier in the day. He could breathe easily. He had parked the Beamer at the south of the overgrown driveway, two huge boulders had been pushed into the middle of the dirt lane creating a natural barrier to prevent any vehicle from going further up the hill towards the cliff. He was a hundred feet or so above sea level already, and the lodge had been at the highpoint of the coast. The road from Port MacDuff had been a long slow steady climb, making the car engine whine and groan, out of its comfort zone.

Anderson had tried to do his homework. He had quickly realized that the Le Adare Lodge was not something that the locals liked speaking about. He had watched the films, seen the exhibition dances of Elenora Haggerty, some relative of George's, Colin presumed, nothing surprised him now. He had watched her dance with a tall handsome man, they did a feature dance, every movement caught on the flickering cine film. He read that she had trained to be a ballet dancer but injured her shoulder. Anderson had hoped it was all going to go a bit Bates Motel after that, Haggerty traumatized by his beautiful mother damaging her shoulder and losing her love of dance and her sanity. But no, she gave up her dreams and settled down to life as hostess and exhibition dancer of the Le Adare Lodge, Dolphin Point, Port MacDuff and had lived a long and content life.

Then Jennifer Argyll had gone missing and the wheel of fortune turned.

It was a long walk, the lane that lead up to where he thought
the house had stood was badly overgrown. The lane wound its
way up a hill, around a crop of boulders to a tall rock stack
right on the headline. Now he had his bearings. He zipped his
anorak, and pulled his hat down over his ears, scarf up round
his neck, gloves on. He trudged on, weaving his way upward
through the thorns and the bushes. Sometimes he found himself
walking along a good concrete road, the tarmac only slightly
cracked, at other times the tarmac was broken and fractured by
the plants growing through. But on the road went, narrowing
slightly. He could feel the change in the air, smelling the sea
breeze, the scent of salt on his face. It was fresher up here,
away from the perfume of the trees and the winter undergrowth,
the bare branches that pulled and tugged at him as he pushed
his way through.

And suddenly he was at the top of the hill, the great rock
stack to the north, the Inner Sound lay in front of him like
undulating grey silk. He stood, gathering his breath. The climb
had been more strenuous than he had thought, but as he walked
into the clearing at the summit, the clouds parted and the sun
came out, warming his face once more, letting him breathe and
appreciate the crystal clear diamonds of light on the water. The
dark grey churn had calmed to a sheet of silver, he could hear
the gentle beat and crash of waves on the shore beneath him.

Mother Nature had welcomed him to her world.

He stood and looked around him, pulling the gloves from
his hands, feeling his fingers so he could dig around in his
pockets for the map. He looked at it again, the small road was
there, winding up to the top of the cliff. He walked carefully
to the edge, fearing that the breeze which was absent one
minute, might gust again and one real blast would push or
pull him right over. Was that what had happened to Jennifer
Argyll? He looked out over the grey water, where the *Jennifer
Rhu* had gone to the depths.

Anderson moved slowly towards the edge and looked down
on to another bank of grass, then another below as if the cliff
had layered itself, tiered to make it easier to get down to the
beach. In the cine film, there had been a wooden stairway
attached to the cliff face. He could still see a few wooden

uprights clinging onto bare rock. The enclosed beach, a perfect semi-circle of a bay with the cliffs reaching out and high on either side, like arms to protect the pure white sand that looked as though it had been sieved onto the beach. A few cracked slabs of rock forked out into the water, waves cutting over them. Jagged fingers that would be treacherous to any boat wanting to land. Dangerous as they were, Anderson could see how they reduced the power of the waves breaking over them, making the beach itself a much safer place to swim.

He leaned over, seeing, on the face of a cliff with its levels of coarse tufted grass, more bits of the wooden stairway, playing join the dots, he could make out exactly where the steps had been. He looked at the photocopy of the photograph of the lodge, it must have been taken from where he stood. The house had faced right out to sea, from high up on the cliff, far enough back to keep it safe from erosion and the worst of what Mother Nature could fling at it.

He looked up and down, from the height of the rock stack to the beach below. No sign of the house was left, no sign it had ever been.

It was the ghost of a house.

What had he been expecting?

This was where Oscar had played as a child. He had spent his life here and he had been a friend of George's, whose mother had danced so elegantly across the terrazzo dance floor. This was the place that George ran back to, but strangely enough, despite the emotional history he shared, he had never brought his wife or child up here. They had never met his father.

Those boys had been formed by this place. They had married the same woman. Now both children of those unions were dead. As Costello had said, something that is too much of a coincidence tends not to be a coincidence. He walked back towards the road, now he could see some outlines of the brickwork, light grey coloured granite stone, a wall only a foot high that would be solid then vanish in the undergrowth as though it had never been. He walked forward, tracing the footprint of the house. He kept turning round to look at the view, to check it was still there and then find himself doing nothing but standing looking, and looking, the view was beguiling and enchanting.

He continued to trace the outline, his feet getting wet. Looking back he could see his path, the footsteps clear in the wet shiny grass, sidestepping to the left and then wandering to the right like the footsteps of a drunk. Then he climbed over a piece of wall, now trying to find his way through drier winter growth.

Anderson realized he was standing on something solid underfoot, more than the surrounding earth and moss. He scraped the sole of his shoe back and forth, removing the dirt to reveal a white tile, edged with black. He scraped and pulled the branches back with his gloved hand, getting his face scratched and cut as the tiles of the black and white terrazzo floor revealed itself. In his mind's eye, he saw Elenora Haggerty glide across the floor in stiff taffeta and sprung heels, he could almost smell her perfume in the air; hear the small dance band in the noise of the wind as it raced up the cliff face.

He pulled out his phone to photograph the few stones that were still standing, then turned to go back to the edge, a wall a hundred yards or so, mentally mapping out the footprint of the building as it had been the day the photograph over Morna's fireplace was taken. It was a well-known picture of the place, he had seen a few versions on the net, on calendars and postcards.

He paused to look at the grass, his own footprints now almost faded in the rain, the blades of grass he had crushed had sprung back to life – on his footprints only, not on the new footmarks that had closely tracked his. The footsteps walked in a straight line, coming right for him, and then they had pulled away to the side, into the trees that ran down the hillside back to the main road.

'Hello?'

No answer, just a buffering breeze warning him not to make a noise up here. This had been a still and silent place for many years. In his mind's eye, Elenora Haggerty lifted a finger to her ruby red lips as she glided past, keeping the secret.

She was a ghost, the footmarks were real.

Whoever it was didn't want to make themselves known, so Colin Anderson put his phone, the print of the house and the map back in his anorak pocket and made his way down the road, a little more quickly than he had come up.

Halfway down the path, Anderson caught sight of him. Somebody, moving ahead, shambling through the undergrowth. The figure started to speed up, running, pushing aside the dead bracken. Anderson shouted at him but the figure, camouflaged in black and dark green, began to melt into the landscape. Anderson gave chase, nearly catching him at the stream where the wet jacket of the man slipped out the grasp of his outstretched hand, but it was enough to put both of them out of kilter and down they went, down amongst the stones, the darkness and the icy bubbling water.

The water went over Anderson's head. He thought no, not again; he was getting too old for this. But he held onto the man he was chasing, taking in lungfuls of water, writhing and twisting as they both struggled for air. Anderson felt his head scrape against a sharp stone, a blow aimed at his midriff made him pull back. The impact this time was hard and brutal. He still held on, trying to push himself up with his legs so the other guy could pull him free of the water when he tried to stand up. But Anderson rolled and he went under again, feeling his head strike something hard again, and that terrible fear of water filling his nose and this throat. Anderson panicked, his clothes weighing him down, he opened his mouth to scream that this could not be happening to him again. Then he felt a hand grab his jacket and pull him clear, the other man got to his feet quicker, staggering, and barely managing to stay upright. He, an older and balding man, bent over, hands on knees, taking in gasps of breath. He reached out a hand to help Anderson up.

'I'm too old for this, pal.'

'Me too.' Anderson looked at the bald head, the weather-beaten face, the straggly beard and subtracted eighteen years. 'Welcome back from the dead, Mr Duguid.'

They sat on the grass in silence looking out over the Sound, both soaking wet. The smell of dead fish rose steaming from his companion. Anderson was about to change this man's world, he could let him say goodbye.

Anderson regained his breathing, he stood up, looking round at the rock stack, feeling colder than he'd ever felt. He looked up and saw that same woman he had seen before. She took her time looking, keeping her distance, a tranquil figure, unmoving. She turned, walking away quickly, heading towards the road, her hand up over her head, holding her hood up. But again he saw another flicker of familiar blonde hair. And, he thought, just for a moment, that she had a gun in her hand.

'Costello?' he shouted, his fatigue forgotten, he was running in an instant. But she was gone. He repeated her name, 'Costello?' quietly, more to himself than for any other ears. 'Did you see her?' asked Anderson. 'That woman?'

'What woman?'

The file from the Scub camera was now available to view after a huge delay about who was footing the bill for the restoration of a video file that might show nothing. Eventually it had been returned to the Complaints team with an invoice.

Mathieson sat down and clicked a few buttons on the computer. She reached round to retrieve her cup of coffee, took a sip, her eyes off the screen for a full ninety seconds. She glanced at it as she rearranged a file from the left side to the right as it was impinging on her view. She flicked it open to check the date on her timeline of Costello's 'last seen'. She hoped this film would tell them something one way or the other as she wanted some closure on Costello's case, they all needed it. Mathieson, despite her reputation, had a lot of empathy for Costello, but the DI needed to be brought back into the fold, no matter what she had done.

Costello did not have the record of a dodgy cop. In some ways, she had a worse issue; she was moralistic and that was an easier recruit to vigilantism. Mathieson could paint that scenario easily, she could understand it perfectly.

She clicked play and let the screen change, still not paying it much attention, somebody shouted from the opposite side of the room about a sandwich order that was going down to Subway. She asked for a twelve-inch wholemeal with avocado, chicken and all the salad, but no peppers, before adding a packet of Doritos. She could be here all night and she could never work with an empty stomach.

Mathieson turned back to the computer and began to watch,

noting the time the film started with a view of a blade of grass glinting and quivering with perfect spheres of rainwater. It was 21.27. A slight frown appeared on her forehead, both in concentration and concern. She had been expecting the long view clarity of CCTV. Due to the incidents on the loch in the recent weeks, all the CCTV cameras at the car park at Inveruglass had been turned along the shoreline or out onto the islands themselves. This was digital video taken by a camera that had been set to film anything it caught in its sightline.

She was worried about what was coming next, watching with a weird mixture of elation and horror in her stomach. She might be a bitch but she knew to admit when she had been wrong.

The camera had been set to look out over the water, moving slightly when buffeted by the wind or when Kieran adjusted its position. Occasionally a white cloth covered the lens, wiping it clear of rain. For a while the screen was filled with an image of the loch, nothing more, nothing moving but the raindrops pattering on the surface. The camera was being switched on and off, the clock changed, moving on only by a minute or so. Kieran was obviously switching it on when he thought he saw some movement, then he would focus in on something in the water that proved to be imaginary. Then the camera would pull back, going in search of something more promising.

Mathieson was trying to think of Kieran lying on his stomach at the top of the hill, a few metres higher than the viewpoint. Instead of the clear view right down the loch, a famous view often seen on postcards, Kieran had picked this spot for the clear view to the island, looking east rather than south east. From where he was looking, the car park would be behind and below him, over his right shoulder.

Then the camera jerked, as if it had got a fright. Mathieson could imagine Kieran hearing something that made him turn. The camera moved along the ground slightly, blades of grass came close as the camera dropped. Kieran was now closer to the ground. Hiding? It was more of a pull back into cover than a fall. Mathieson frowned. The film of grass getting wet with raindrops continued, with no further movement. Was that it? Kieran had dropped the camera at the first sign of trouble and the film had caught nothing more?

But the camera kept filming, minutes passed. Mathieson was about to sip her coffee when she saw something. She could make out the top of a figure on the right side of the frame, a mound of dark, the head and shoulders swaying from side to side with the effort of climbing the steep hill up from the viewpoint. She wished she had visited that scene herself, then she might have a better idea of the lie of the land. The camera was near the water's edge but in an elevated position, the walker was coming up from the car park, she thought. The figure stood at the top of the hill, looking out over the water with no idea he was being filmed. So that meant the camera had already been abandoned or Kieran was very well hidden. Or this visitor had no notion to look around for a covert cameraman. From the darkness of the film she couldn't make out who it was, but he was well dressed for the weather and didn't really seem bothered about being seen. Then someone else appeared, quickly from the left screen.

The attack was swift and brutal, three low level stabs before the first figure had time to turn around. Mathieson let out an involuntary squeal, and pulled back, her colleagues turned to look at her. The first figure was now on his knees, the camera caught the flash of a blade. She put her coffee down.

Bannon came over, to stand behind her, looking over her shoulder, watching as the knife went in again and again. She pressed pause as the man in the anorak turned towards the camera, trying to get away.

Mathieson took one look at his face.

'Donnie, Donnie. What the hell did you get yourself into?'

Anderson sat on the side of the table, perching himself there, comfortable with the situation. Alastair Patrick was standing in the corner, his legs locked at the knee, arms folded, his jaw tight, unreadable. Anderson was wary where Patrick's allegiance lay. His demeanour was not that of a detective who had just bought into custody a murderer, or a rapist. It was more like the local drunk had been brought in for pissing into the harbour again.

Anderson was keeping his own allegiance neutral. Mathieson had updated him on the contents of the file using the word 'military' to describe the stealth of the fatal assault on Donnie McCaffrey on Loch Lomondside. His eyes swivelled to Patrick as he updated her on the orange carpet and that it might be worth a look at the HikeLite website, he said quietly when Patrick's own mobile had distracted his attention.

Sometimes the better dance was with the devil.

Anderson handed over a mug of soup made by Patrick's wife; Oscar Duguid looked like he needed it.

'So, welcome back from the dead, Oscar. How does it feel?'

'I'm not proud of what I did. But I did need to do it.' He sipped his soup savouring it, his lips making smacking noises. Anderson heard Patrick move behind him, readjusting his position. He could feel the tension from the other man's body. Somebody here had a secret.

Oscar Andrew Duguid, clean, beard trimmed, sat in the small interview room at Port MacDuff, he seemed to have shrunk from the ambling man that rolled out of Anderson's arms, then helped him out the icy waters of the stream.

Anderson was patient, waiting for Oscar to feel comfortable enough to start talking. Starting at the beginning and working his way to the end. Anderson was interested in where Oscar was going to start, suspecting that the story might start much further back than Oscar might be willing to reveal. Maybe as far back as Jennifer.

There was no talk, no eye contact so Anderson thought he had better jumpstart the conversation.

'Whose idea was it to fake your own death?'

Oscar screwed up his face, rubbing his thumbs deep into his eyes and shaking his head. But there was no answer.

'You do remember Mary Jane.'

'Of course I do.' The voice was strong, sounded intelligent and eloquent.

Anderson pushed a picture across the top of the table to him, the picture George had given to him. Oscar didn't look at it before turning it over and pushing it away.

Anderson tapped the back of the photograph. 'That was my daughter, that girl you adopted was my daughter. You going missing sparked off a chain of events that led to her death, so don't give me any shit about what a hard life you have had.'

'Sorry for your loss,' said Oscar. 'It's my loss too.'

'Of course, but you did know that she had died.'

He nodded.

'And how do you know that, if you are living in the middle of nowhere, out of touch with society?' Anderson leaned back in his seat. 'Who told you? You are no Bear Grylls, so somebody is helping you. Who?'

Oscar Duguid closed his eyes in a very deliberate slow blink. 'This is a place where people come to run away, they are very good at hiding you here. Walking around, how many different accents have you already heard? All those home counties professionals that couldn't take it anymore and had to get away.'

'Very few went to the lengths of faking their own deaths.'

'I just wanted to disappear.'

'So how did it go, you bought a small dinghy.'

'No, I didn't.'

'OK, somebody did. Somebody bought one for you, from somewhere. Might be a bit obvious if they found the *Jennifer Rhu* burning, the small boat still attached but a second boat you had just purchased was gone. Nobody had to know about the second small boat that actually got you off the *Jennifer Rhu* and back to shore. So who bought you that? Who was your partner in crime?' Anderson folded his arms. 'And to be clear, it was a crime.'

It was a guess but he knew he had struck gold. There was a mastermind in this and it wasn't Oscar Duguid. His gut feeling was that Oscar was a man in search of nothing more but a quiet life.

'It's all nothing to do with me. I'm happy sitting in the corner of the pub, or in the back room, eating the leftovers, having a shower, moving around but mostly living up there near the lodge. It's fine in the summer, not best in the winter. The winters are tough,' he said, touching the reddened skin of his cheek, as if it was still tender. 'I have a hut. It's fine.'

A look passed from Oscar to Patrick. All he got back was

a brief nod. It was not returned. Anderson made a note to search the hut.

'Who bought the second boat? We need a name?'

It came as no surprise when Oscar Dugiud's lips opened to form the name. 'It was George Haggerty.'

The story that Oscar Duguid told was frightening in its simplicity. He had a boat and he was a good sailor. George Haggerty had bought a small boat with an onboard motor months before in Glasgow. Nothing that could be traced back to either of them. Oscar sailed out, set his boat on fire before returning to shore on George's boat. Then he tied it back up again behind the yacht George had owned at that time. He left his own dinghy tied to the burning remains of the *Jennifer Rhu*.

'The *Jennifer Rhu*?' asked Anderson, 'Named after?'

'Jennifer Argyll,' he said through a painful smile. 'She was a crush of mine. She needed to be remembered.'

'More than Abigail?'

'Yes. Oh yes. If I had stayed married I would have died. My life was managed from the minute I got up to when my head hit the pillow. The life of being a husband and father wasn't for me. I had to bail out. Nobody's fault, I'm just no good with four walls, pension schemes and thirty-five hour weeks. At the time, nobody said anything apart from how sorry they were. We got away with it.'

Oscar was used to sailing off on his own, it raised no suspicions. They found the boat still burning and the presence of the dinghy alongside suggested he had tried to free it but had fallen overboard. Search and rescue found nothing. There was nothing to find.

'Who insured your life for two million pounds?' asked Anderson, and saw Patrick's eyes narrow and flicker. He hadn't been expecting that.

'I did.'

'Who advised you to do that?'

'A friend.'

'A particular friend?'

Patrick was paying a lot of attention now.

'George Haggerty.'

'Of course it was. And what did you think when Abigail

was insured for two million and she was then murdered, with all that money going to . . . oh yes, her husband. George Haggerty.'

'I didn't get a penny.' Oscar looked a little confused.

And looking at him, Anderson believed him. 'Of course you didn't, you were dead. Abigail got it, and now George has it.'

He had escaped the madness of his married nine-to-five life to escape to a different madness of this life up here. This was where he wanted to be, where he was born. And then he started mumbling about wanting to be here with Jennifer.

He heard Patrick sigh, Anderson felt that he was kicking a puppy. This man needed help.

'Do you want to rebuild the lodge, Oscar?' he asked gently.

And then Oscar began to cry.

Patrick tapped Anderson on the shoulder, time to call it a day.

'Was it all back to bricks and mortar?' he muttered as Oscar was taken away.

'Life's loss but I bet the money will be useful, though not to him,' said Patrick in response. 'Not bricks and mortar. Cocaine.'

'What?'

Patrick's voice was low. 'Look, the North Coast 500 is a gift to a dealing network. The place floods with tourists. Then consider that anybody who builds on land on that route is on the gravy train for life. Somebody couldn't see a way of bridging that gap between what they had and what they needed. So they killed until they got what they wanted. The oldest motive in the book. Money. Pure greed.'

'They killed Abigail and Malcolm for that?' Anderson sat back down.

'Looks like it.'

'Do you know who they are? Anything to do with a company that might be driving luggage around the North Coast 500, specifically?'

Patrick gave a short sad smile, 'Yes, but it will break some-body's heart.'

\*    \*    \*

One of the men looked right into the camera. The camera jumped, and rolled to the side, the world tumbled making Bannon and Mathieson both twist their heads as they tried to make out what they were seeing. A dark figure moving toward it very quickly, and then veered off to the right.

'I think that's where the boy makes a run for it. He gets chased and we know what happens next.'

The camera was still moving, sliding to the left towards the drop to the water where it was found. There was a jerky image of the female figure walking backwards, then dropping to the ground, and clumsily getting to her feet again. Then the screen filled with movement of limbs and shadows, that image was lost as the camera became airborne and started to film grass and sky. Then the screen filled with dark, murky water.

'Bloody hell, what was that about? What were they doing there?'

'Diane, you need to get that middle section slowed and analyzed.' Bannon realized that the DCI was shaking. It wasn't easy to watch the death of a colleague, unable to do anything about it. Except catch the man who had used that knife.

'Why don't you go and put the kettle on? I'll get a note of the timings, there's one bit where the second attacker looks right at the camera. The tech boys will be able to catch that and work it up. We've got one of them, Diane. He's on a shoogily peg, it's a matter of time.'

'They might be able to do something, but the lower part of his face is covered. Don't get your hopes up. They killed McCaffrey. That student was very lucky to survive and I don't think Costello, if that was Costello, would have been able to get out of there alive.'

They were settled down for a second viewing of the film, fortified with black coffee and the knowledge of what they were about to see, they hoped they could watch it this time with more analysis and less emotion.

'That look like McCaffrey to you?' asked Mathieson.

They watched as the guy on the ground tried to get back up before they saw the blade again. The guy on the ground then stopped moving.

'Was he dealing? That looks like an organized take down,' offered Bannon.

'There's no evidence of that anywhere in his life, he was a normal young man with a wife and kids. How the hell did he get into this? Shit! Who is that?'

Another figure appeared.

'That's a female. What the hell is she doing?'

'Walking backwards? There's somebody behind her, she's talking to them, hands up trying to appease them. The camera has moved to follow, showing that Kieran was still filming. He got the murder on film.' Only seven minutes had passed. They both leaned forwards, watching carefully as the smaller figure turned to the camera and seemed to fly through the air with such force that her body juddered as she impacted the ground. The bigger figure, walking up behind her, was still bringing his arm down, following through from the strike to the back of her head.

The enhanced film moved frame by frame showing two dark figures started moving, pulling at clothes. They took their time, confident that they would not be seen, unaware of the low light camera watching from the undergrowth. They had on gloves, their faces covered, clearly very forensically aware. They were wearing something like black boiler suits.

'What is going on here?'

'Mixing the blood, the DNA? I don't know. So we have Donnie, two assailants and one other unidentified . . . victim? He's pouring the contents of a bottle. Do you think that's cheap whisky? And what's he doing?' One of them had pulled back Donnie's face and was tapping something in it. The taller one kicked the prostate small figure with his foot, the hat slid slightly to reveal some short blonde hair. Mathieson groaned.

'Well we know what happened,' said Bannon over her shoulder. 'We need to know who those two are? Any ideas?'

'Too clean to be regular drug take downs. That looks military to me.'

'Let's go through the file again. And you'd better phone Anderson and tell him, I'm sure he'd like to know.'

# THIRTEEN

*Friday, 1st of December*

Morna got up, thinking how cold and damp the house was. She walked into the shower, letting hot water run over her, wondering if they had enough bread left to make toast for breakfast. Neil had forgotten to get any shopping. She needed to feed Finn before she delivered him to her mother's so she could get to work.

When she got dressed, she walked into her son's room to start the difficult task of waking up her six-year-old. The room was very cold, the air damp, the curtains at the window billowing, lifting the hem from the carpet. She turned round, looking at the bed, the shape of the duvet, ruffled up on the bed like a small log. Before she reached out to it, she knew her hand would go right down until it reached the mattress. The bed was empty.

Morna looked at the curtain, still shifting with the wind and rushed out the room to get her mobile. She phoned Neil, left a message and then called Patrick who answered immediately, and told her to keep calm. He mentioned an amber alert, told her to keep her mobile phone with her.

She said she had to get out and search, she wasn't staying here.

He said he would get a team organized when he thought it was pertinent to do so.

*What?*

'He might have climbed out the window, Morna. We have to be sensible here. Go round, ask Lachlan, check Finn's friends, phone round, be logical and don't panic. Everybody round here knows Finn. He'll have gone off on a Star Wars adventure. They will spot him, don't you worry.'

And with that the phone was cut off leaving her staring at the screen.

\*    \*    \*

Patrick looked around, standing on top of the hill, watching
the lie of the land, binoculars at his eyes. He was close into
the side of the wall, a small cliff face, scanning the horizon
down towards the water, watching. He checked his watch; it
was half past three. Finn had been missing for eight hours.
People were predictable and he was sure Morna was no
different. She had spent most of the day with Lachlan, being
driven around, leaving her mother at Constance House to watch
the phone in case there were any sightings. Patrick knew that
wasn't going to happen. The lack of sightings would drive her
to look round Dolphin Point eventually, within the next hour,
he reckoned. People really could be that predictable.

Ten minutes later he saw Morna walk along, hearing her
shouting for Finn, on her own. No Neil with her, that suited
Patrick fine. That useless piece of crap would be out doing
his own dirty business. He had been worried that Anderson
might get involved but Patrick had made sure the city boy was
where he belonged, wrapped up in the office, dissecting the
video from the loch.

He took no pleasure in watching Morna, listening to her
hoarse voice shouting, the heartbreak she had been going
through that day. In every way, she was on her own. Slowly,
he lifted the phone and called a number and gave a set of
coordinates. She was on form, she wasn't going to be going
anywhere fast, the guys would move in and take her, easy.

He waited, motionless. He was a man who could wait for
a long time. Occasionally pulling back into the shadows when
he thought Morna might be looking up his way. How pathetic
she was, how programmable. One word from Lachlan about
how the boy had believed Chewbacca lived up here, that the
boy believed Neil when he told him the tall stories of this
magical place and this might be the place a boy would run
to. Morna had really accepted their reasoning. She had checked
everywhere else, and now she had been brought to where her
son might be. So she thought.

It had been easy to take the boy.

Taking the mother would be easier.

He waited until he saw the man approach, forty degrees
behind the target, downwind, so she wouldn't catch the stink

of dead fish. It was going to be a simple take down. Patrick didn't stop and watch, he didn't need to. Seen too much of that in his time.

He slipped his binoculars into his pocket and walked away.

Morna was looking for her son, meandering over Dolphin Point, no plan to her search. Neil was going round the town, asking in pubs, like that would help. She was walking south out towards the lodge. It wasn't like the wee boy to wander away, but her mind didn't want to think past that possibility. She'd had eight hours of tears and screaming and doubt.

DCI Patrick had taken charge. He was organizing the search teams. The helicopter would get called out, the dogs, everything for wee Finn. Patrick adored her wee boy. She couldn't work out why she had heard nothing so far, the sky was quiet. Even Anderson had given her nothing but platitudes, leave it to Patrick, he knows what he's doing.

She checked her watch, it was mid-afternoon. Where was a search team? What was holding them up? She should have brought the dog, but she didn't want to interfere with the search dogs. But she couldn't sit at home doing nothing. Morna turned, thinking she heard somebody coming through the hedgerow behind her. She called out, shone her torch around for a bit of extra light, but it was just the bushes waving, only the wind. She shouted, calling out again and again, the breeze catching her words and taking them out to sea.

Then she stood very still for a moment, in windblown rain; she pulled her jumper round her, zipped up her jacket. There were sounds out here in the half-darkness; she shouted her husband's name louder, then quietly. Then she called for her son.

She tried to ease the beating in her heart. There *was* somebody up here with her.

She stood very still, very still indeed. Listening. Then the thought struck her that now Finn was gone, they might be after her. But why?

Her car was down at the road so she turned and started to walk, then ran, her arms pumping. The sound of her throat rasping for air, she heard her footfall, but nothing following them. But she felt she was running for her life. She believed in the instinct of danger, she needed to find Finn and she needed to be alive to do that.

She ran through the undergrowth. It was getting thicker, holding her back. She thought she was running down to the road but looking back she couldn't see the rock stack. She couldn't see it against the darkening sky. Had she come down the wrong way? Her wet red hair was straggling behind after her. She stumbled as she ran, her arms windmilling to stop her falling. There was somebody there now, she could hear their feet behind her, they were getting closer. She was being chased down. She risked a quick look over her shoulder, managing to run forwards while looking back.

She ran straight into his arms, a fist to her stomach. She was down, winded.

Morna lay in the undergrowth, sleeping in a nest, comfortable and still. They circled round her, people like vultures. She lay in the middle, a tiny form in a big spinning wheel. The man looked down at her and smiled.

Easy.

'What do you mean, you let him go?'

'Nothing to hold him on,' said Patrick, tapping angrily at the enter button on his laptop.

'Well, fraud for a start, he defrauded his insurance company out of millions of pounds. If we don't get Haggerty for the murders or for facilitating those rapes, we could at least hold him for fraud.'

'DCI Anderson,' Patrick began, ready for a speech, 'in the whole scheme of things, of life and death and the universe and the glory of a sunrise, nobody cares. Joe Bloggs out on the street would clap at that fraud, bravo they would say. Sometimes better to go with that, eh? What good would it do? Ask yourself, what good would it do? Let Oscar be. Anything else would be cruel. And Morna's boy is missing. Did you know that? And now we can't find her either. I'm worried, DCI Anderson.'

'Sorry. Surely Finn's just wandered off and got lost? Morna is a trained police officer, any idea where she has gone?'

'Do you?'

'No. Has she just upped and left?'

Patrick had his chin on his hands, deep in thought. 'Her son was abducted, she has been abducted.'

'So why are you not out there looking for them. Get an incident room set up, call in the squad for a house to house.' He was appalled. 'If that's what you think why are we doing nothing?'

Patrick raised an eyebrow. 'Just as you are turning over every leaf to find Costello and Abernethy?' He gave a trite nod. 'We have the situation in hand, believe me.'

It sounded like a slight threat. This was Port MacDuff. Anderson needed to be careful, he wasn't going to be burned in a wicker pyre. He had missing people of his own to look for so he excused himself and went to phone Mathieson for an update. 'Fine,' he said, as he went out the office door, 'your turf, your rules.'

# FOURTEEN

*Saturday, 2nd of December*

Morna woke up, slowly. Looking at a ceiling she didn't recognize, a wooden slatted roof with the cross beams stuffed full of some yellow packing stuff that looked like fluffy clouds or dandelion heads. She was under a warm duvet, she was fully dressed, except her boots that she could see paired neatly on the floor beside the bed. Her head hurt but she wasn't injured. She eased her limbs one by one. And she could smell dead fish.

She had been found by somebody and brought here; she slid out from under the duvet thinking about finding Finn, and finding a toilet. She looked around, she had her anorak on when she'd been outside, and in the pocket was her mobile phone. She looked out the window, nothing there just trees and brown ferns, no sign of the cliffs, no sign of the rock stack. She pulled back the curtain that served as a door, it covered nothing more than a fire and a chair, an ancient chair piled up with dirty cushions. There was a radio on a shelf, some electric equipment, and a pile of blankets on the floor. She recognized it immediately as a dog bed. There was a Calor gas cooker in the corner, a plastic bag from the local co-op.

This was somebody's secret hideaway? Or did they live here? Her anorak was on the back of the chair and her mobile was on a shelf. She grabbed at it but it felt too light, somebody had taken the battery out.

She looked around; there was no sign of life, nothing.

Morna wasn't staying, so she slipped her boots on. She opened the door and pulled her hood up, the wind had got up but it had stopped raining. She made her way round the back of the hut and squatted to empty her bladder, hoping the relief would help her think clearly.

Looking at the sky, the cloud cover had lifted a little so she could see the flat peak of the rock stack, and from that, she knew roughly where she was, inland to the south of the stack, so the coast road would be right in front of her as she stood here. She needed to make her way down there. But she didn't, she turned round and went back in, switching on the radio, being careful not to untune it to the station it was already on. She knew it would be local, for the weather if nothing else. She listen for a few minutes, realizing the time, hearing the news, the local news. Nothing about Finn, nothing about her boy.

She felt sick. She was on her own, there was some conspiracy going on. DCI Patrick and his little smiles. He had done nothing. She was a cop and she had been abducted, just to get her out the way? Why? To get Finn out the village?

She looked round, searching for clues, opening bags, looking under the bed, the person that lived here led a very simple life. There was an old bookcase, shackled together, stuff that a charity shop would throw out; there were a few tattered books, a couple of candles. A battery-powered lamp, a good torch. And at the bottom, yellowed and musty was a curled page on a pile of old newspapers. She bent down and looked at them, thinking she might see a headline of other children that had gone missing, children she knew nothing about. Other victims. These papers were old.

She lifted the top one, Jennifer Argyll, November 1987. A beautiful photograph of Jennifer, on the front page, curled and fragile with time. It was a familiar picture for her, the official press photograph. And a clipping, the name of the newspaper cut off the top. An attack on a mystery woman, raped, a twenty-three-year old. The following newspaper carried the same story; a story that went nowhere. Then Sharon Sixsmith, the one found at the bottom of the gorge and then one she didn't recognize, Patricia Sandyman. The article was cut out. No date. Morna looked round until she saw a small army knife on top of the pile of books.

It would do. She slipped it in her pocket and ran.

There is some comfort in knowing that today is the last day of your life.

No better player than a woman with nothing to lose.

There had been a lovely item on the news that morning, a still from CCTV six weeks before, on the Kelvindale walk. A picture of a person, walking, probably a man, just a person the police hoped might be able to assist them with their enquiries as they might have seen something pertaining to the murders of Abigail and Malcolm Haggerty. To anybody else watching it looked like a bloke walking home with a package under his arm. Thirty-three inches long, twenty-two inches wide, carried on its side so it fitted under his arm.

She recognized it, she had built it.

Valerie had paused the TV screen, and looked closely. She knew that shape: the Millennium Falcon.

She had known that she had to move and move fast, Mathieson was close to the truth, but she was closer, so she rolled the white Fiat into the trees and down into the thick bracken. There was only dense undergrowth in sheltered places, and there was little shelter on the headland, up near the lodge. She'd do the last bit by foot. But she had her boots, her jacket and her gun.

She was going to end it now. She'd been following Haggerty for a couple of days now. He had been doing nothing but lazing around, drinking, meeting his friends and socializing, constantly on his mobile to somebody. The one place he had not been was the care home where his dad was. This morning was different though. Haggerty had been up, ready and was moving quickly. She could sense things were coming to a head. He would have seen that footage from the bridge and she was going to get him before he boarded a ferry and slipped away.

Her decision was made.

Valerie Abernethy felt the happiest she had felt for ages.

DCI Alastair Patrick was back at the rock stack, standing in the shadows, as motionless as the standing stones. His utter stillness made him invisible, the way an aboriginal standing can be mistaken for a tree. His background of grey rock matched the pallor of his face.

'Is this where Oscar lives? Up here at Dolphin Point?' asked Anderson, sotto voce.

'Be quiet and keep your eyes open. And don't move, if you move you will be seen.'

'But is this where—'

'Quiet.'

He had got a similar answer when he asked, 'What are we doing up here?'

They had been there for two hours, at Dolphin Point, on the far side where the outer limits of the house used to be. Anderson was in awe of Patrick's ability to remain motionless. He tried to amuse himself, keep himself warm, closed his eyes and tried to keep standing up, got cold and numb. He wanted a hot coffee and his bed, a cooked breakfast, anything but to be here. But he didn't really trust Alastair Patrick. Not one bit.

'Hear that?' whispered Patrick.

'What?'

'Vehicle coming.'

'You can hear that?'

'I can if you don't speak.' Patrick's head was down, looking at his feet, as if he was concentrating on his ears.

'We should be out looking for Morna and the boy. Abigail and her boy were killed, now Morna and her boy have gone missing.' It was the fourth time he had said it.

Patrick said, 'Huge difference between being missing and being dead.' Then he ignored him.

The noise of the engine stopped. To Anderson it only sounded like the wind dropping a little. Patrick held his hand up, telling him to wait. And pointed to the Sound, where the land flattened off. In the cine film this had been where the tennis courts were, flat all the way to the cliff with a gentle seaward fall. Anderson suddenly got a very bad feeling about this, he watched where Patrick had indicated to look, and saw a disturbance in the trees. He dropped down a little to stay out of sight as they walked into view. The two of them.

'Who is that?' he whispered.

'If there is a god it will be Haggerty and Taverner,' whispered Patrick, then turned to look straight at Anderson. 'Why? Who were you expecting?'

'The Argyll and Sutherland Pipe Band for all I know.'

Anderson grew silent, fascinated as he watched the two men; Haggerty, the smaller figure out in front, walking through a plain flat field of grass but following a definite path. Neil Taverner, taller, at the back was less certain, he kept turning round, checking the horizon. Alastair Patrick didn't move, he stayed very still against the rock face. Neil Taverner's eyes passed right over them. Anderson wondered how often Patrick had stood here, watching.

'Who is that?' asked Anderson as a smaller figure came walking over the hill, from behind the rock stack. They too, were heading towards the sea.

'I have no bloody idea,' replied Patrick, almost in admiration that something was going on that was unexpected.

'I think I do, I think that's my DI.'

'The untraceable Ms Costello? Well, she's come ready for the party. That's a firearm in her right hand.' Patrick raised his binoculars. 'Bloody hell.'

'She can't be allowed to do this, she can't risk everything to take Haggerty out. We have enough on him.'

'She doesn't know that though.'

Patrick remained immobile so Anderson made a decision and ran, slipping out from his hiding place and moving fast across the ground, losing height with every forward stride, gaining on the two men from behind. They both took off at the sound of footfall without looking round, but they had seen the woman with the firearm. They were caught in a pincer movement. Both ran towards the edge of the cliff, trying to outrun them before they ran out of land.

Anderson could hear Patrick behind him, shouting, and then the woman held the gun up as if to fire it. She took aim and seemed to pull the trigger. Anderson yelled at her, holding his arm out.

It all happened in perfect slow motion.

Absolutely nothing.

The woman tried to pull the trigger again.

Nothing.

Anderson was still shouting Costello's name. *He's not worth it.*

She didn't seem to hear, but he had no idea if she could

hear him. Then she was running, still holding the gun, making for the smaller of the men. She was going for Haggerty, getting closer before she tried firing again. Anderson saw Patrick cut off to his left, blocking any escape that Neil Taverner might think he had.

The two men backed up, Anderson noticed how much land they had covered, how little grass was left between them and the cliff top. Then he saw the hand rise again, gun perfectly level, this time in a double-handed stance, like a police officer. She stood firm, and pulled the trigger, nothing happened.

Haggerty stopped and turned towards her. Facing her, he brought the palms of his two hands together.

*Clap clap.*

Then he turned, resuming his flight.

Patrick was running up fast behind her, reaching for the gun. The woman screamed as it was wrestled from her hand, she twisted free and started running, running as if the devil himself was after her. The look on her face was one of intense concentration, beyond human, she was a killing machine.

And she ran. Heading for Haggerty.

Anderson stopped, watching in horror as she kept moving, grabbing Haggerty round the waist. He had been expecting a punch or a blow but not to be held, so low, her arms round his waist, her shoulder pushing him off balance. She was light, but quick, and she had the momentum of the roll of the land to carry them both stumbling towards the edge of the cliff. He saw Haggerty's heels dig into the soft ground, his hands trying to prise himself free from her, but she had her prey. She wasn't letting go now. Anderson thought he saw Haggerty manage to force up her head, forcing her to choose between releasing him or having her neck broken.

Anderson didn't know if they went over the edge together or apart. He saw, he thought, blue sky and grey sea between them, before they hung in mid-air for the briefest of moments. Then they plummeted from his view.

Anderson stood shocked, blinking, thinking about running forward to make sure, but his legs didn't move. He heard the waves, somebody screaming and somebody shouting. He turned. Patrick was pointing it at him, right at his forehead.

'Drop! Drop.'

Anderson opened his mouth but dropped to his knees, this had all been so, so wrong. He heard the gun fire once, a bang so loud even the wind stopped in shock. Anderson felt himself fall. Face down into the grass, it was wet on his skin. He heard another blast then another two. He felt the rain fall on the back of his neck, a dribble leaked from the corner of his mouth. He heard Patrick approach. He thought there might be another bullet in the chamber; the muzzle would be cold against the back of his head. Military precision, Mathieson had said that. Why had he not listened?

He thought about Moses, about Claire and . . . then he felt a hand on his collar, pulling him up.

'Silly bastard. That piece of shit was right behind you.'

Anderson raised himself up on his elbows and looked behind him. Neil Taverner, lying with bits of him missing, staring at the sky. Glinting in the grass was a knife, with a long thin blade. He was less than two feet away. Anderson had seen the damage that knife could do.

So very close.

Anderson put his head back on the grass, He wasn't going anywhere for a wee while yet.

Anderson had to crawl the first few yards before he was up on his feet, walking towards the edge. His shoes slipped on the damp grass as he neared the precipice. Slowing, he stepped carefully, the edge was unstable, broken, land slips, mini cliffs, bites taken out here and there. He got back on his knees, hearing a warning shout from somebody behind him. He crawled to the edge, looking, his dirty fingers clawing through the mud then over at the waves crashing on the rocks below. Down near the narrow band of soft white sand lay the body of George Haggerty spread-eagled on the waterline. His head in the water being buffeted, rolling back and forth with the advance and retreat of the smallest waves like a nodding puppet. If the fall, over a hundred feet, had not killed him, then the sea surely would.

Anderson steeled himself to look along the water's edge. Nothing. Then he moved closer, looking directly down, scanning the cliff, then he saw her, caught on a ledge. He shouted down but there was no reply, no response at all. He looked past her to the mass of blonde hair caught on a grassy ledge further down.

Not Costello.

Back at the Exciseman, Anderson had spent a long time in a hot bath thinking about Costello and where she was. As Valerie had been lifted from her narrow grassy hammock on the side of the cliff onto a cradle and winched up the cliff face, her eyes had sought out Anderson. They suspected a spinal fracture and a few broken limbs but as they carried her past she had weakly pointed a finger at him. He had lifted her oxygen mask just enough for him to hear, 'Costello's fine. She did good.'

He whispered in her ear, 'And so did you.' He replaced the mask, her eyes closed with a sense of peace. Mission accomplished.

He had felt like crying, Patrick had stood back, giving him a moment.

At the Exciseman bar, the owner was now very friendly, telling Anderson to get his jacket, there was a double measure of eighteen-year-old Glendronach waiting outside.

'Outside?'

Beyond prying ears.

Alastair Patrick was sitting alone, on a bench on the seafront, two crystal glasses cradled in his gloved fingers. Without looking, he passed one over to Anderson and for a moment they sat in silence, the wind had died, the rain had stopped. They looked out over the dark water of the Sound, it merged into the darker sky somewhere beyond the horizon. Patrick seemed hypnotized by the rhythmic sweep of the beam of the Rua Riedh lighthouse.

Anderson felt comforted by it. How many sailors out there in the unseen darkness, were watching.

'So, what are you SO14? SO15? Any other number we mere mortals are not allowed to know about?' asked Anderson, sipping the malt. It warmed his heart.

'SO 15? Do I look like a tosser?' Patrick whispered. 'Anyway, all this almost makes you believe in the Good Lord,

now that the demons have been chased, the resident evil is no
longer . . . resident.'

'That was some shooting you did.'

'Not that difficult. I wasn't caring if I hit you.' Patrick kept
his eyes on the water.

'You a weapons man, somewhere?'

'Some might say.'

'Was Valerie trying to fire that gun? Did it jam? How did
you know it would fire?'

'Ruger. It fires OK if you release the safety.'

Anderson smiled.

Patrick continued, 'And for your paperwork, you need to
know that Kieran Cowan was never left alone after he was
discovered. The chain of evidence was kept intact, your little
orange fibres are safe evidence. And he's alive to testify that
it was Haggerty who attacked him.'

'Would I regret asking who was watching over Cowan on
the Bealach that morning, if I needed a statement?'

'No, you wouldn't regret it. But you wouldn't get an
answer.'

'OK. Is something going on up here? Something important?'

'Some folk might say that. Preparation. Exercises. You've
seen the news.'

'The Yemen? Are they going to—'

'I wouldn't know.'

Another silence felt between then.

'You saved my life, Neil Taverner was going to slit my
throat.'

'You would have survived. He's watched too many
Hollywood films to do it properly.'

'You knew for a while though. About them both.'

'They were clever but it was a house of cards. We needed
a catalyst, after we found Cowan, I knew it was game on. It
was stepping stones after that. The McCaffrey boy. Then the
Abernethy woman came here, stuck out like a sore thing. We
were watching, of course, waiting. And she was following
him. He wasn't expecting that so his guard was down. Sneaky
woman, Abernethy, surprised me.'

'He thought he had killed the woman who had been

following him. Haggerty must have thought they got away with it.'

'Feeling secure made them sloppy.'

'Why did you take Finn?'

'For his own safety. Morna said she was doing her sergeant's exams. Neil immediately increased her life insurance. Then there were a couple of accidents, incidents? Nothing was going to happen to Morna on my watch. Easier to lift them and contain them. She'll forgive me when she calms down. She has more to concern her.'

'It was not lawful. And what happened to Neil Taverner wasn't lawful.'

'It was quick, better than he deserved,' Patrick's voice was hard.

'What happened to his body?'

A shrug.

'I thought you might have an idea.'

Patrick ignored him. 'The Millennium Falcon is in Taverner's garage. Abernethy's fingerprints are on the inside which is perfectly natural as she's on record as saying she built it with Malcolm last Christmas.'

Anderson nodded, glad of solid evidence.

Patrick said quietly, 'Did you not see Neil Taverner roll down that hill? I think his body got washed out to sea.'

'I saw him lying . . .'

'You saw nothing, you were chewing the grass.' Patrick looked along the water, watching the light sweep. 'Aye well. They'll be a wee hiatus in the efficiency of drug running for a while. Hope the drug squad try to capitalize on that. Slip in someone undercover, somebody good.'

'Sounds like you fancy the job yourself?'

'Twenty, thirty years ago nae bother.' Patrick took a large slug, smiling. 'It's always the same. You need balls to do that kind of job.'

'Who dares wins?'

And Anderson thought that Alastair Patrick might have winked at him.

# FIFTEEN

*Sunday, 3rd of December*

Costello was in her hospital bed, sitting up like a posed doll, stiff against the pillows. The bruising around her eyes had blackened. Her hair was sticking up. She looked like a drunk raccoon.

She was wondering when the pain would cease when the door opened. A tall blond man walked in followed by a small man, better dressed, with salt and pepper hair. OK, maybe not better dressed but he carried his clothes better, as if he owned them. With the taller man, it was the other way round.

'So here you are,' DCI Colin Anderson said, not keeping the bite of anger from his voice. Just because she wasn't fit enough to hear it, didn't mean that he wasn't going to say it.

'How's Valerie?'

'Three vertebral fractures, both femurs broken. She's in Raigmore.'

'Did you really think it was me?' asked Costello.

'I hoped,' answered Anderson. 'Especially when she went over the cliff.' He resisted the urge to lean forward and pat her on the head. The fracture at the rear of her skull was covered by a dressing. He had seen the film now, Costello running forward to help a fatally wounded McCaffrey. Not hearing the second man, Taverner, arm raised ready to bring a tyre lever down on her head. O'Hare said she had been lucky. She had her hood up and a hat on under that. The cushioning had saved her life.

Costello's eyes looked at Anderson then to Walker, back to Anderson. 'And who are you, exactly?' She wasn't laughing; there was no sarcastic humour in her face.

Now it was Anderson and Walker's turn to look at each other.

'You two are so easy to wind up.' She smiled. 'Getting a bit of memory back every day.'

'I've brought you some grapes,' said Walker, pulling up another seat.

'How long have we worked together?'

'Must be about twenty years, maybe more,' said Anderson. 'It seems like a life sentence.' Injecting a sense of their normal relationship into a conversation. 'How is your memory really? Do you remember resigning?'

Costello tried to shake her head, then stopped as it hurt so much.

'You told the big boss to stick his job up his arse.' Anderson said gleefully. 'But Mitchum didn't process it as he thought you . . .'

'Weren't serious?'

'No, he thought you were barking mad. There will be an investigation but I think Police Scotland will have you back. So how is the memory really?'

She shrugged. 'Patchy. It's not so bad, living in this world in my head. Things are very clear, very cut and dry, I know the essence of somebody, nothing else. It's useful.' She chewed on her lip, looking out the window, a slow smile formed on her lips. 'So Valerie got him. Our plan worked.' She closed her eyes now, as if with that knowledge, she could sleep more easily. 'She's paying for me to be here you know.'

'Well she can afford it, she's going to inherit the house.'

Her eyes flashed open. 'You were with me.' Her forefinger drifted towards Walker's face, seeing a small nod of agreement. 'When we found the bodies. Haggerty killed them both.'

'He couldn't have, he was on the A9 at the time. He got his sideman to do it for him. Haggerty helped Taverner with the rapes. Taverner did Haggerty's murders for him. As you guessed, he was in the garage all along.'

'Bastard. I knew Haggerty was behind it. You lot were doing bugger all about it. So I did something myself. Poor Abigail, targeted by George after Oscar disappeared.'

'You were very sure, on very little evidence.'

'I was on the receiving end of his taunts. I have a very clear memory of that. I have a clear memory that he had persuaded you lot not to listen to me, he wanted to discredit me. Though I doubt he thought I'd get suspected of murdering Donnie.

He must have loved that. You can't protect yourself against gossip and lies, so in that way, he got me. And he got me good.'

'Why were you there at the lochside? Whatever it was, you could have come to us,' said Walker delicately. 'We would have listened.'

'You didn't. You told me to get lost. All anybody could talk about was his alibi. Donnie was the only one who listened to me. And that got him killed.' She blinked back a tear. 'George was tailing me at times after Abigail's death, I did tell you that. And what did you do? You told George.'

Anderson closed his eyes. Had he really done that?

'George was off his work after the murders, he had all day to annoy me, and you lot were happy to stand aside and let him. I was following him as much as he was following me. Donnie and I were nowhere near careful enough. It had become comical almost, it made us forget how dangerous he was, and I will never forgive myself for that. But we had no choice. But you know . . .' She was getting angry. 'It took us ten minutes looking into George's life up north to come to Neil Taverner as the man with the opportunity. Donnie and his love of the sidemen, he almost profiled Taverner before we got near him. An adoring wife who earns more than he does, whose value goes up as a mother, yet the father is not close to the child. You do my crime and I will do yours, not an uncommon thing when there is a long-term bond between two people. The bond between Taverner and Haggerty was much stronger than the bond between Taverner and his wife, or Haggerty and his wife.'

'Costello? What were you doing at the lochside?' Anderson asked again.

'We met to go to the campsite, it's only four miles up the road, and wait for Taverner to do his pick-up of the luggage. That was all. We met at the loch so we were only in one car, to look less conspicuous. But we didn't think they were following us, we didn't think.'

In hindsight, Anderson had thought it through. They hadn't been as careful as they should have been. Costello had believed that Haggerty thought she would accept his warning off, but Haggerty had realized that she had taken it as a sign to freelance her investigation. He had made her more dangerous. Anderson might have told Haggerty that himself. Donnie had thought Cowan was Taverner and had followed him up to the viewing point. Cowan had been in the wrong place, wrong time.

Walker filled up the gaps. 'So Taverner and Haggerty realized there were three of you and only two of them, so they placed a stop box on each vehicle in the car park. They came prepared to clean up the situation. As you were left alone, they presumed you were dead. Haggerty goes after Kieran, and waits for him to pull over. Taverner takes Donnie away from the scene and drives up north, as he was scheduled to do. You were in the grass bleeding. Haggerty had to retrieve your phones, mix the blood, spill a little cocaine, pour some drink around the scene. They wanted to destroy your reputation. Cowan made them panic, it made them careless.'

Costello settled back into the pillow on her chair. She closed her eyes, her eyelids pink islands in the bruised patches around her eye sockets. 'I think I can see Donnie on the ground, I was coming up the hill, my thighs are sore because of the climb. I remember trying to get away. I ran forward to help but . . . Then I don't remember. I was on the ground at one point. I tried to get up, I remember wet hands round my neck. There was a blow on the back of my head, not sure what happened then. I don't recall much but being in here.'

'You crawled away, through the undergrowth. You got out.'

Walker said, 'The doctor explained your thinking brain shut off, your deep brain was looking for patterns, for safety. People do the weirdest things. So by the time you were picked up in the middle of Glasgow, you had changed, showered and gone back out. You left your car at Lochmaben Road.'

'Where my grandmother used to live.'

'You drove it there, ignoring the clatter of the ball bearings. You sat in the park then ran off when the police were called. Then you walked home, then out to Buchannan Street, we have you on CCTV. Do you know why you did that?'

She shook her head. 'I have no idea.'

'You could have come to me,' said Anderson.

'George was at your house, so what good would that have done me?'

And it was true, he'd lost count of how many times George asked him if he'd seen Costello.

And George had known she was onto him. He knew they could be intercepted and caught red-handed at a baggage pick up or drop and the one closest to Glasgow seemed most logical. He wondered how many times they had watched Costello and she had not moved, but when she did they were ready. She had been arrogant and stupid, and because of her, three wee boys would grow up without a dad.

'Taverner was picking up and distributing drugs, mostly cocaine. The big bags, like a golf flight bag, well they contained the luggage for transportation to the different sites, and they were lined with old carpet, orange tri-lobular fibres. That puts a lot of connections together.'

'So George wasn't the rapist,' asked Costello.

'He wasn't. He was the facilitator of the rapes. There's a team on it now. They have already proven he knew Sally and that Haggerty and Taverner were in Glasgow when she was raped.'

'But it was very useful for him to have us pursue him on something he was innocent of. The "Clapping Song" playing. He clapped at me at the funeral. So no I did not work it out, he told me. The clapping is in Sally's notes, it's in the case file of Gillian Witherspoon as well, and there will be more, there will be more out there. Haggerty clapped, Taverner raped, Haggerty probably watched.' Costello thought about shaking her head again.

'We think Taverner had a bad shoulder, there's anecdotal evidence of a young woman throwing him at karate, breaking his shoulder. That might have annoyed him a bit.'

'Easy for Taverner to drive around, early morning, late at night. He had a right to be everywhere. Woman walking, hiking, camping on their own.'

'So it was all for money, and the nice little line they had running cocaine about the country. I wonder how many of their hikers are extremely regular. And sniff a lot.'

'All small fry compared to the murder of Malcolm and Abigail.'

'You were right about the MO. Haggerty came home the previous evening and drove in to the garage. I think Taverner was in the boot. Taverner stayed in the garage, then walked in the back door, killed them. The guy on the CCTV on Kelvindale path is the right height for Taverner, not for Haggerty. There is no DNA because of that outfit he wears, it's like a boiler suit, with the name of the company on it. He killed them, slipped a jacket over his easily recognizable suit and left. Walked back to wherever he left his car. It wasn't sophisticated, it wasn't even that clever. It was merely effective.'

'Haggerty had been using that path for years, he was a secretive man and the path had been closed from his end, so it's likely that he "allowed" naughty Malcolm to open the path again knowing that it would give Taverner a way out in the early hours of that morning largely unseen. Nobody else knew about the path at the back, Haggerty would deny it. Mathieson and her team missed it, they didn't know where to look, a small gap in an overgrown hedge. Heads will roll that the search team missed that.'

'And Oscar Duguid? The first husband? What's his role in all this?' asked Costello.

'I think something happened to Oscar Duguid when he heard about Mary Jane's death. Her murder shocked him, just because he walked away from the marriage doesn't mean he stopped loving his daughter, my daughter,' said Anderson. 'He thought he had left them comfortable and safe, his friend moved in as role of father and protector. He knew about the attacks on women, that was his insurance to keep them quiet about his disappearing act. They didn't stop the attacks. Haggerty is a man of intense cruelty, Oscar was OK with faking his own death, but he must have had a serious rethink when Abigail was murdered. And maybe when he worked out what might have happened to Jennifer Argyll up at Dolphin Point. His Jennifer, thirty years before. That's still under investigation. Lachlan McRae was the SIO on her disappearance.'

'Where is he now? Oscar?'

'DCI Patrick is saying nothing. You can attach electrodes to his testicles and you'll get nothing out of him,' said Anderson smiling.

'Reading the reports. I fail to understand why Taverner's body was washed out to sea,' said Walker.

'You had to be there,' said Anderson blithely. 'I'm more interested in the psychological hold that house held over them, it became a focus for memories. That's why people have cenotaphs set in stone, I suppose, so their memories are also set in stone. Happy days at the lodge, the three boys growing up there. Then Jennifer Argyll went missing, Oscar's heart was broken and from then on, it was all downhill.'

'Memories, eh? Powerful but untrustworthy.'

'They are useful,' added Costello.

'Well, I had better get home before I get forgotten about,' said Anderson.

'And I'm going to visit my sober god-daughter,' Walker shrugged, 'now that she's therapeutically plastered.'

'Oh very good,' laughed Anderson. 'I'm going home to a kitchen which is slightly busier than Sauchiehall Street in the Boxing Day sales.'

'And does that not make you yearn for the ruggedly beautiful isolation of Dolphin Point?' asked Walker.

Anderson appeared to consider it carefully. 'Nope.'